The elven maid merely laughed. 'Your petty magics cannot harm me now – for he is almost mine.' She stretched out her hands again and Conla reached for them. But on the beach Conn and the druid could only see him reaching into thin air.

Tiny spots of green fire darted before the youth's eyes and flickered in long traceries of light across the space that separated him from the banshee.

'Your power is spent, Druid,' she called. 'You are a dying breed; soon a new race of magicians will challenge your power and they will cast you and your elemental gods back into the Abyss whence they came.' And the maid gestured, shattering the green fire like so many pieces of broken glass.

'Come Conla.'

And out of the waves rose a longship of white crystal, without sail or oars and its name cut into the side in red gold.

'Come, Conla and we will rule in Tir na nOg for all eternity.'

Irish Folk and Fairy Tales

MICHAEL SCOTT

SPHERE BOOKS LIMITED
London and Sydney

First published in Great Britain by
Sphere Books Ltd 1983
30–32 Gray's Inn Road, London WC1X 8JL
Reprinted 1985
Copyright © 1983 by Michael Scott

Set in Garamond

Printed and bound in Great Britain by
Cox & Wyman Ltd, Reading

This book would not have been finished without the help of:

Claire and Harry for their patience, Johanna and Bill for their assistance, Patricia and Tommy for their time and co-operation, Jim White because he asked for it.

And,
Anna, without whom it would not have been finished, with love.

CONTENTS

CHAPTER 1

THE SONS OF TUREEN
(The First Sorrow Of Irish Storytelling)

Brian loosed his sword in its sheath and called over his shoulder to his brothers. 'Rider coming!'

They edged their horses up beside their elder brother and stared across the flat expanse of the Plain of Muirthemne. A lone rider was racing towards them, his armour and weapons flashing in the early morning sunlight and his crimson cloak streaming behind.

'A Fomor?' wondered Urchar.

'Too tall,' replied his twin Iuchar, drawing his sword.

Brian reined his horse to a halt. 'We wait; let him come to us.'

The rider came closer, his tall white steed galloping effortlessly across the flat plain. He suddenly caught sight of the three mounted warriors and, pulling up short, stood in the saddle to stare across at the sons of Tureen.

Brian slipped a throwing spear from its sling alongside his boot, whilst his brothers drew their swords. In these troubled times, one was always wary of strangers; and even now the three brothers went to join the gathering of the De Danann lords at Tara for the coming war against the deamon Fomorians.

The war arrow had come three days previously. Lugh of the Long Arm - an arrogant trouble maker - had slain a score of the Fomorian tax gatherers; and Balor, the one-eyed king of the northern men, had declared war on Banba.

The three sons of Tureen had gathered their armour and honed their weapons before setting out for the High Court

1

to offer their services to Nuada, king of the Tuathe De Danann.

Already they had been attacked twice on their journey east; once by the great black wolves that men whispered were controlled by the wizards of Balor, and once by bandits. They had slain a score of the wolves and the corpses of the bandits littered the woods.

Suddenly Urchar and Iuchar cried aloud and pointed – the warrior had disappeared!

Brian gripped the spear until his knuckles whitened about the shaft and without a word rode towards the riderless horse. The ground dipped into a slight hollow and in the hollow a herd of swine rooted amongst the gorse and bracken.

'Where did he go?' wondered Iuchar.

'Disappeared,' said Urchar.

Brian pointed down into the hollow with his spear. 'He's there amongst the pigs – and a right fitting place for him. Did you not recognise him?' He turned to his brothers. They shook their heads.

Brian laughed grimly. 'Fine warriors you make; you would have to wait until your enemies were on top of you before you recognise them. That was Cian, father of Lugh.'

'Cian!'

'Aye, Cian, that foul-mouthed black-hearted bitch's cur. The dishonour he and his two brothers, Cu and Ceithne, brought on our sister, has not been resolved. But now we shall have our revenge.'

Iuchar hefted his sword and swung it whistling through the air. 'He had obviously recognised us and assumed the form of a pig.' He turned to his twin. 'Shall we go a-slaughtering, brother.'

Urchar bowed mockingly, his blue-black hair catching highlights from the morning sun. 'Yes, let's butcher a pig.'

'Wait!' Brian snapped.

They turned to their older brother. 'There is no need to slaughter good bacon in search of a lizard. Put up your weapons and I will work an enchantment.'

2

The twins obediently sheathed their swords whilst Brian slipped a short alder wand from his belt. Concentrating intently and calling upon the Dagda and Danu, he passed the wand over his brothers. Their forms seemed to liquify, and tremble as if seen through a heat haze ... and then in their place stood two of the great war hounds of Bamba. With yelps of joy the dogs ran down through the swine which rapidly dispersed in all directions squealing shrilly. But the hounds had one target; for under the enchantment the twins could easily recognise Cian in his true form. Deftly they cut the pig out from the main pack and drove him up the incline towards their waiting brother.

Brian crouched at the top of the hollow, his arm cocked, the throwing spear lying flush against his cheek. As the pig came over the top of the rise Brian threw. The spear caught the pig just below the throat, the force of the blow flipping the animal backwards into the pursuing hounds. Brian slid down the incline, the alder wand already in his hand, muttering a reversal of the shape-changing spell under his breath.

By the time he reached the bottom, his twin brothers had already resumed their human forms. Both had swords in their hands and were prepared to finish off the animal.

'After you,' said Iuchar.

'No, no, I insist, the honour is yours,' replied Urchar.

'He is mine,' said Brian joining them. 'I will avenge our sister's honour.' His sword rasped as it slid from its scabbard. Holding it in both hands he brought it above his head and prepared to cut the pig in twain ... when it spoke, 'No ... no ... you cannot ... cannot slay me ... thus. Upon your mercy ... let me regain the form ... of man so that ... I might die honourably.'

'Does he deserve an honourable death?' wondered Iuchar.

'He is without honour,' said Urchar. 'Slay him now like the animal he is.'

'You are ... men of ... honour. You cannot ... cannot slay me,' gasped Cian.

'Resume your true form,' said Brian wearily.

3

'Perhaps that is his true form,' whispered Iuchar to Urchar.

The pig suddenly grew indistinct, as if it was covered with a thick blanket of gauze ... and then the blanket fell away, revealing the true form of Cian. He was tall, nearly the same height as Brian, his sandy coloured hair now flecked with grey, and his strangely colourless eyes were lined and sunken. But the haughty arrogance that had earned Cian and his brothers their reputation about the Duns and Forts of Banba, the arrogance that he had passed on to his son, Lugh, was still stamped on his proud face. Ignoring the wound which trickled blood from his chest, he attempted to stare down the three sons of Tureen.

'You have made a grave mistake,' he informed them. 'My brothers and son will have your heads for this act.'

Brian struck him a blow which sent him sprawling. 'You presume a lot, my lord. You presume we are about to let you go free. You presume we fear you, your brothers and your son. You presume we are not men of honour. And you presume we will not avenge the dishonour you and your brothers brought upon our sister. But you presume wrongly, my lord. For you are not about to leave this place alive. We will take your death in part payment for that foul deed.'

Cian staggered to his feet.

'I am of the De Danann, steel cannot kill me.'

'My lord,' said Brian coldly, 'I would not stain my blade with your blood; I would rather have the blood of the Fomorians upon it than yours.' He stooped and plucked a stone from the soft earth. 'Let the earth that spawned you slay you.'

Brian threw the stone with all the force of his arm. It struck the De Danann lord high on the shoulder, numbing his arm. The next rock struck him across the head, dazing him. He raised his hand, either to ward off a blow or to beg for mercy, but the third stone struck him full between the eyes and he fell to the ground - dead.

'Thus is vengeance ours,' whispered Brian.

The sons of Tureen dug a shallow trench in the damp

ground and buried the body of Cian, covering it with large flat stones. As they stood over the grave, Iuchar said, almost to himself, 'No warrior should die like this.'

'A warrior must have honour,' reminded his twin.

'And Cian was a man without honour,' added Brian.

It was the evening of the third day after the battle. The remnants of Banba's host had returned, and were now gathering about Tara's halls where a great victory feast was in progress. In Maecadre, the main hall, the atmosphere was slightly more subdued, for the princes of the De Danann realised by how close a margin they had beaten the northern deamons; next time they might not be so lucky.

Lugh stood beside Nuada, king of the Tuatha de Danann.

'Our men celebrate victory,' he shouted above the raucous cries that drifted through the thick walls.

'As well they might; they have all felt the Morrigan's breath these last days.' He turned to Lugh, poking him gently in the ribs. 'You fought well. If you keep collecting heads at this rate, soon you'll have to build a separate room for them.'

Lugh spat. 'I do not collect the heads of deamons.'

Nuada gripped the young man by the shoulder. 'You are foolish to mock the Fomorians; they are brave warriors. Aye, their ways are not our ways, and we call them deamons for their swarthy looks and curious mannerisms, but they are many and the days of the De Danann are numbered. Even now our people dwindle, some have already retreated to the lonely places. Some day ... some day ...' he paused and shook his head. 'Enough of this. How fares Cian? I did not see him in battle.'

Lugh spun and faced the king. 'What do you mean, "*you did not see him in battle?*" Surely he fought beside you?'

Nuada shook his head. 'I thought he fought beside you and his brothers.'

Lugh abruptly brushed past the king and pushed his way through the crowded hall searching for Cu and Ceithne. A dark premonition which had haunted him since the eve of battle now returned, a premonition in which he saw the ground seep blood and the stones run red.

He found his uncles in one corner of the room recounting their exploits to a group of wide-eyed youths. Lugh called them aside.

'Have you seen my father? Did you see him during battle?'

'I thought he fought with you,' said Cu.

Ceithne shook his head. 'I have not seen him since he set out six days ago to raise the families of the west.'

'He seems to have disappeared. I fear for him,' said Lugh.

'Let us see if his horse is in the stables,' suggested Cu.

They made their way out of Maecadre, out into the long winding halls and down to the stables at the rear of the palace. The area was bustling with activity, some of the knights only now returning, slack-jawed and bulbous-eyed heads dangling from their saddles.

They searched through the stables, looking for Cian's snow-white steed. Cu grabbed a passing stable boy and questioned him, but he had seen neither the horse nor the lord.

'Something has happened to him,' said Lugh. 'I am going in search of my father.'

And as the moon rose over Tara's halls three riders galloped from the high gates and rode into the west.

They reached the Plain of Muirthemne the following evening. The day had turned cold and a chill ice-laden wind whipped across the flat plain. They had stopped at every Dun and Rath on the road and in every case the story was the same. Cian had passed that way, calling forth the families for the coming battle, but no-one had seen him return.

Lugh and his uncles camped that night in a slight hollow which at least afforded them some protection from the chill wind. Lugh's sleep was troubled. He seemed to hear his father calling on the wind and he was once again troubled with visions of the earth seeping blood. He tossed and turned the whole night unable to find sleep and he arose with the first light of dawn.

He climbed out of the hollow and stood staring into the east where the first crimson tinge of the sunrise was lightening the heavens. He lifted his hand to push back his yellow-gold hair and noticed his hand was stained with red also ... then he realised the wan sunlight had not yet reached him.

He looked closely at his hand in the grey light of dawn. It looked like ...

Blood!

Lugh turned and stared down into the hollow where he and his uncles had passed the night. The rich green earth was dark - stained with a thin covering of blood-red dew. Even as he watched it welled up from between the stones and ran in slow turgid trickles. The hollow was awash with blood - it resembled a battlefield or slaughterhouse.

He raised his bloody hands to his face and screamed aloud.

For he knew. He knew.

Scrambling down, he fell to his knees and began to pull up the stones from the soft earth with his hands, whilst his body shook with an icy fever. Cu and Ceithne awoke and stared in horror at Lugh, his clothes and hair matted with dried blood, tearing at the ground like a madman. And then they looked about at the blood-soaked landscape, the like of which they had never imagined.

They dragged Lugh to his feet, even though he struggled and raved, and kept shouting, 'He's here, he's here.' Cu struck him unconscious, whilst Ceithne rode to the nearest Rath for help. He arrived back about mid-morning, a band of warriors trailing reluctantly behind. The morning sun had dried the blood and now it crusted the earth in a reeking film. In places the yellowed grass peeped through, giving the hollow the appearance of a gaping, infected wound.

The warriors began to remove the befouled earth, passing

it out of the hollow, digging slowly deeper.

Lugh meanwhile, had awoken and stared morosely at the ground, his eyes flat and expressionless. At last, stirring himself, he pointed to a spot to one side of the hollow.

'Dig there,' he commanded.

The warriors looked at Ceithne for orders. 'You heard. Dig there ... and on your lives take care.'

Shortly thereafter they unearthed the partly decomposed body of Cian.

Cu and Ceithne gently removed the body, whilst the warriors stood nervously about, keeping as far away as possible from the two older men and the wild-eyed youth. Wiping away as much of the grime as possible, they examined the corpse so that they might see how he had been killed. That he had been murdered was plain, for even the earth itself refused to hold the blood of the slain man. He had not been robbed, for his weapons, wand of power, armour and gold were still with him. There was a single wound high in his chest, such as might have been made by a thrown spear, and the bone in his shoulder was splintered and showed through the putrescent flesh. But the major wound - the one that had killed him - was upon his head. Something - possibly a stone - had struck him full between the eyes, crushing the front of his skull like an eggshell.

The brothers stared in horror at the wounds. It was almost inconceivable that a warrior, and a warrior such as Cian, should have been stoned to death, a punishment fitting only for dogs and slaves. Cu attempted to stop Lugh seeing the wounds, but he was pushed roughly aside and the young man went to kneel before the battered corpse of his father.

'Who has done this?' he whispered in anguish. 'Who has done this?' He suddenly screamed, his head thrown back. He fell forward across the mutilated body and sobbed like a child.

As his tears soaked the shattered face, the slack jaw suddenly moved. With a cry of horror, Lugh fell backwards whilst the assembled warriors fingered their weapons, prepared to cut the animated corpse to pieces and burn it.

The jaw moved again, whilst the fingers of one hand convulsed in the earth. Again and again the jaw moved as if it sought to speak.

Lugh crept forward on hands and knees and whispered to the creature, 'Who did this?' He placed his ear close to the cracked and flaking lips. For a moment he could hear nothing and then the jaw moved again. A charnel reek, the stink of decay and offal emanated from the corpse and deep in its dessicated throat Lugh could hear the muted grating rumble of words.

'The … sons … of … Tureen.'

The atmosphere in Maecadre, the Great Hall of Tara was tense and subdued. The kings and lords of Banba in their full armour and finery sat in silence listening to Lugh of the Long Arm finishing his tale of the discovery of his father's corpse. The only part left to tell was the identity of the killers.

'And your father,' Nuada paused, 'your father's corpse, it spoke to you?'

Lugh nodded. 'It is not uncommon for the shade of one foully murdered to linger on in an attempt to communicate the identity of his killers.'

'So you know who killed your father?' persisted Nuada. 'I do.'

'And that is …?'

'I killed Cian!' said a voice from the back of the hall.

Lugh half rose from his seat of honour and pulled his sword from its sheath. 'Yes, yes, you did, Brian MacTureen, you and your bastard brothers,' he hissed.

Brian shook his head slowly. 'No, my brothers were not involved in the slaying, the actual blow was mine.'

Urchar and Iuchar pushed their way through the crowd and stood beside their brother. 'We are all guilty,' said Iuchar.

'And we freely admit our guilt,' added his twin.

9

'Although I do not think it a crime to slay animals,' said Iuchar into the silence.

With a cry of rage both Cu and Ceithne came to their feet, weapons in their hands, but Lugh only smiled coldly and sheathed his sword. 'Put up your weapons uncles, they do not deserve honourable slaying.'

Lugh rose and walked the length of the wall, 'You deserve death,' he said, 'but I think death is too good for you.'

A murmur of assent rumbled about the hall. And whilst many of the assembled lords had little liking for either Lugh or his kin, they were all in the main honourable men, and the code they lived by was unbreakable. The sons of Tureen had slain and therefore they must be slain or pay whatever fine Lugh might levy.

'We avenged our family honour,' said Brian simply.

'By stoning my father to death?' shouted Lugh.

'It was what he deserved.'

Lugh shook his head slowly. 'No, no, you will not rise me to anger.' He stood by his seat and stared into the shadows which lingered in the corners of the great hall. 'Killing you is too easy.' He gazed at them and added softly, 'Too easy. You are now bound by whatever honour you possess to pay the fine for my father's foul murder.'

Brian nodded. 'Never let it be said that the sons of Tureen were without honour,' he said looking at Cu and Ceithne.

'The fine is in eight parts and each part must be accomplished before your debt is paid in full.' He sat in the high-backed chair and looked closely at the three brothers. 'You understand; all the parts to be completed?'

They nodded.

'You will bring to me three apples, a pigskin, a spear, a chariot and two horses, seven live pigs, a whelp, a cooking spit, and you will complete your fine by shouting three times upon a hill.'

'A curious litany,' said Nuada.

'He places a high price upon his father,' said Iuchar.

'No more than he was worth,' said Urchar.

Brian quietened them with a glare. 'There is more to this I'll wager. Explain your fine.'

10

Lugh laughed grimly. 'Yes, there is a little more to it. But let me explain that I do not choose these items at random. We will need them in the coming battle against the Fomorians; you can take some pleasure in that, if you wish.

'The three apples,' said Lugh 'are from the Garden of the Hesperides in the Orient. You will recognise them by their colour, for they are warm-gold and the size of a helm. A bite from one of the apples will cure all wounds, however serious.' He looked across the silent table at Brian. 'And they are well guarded, you will not come by them easily.'

'The pigskin,' said Brian softly.

'The skin of the boar is held by Tuas, King of the Land of the Greeks; it has the power to cure all ills; even incurable diseases are not beyond its power.

'The spear,' continued Lugh, 'is from the land of the Persians. It is called the Destroyer. Pezaer, Lord of the Persians guards the spear.

'From Persia you shall go to the Kingdom of Sicily, where you shall find the two horses and chariot of King Doabre, which is capable of travelling on both land and sea.

'Then you shall sail west to the Pillars of the Sun, and capture the seven swine of King Aesal ... The swine are the beasts of the gods – they are immortal, like their masters. They are an inexhaustable supply of food. Even though three or four or five might be slain for the evening meal, there will be seven pigs in the morning. Their flesh is said to heal even the most grievously wounded.

'The whelp you shall claim from the King of Irouad. It is destined to grow into a beast even the fabled lion will follow and an invincible warhound.' Lugh paused and added, 'Although these are part of the fine, yet are they also weapons to be used in the coming war. But the last part of the fine is payable only to me. You must bring me the cooking spit of the water maidens of Fioncure Island, which is said to lie between Bamba and Alba, but which has yet to be found.'

Iuchar opened his mouth to comment, but Brian gripped his elbow hard, causing his brother to bite his lip in pain.

'And the last part?'

11

'Ah yes, the last part. Assuming that you have survived thus far – and have found the cooking spit ...'

'And have not died of old age in the meantime,' murmured Urchar.

'You will then,' continued Lugh forcefully, 'make your way to the hill of Midcain in the land of the Fomorians. Midcain and his three sons, Conn, Corc and Aedh, guard that hill and they are under a geas to let no voice be raised in joy nor anger upon its slopes until the New God has come to our land.' He grinned maliciously. 'This then is your task.'

Brian, Iuchar and Urchar bowed and then turned and left the silent hall. Lugh turned to Nuada and grinned boldly. 'Is it a fitting fine my lord?'

The High King nodded solemnly. 'Your father would be proud of you.' He rose to leave and the entire assembly rose with him. 'But though the deed of the sons of Tureen was evil, I'll wager the bards will remember their tale and name more readily than they will remember yours.'

Brian, Iuchar and Urchar stood at the bow of the *Watersprite* watching the waves slip by with ever increasing swiftness.

'This craft chills me,' said Iuchar.

Urchar nodded silently, sharing his brother's discomfort. The *Watersprite* had been lent to them by Lugh, '*to aid then on their way*', he said, and to show that he held '*no ill feelings*'.

It was an elven craft, long and slim, high in the bow and stern, with a single sail set amidships. It was constructed entirely from the white-wood of the forests of Tir fo Thuinn, the Land Beneath the Waves. Its sail was woven of the hair of the Dagda, the Father of gods, and billowed in winds that blew not from this world. At the prow was a figurehead in the shape of a great gape-mouthed, long-fanged serpent, whose eyes burned with an unearthly fire. When one wished to set the craft in any direction, one merely whispered the destination to the figurehead and at once the craft would set forth, skimming the waves.

Lugh had come down to the shore as they set out. He had stood on the white sands and silently watched them loading the magical ship with the food and weapons necessary for their journey. Tureen himself had come with his daughter Ethne to see his sons set forth on their quest. Lugh had bowed mockingly to them.

'What honour this will bring to your family,' he remarked.

'What do you know of honour?' spat Ethne. Tureen laid a hand on his daughter's arm and quietened her.

'Say farewell to your brothers,' he commanded. When she had gone and stood by the water's edge, he turned to Lugh. 'Have you come to mock?'

'Mock; no, not I my lord. I have come to see your sons depart safely.'

'They will not shirk their responsibilities. Your fine - which will be remembered as the heaviest laid on mortal man - will be paid in full.'

Lugh nodded silently, and walked towards the shore.

'Why, here is our benefactor come to wave us farewell,' said Iuchar.

'His concern is touching,' added Urchar.

Brian nodded to the De Danann lord solemnly. 'We are grateful for the loan of this craft. Of course, had you not given it, we might not be able to return with your weapons and talismans in time for the coming battle, eh?'

'You understand the workings of the craft?' Lugh asked gruffly.

'We do,' said Brian. He turned and shouted towards the figurehead. 'The Garden of Hesperides in the Orient.' The figurehead's golden eyes blazed, and slowly, silently, the craft wheeled and made its way from the bay.

'It reeks,' said Iuchar, sniffing the rich dark perfume of the island in the distance.

'It is foul,' agreed Urchar, pulling a corner of his cloak across his face to cover his nose.

The *Watersprite* bobbed unmoving just in sight of the

13

shore. It had taken them barely three days to reach it and Brian estimated that they had come almost to the edge of the world. The sun no longer rose in its usual place and even the stars were gone, replaced by strange new configurations. The days here were longer also and the sun burned from a brilliant blue sky, the like of which was rarely seen in Banba. But the nights were as cold as home and sometimes before the dusk fell, great massed clouds would roll in swiftly and then it would rain with incredible ferocity, until it seemed as if the gods themselves wept.

Brian had ordered the craft to halt when it became evident that the shore ahead was its ultimate destination. All that now remained was to claim the three apples.

'We could, I suppose, just ask for them,' suggested Iuchar.

'We could, I suppose, just lose our heads just asking for them,' mocked Urchar.

'This is a barbarous land,' said Brian softly, leaning over the edge of the craft. 'Its manners and customs differ greatly from our own and whilst I have some knowledge of the lands that border and lie to the east and south of Banba, I know very little about this land. Therefore,' he said, taking his short alder wand from his belt, 'we will take refuge in enchantment. We will assume the shapes of hawks and circle over the gardens and spy out the defences. Maybe it will be possible to snatch the apples.'

He shrugged and raising his hand high above his head began to work the enchantment. But the spell seemed to take longer than usual to work. Perhaps, thought Brian, the power of the Dagda and Danu is not so strong in these foreign waters where none worship them. Do the gods live by the faith of men? he wondered.

Slowly, and with a gritty uneasiness, they assumed the shapes of hawks; huge golden winged, razor taloned birds, who took to the air with slow ponderous, powerful beats of their great wings, and headed north towards the lush green land, and the Garden of the Hesperides.

Once they passed beyond the golden sands of the shoreline they were over the rank and impenetrable forests of the interior. They flew over the almost obliterated ruins of cities that had been great before the first invaders had come to Banba.

Huge rivers wound their way through thick forests, rivers which made the Sinann, the longest river in Banba, seem little more than a stream. Away to the north and west loomed great purple mountains, snow-capped even at this late season, and in the east a single great cone belched smoke and fire as if some angry deamons laboured therein. Tiny villages disappeared below, their houses constructed of yellowed grasses, not like the wood and sod dwellings of home. And everywhere there were roads.

In Banba, Nuada was constructing the first of the many roads that would link the country to Tara, but there the roads were rough affairs, indeed little more than tracks, whilst here, huge highways glittering white in the sunlight cut across even the most distant parts of the country. Broad roads also, wide enough to allow two or more of the curious chariots of these people to pass abreast.

The sons of Tureen swooped down towards the largest city they could see, a great sprawling affair that dwarfed Tara. It was surrounded by a large wall of black stone, and its gates were heavily guarded. The buildings were all constructed of pale white stone and some of the domes of the larger buildings were sheathed in gold or a thick black stone, that glittered with shimmering rainbow hues in the sunlight.

As the three hawks flew low over the broad streets, the colourfully clad inhabitants stopped and stared for great birds were not often seen in this part of the world. Guards posted about the city walls noted the growing disturbance and one set out to bring word to the Emperor.

Meanwhile, the sons of Tureen had found the Garden of the Hesperides. It was almost in the centre of the city, attached to a great building of green stone, set with many precious and semi-precious stones. The Garden was surrounded by a barbed-topped wall and guards in laquered armour with hooked pikes patrolled outside the walls. In the

centre of the Garden was a single tree. All other vegetation
had been cleared away from it and it stood alone on a little
knoll. It was tall and thin, its wood a rich dark shade of ochre
and its leaves a shimmering emerald.

And growing on the tree were three huge golden apples.

About the base of the tree lolled seven guards, huge men
in green-laquered armour, carrying swords and spears.
Thick recumbent bows lay on the ground beside full quivers.
The guards were engaged in a game which they played on
two small chequered boards, moving the tiny ornate pieces
from one board to the other.

Without warning the brothers swooped. One of the
guards glanced up; his cry brought the others to their feet,
their weapons in their hands. A thrown spear hissed by
Iuchar, causing him to swerve suddenly in flight, nearly
tumbling him from the skies. Two arrows flashed by in
quick succession, and the guard was notching a third, when a
huge hawk almost tore the top off his head. Iuchar and
Urchar followed their brother in the attack – clearly they
would not get the apples unless they slew the guards first.
One of the guards turned, but not to flee, for attached to a
low wall beside the appletree was a short, squat bell. Beside
the bell lay an ornamental hammer. The guard had almost
reached the hammer, his outstretched fingers brushing its
surface, when he was struck a powerful blow on the back of
his head. The force of the blow propelled him into the hard
unyielding wall with a sodden crunch.

An arrow parted the feathers of Brian's left wing.
Abruptly he folded his wings and fell, talons outstretched
onto the upraised face of the crouching archer.

Of the three remaining guards, two had decided that they
had had enough and turned to flee through the gardens.
They had barely gone a hundred paces when Iuchar and
Urchar struck like levin bolts, snapping the neck of one with
a rotten crack and driving a razor beak into the base of the
other's spine.

The remaining guard stood at the foot of the tree. A
notched bow was in his hands and driven into the soft earth
at his feet were two long lances. He watched the two great

bloody hawks lifting from the bodies of his felled companions. These were no ordinary birds. They were twice the size and more of any hawks he had ever seen and the uncanny precision and co-operation they had shown during the attack hinted at only one thing: Sorcery.

And then he paused. Surely there had been three of the large birds? But now there were only two of them before him. Had the third been slain during the brief encounter?

He never even saw the great bird that crashed into his face, driving him backwards into the tree.

Brian, Iuchar and Urchar carefully plucked the apples from the tree and set off for the distant shore, their great wings beating slowly with the unaccustomed weight, and the exertion of battle.

The Emperor regarded the cowering guard through slit eyes. 'Stolen?' His voice rose to a scream. 'Stolen? And you dare to stand before me and tell me that one of the Treasures of my Empire had been lost and you have not died in its defence?'

'Majesty, it was sorcery,' whispered the guard.

'Sorcery,' the Emperor's voice dropped to a hiss.

'These were no ordinary birds sire. They were greater in size and their cunning was preternatural ...' the guard trailed off. The Emperor's eyes had unfocused and he stared intently into the vastness of the presence chamber.

Abruptly the huge crystal doors opened and three slim figures entered and glided to the Dragon Throne.

'Yes father,' they whispered as one.

'Shape-changers have stolen the Apples. They were last seen heading towards the coast; I want them stopped.'

The Emperor's daughters bowed silently and turned and glided from the chamber. As they reached the crystal doors, their forms seemed to shiver and tremble on the scented air. And before the great doors closed the shaking guard could have sworn that three large ospreys had taken flight where the three young maidens had stood.

The brothers rested in the topmost branches of a tree that

would have dwarfed the great world-tree of the northern folk. It rose up for many lengths, bare of both branches and leaves. Its crown, however, spread out in a flat expanse of green. The broad upper branches supported whole colonies of birds and even a small family of tiny men-like creatures covered with fine fur. Several times these creatures had attempted to steal the Apples, but Brian had struck one with his huge pinion, sending the animal tumbling and screaming to the ground far below.

Brian stood and stretched his wings, opening them to the golden ball of the sun. Suddenly he stiffened. Three tiny specks were angling out of the sun. He squinted into the harsh light; these birds moved with unusual determination ...

His cry brought his brothers to their feet. 'Ospreys. Changelings!' He gripped the large Apple in his claws and set off for the shore as quickly as his heavy burden would allow.

The ospreys had recognised their target. Their flat yellow eyes narrowed, and their metallic claws flexed.

It was a race for the shore and the *Watersprite*. The brothers pushed on, but they were exhausted with the weight of the Apples and the battle, whilst the ospreys were fresh and unencumbered. Gradually, length by length, the ospreys gained on the hawks.

As they reached the shore, Brian dropped from the skies, falling downwards in a slow spiral. The larger of the three ospreys broke formation and followed him down, claws outstretched to rend and tear. Abruptly, Brian folded his wings and plummetted, and the osprey, already angling for the kill, overshot, and was now in front and a little above him. The hawk's great wings opened and beat air, once, twice, thrice, and lifted. Its razor bak flashed golden in the sunlight and came away crimson and the osprey crashed to the beach in an untidy tumble of wings. As it struck the golden sands, its shape dissolved and the shattered body of a delicately pretty maid lay broken upon the shore.

The remaining two ospreys had almost caught the hawks,

18

unaware of their sister's demise. With claws wide they prepared to strike, but suddenly they were buffetted from behind by a powerful pair of wings. Dazed and unco-ordinated they tumbled about whilst getting their bearings ... but in that time, Iuchar and Urchar were upon them and two bloody carcasses fell to the sands below. They too, like their sister, resumed their original shape.

The three brothers hung motionless above the slain maidens on the beach.

'We have paid a high price for these Apples,' said Iuchar sadly.

'Will all the talismans be as expensive?' asked his twin.

'Let us hope not,' whispered Brian softly. 'Let us hope not.'

A day and a half later, the *Watersprite* rested in the sparkling waters of the Aegean, the purple and gold cliffs of Greece shimmering in the early afternoon sunlight.

Brian stood at the bow of the ship staring out across the waters; his brothers joined him.

'We will try a different ploy this time,' he said, 'and perhaps we can avoid bloodshed.'

Iuchar shook his head. 'This quest was founded in blood ...'

'... And in blood it will end,' finished his brother.

'Well then, let us make sure that it is not ours,' finished Brian. He turned to the figurehead. 'Take us into the shore.'

The sons of Tureen took the guise of poets and bards and made their way to the court of Tuas, King of the Greeks. And there they were made welcome, for Tuas was a man of learning and delighted in the tales and sagas of distant lands.

The three brothers waited their turn in the outer chambers whilst the bards and minstrels, poets and harpers of many lands and many colours made their way through the court, each one entertaining the king for one night with their tales of music, poetry or song. If the king found their

19

work acceptable, they were richly rewarded, but even if it did not, he often spent time with the artist correcting errors in his work, a note here, a rhyme there, until both Tuas and the artist were well satisfied.

At last came the brothers' turn. They made their way through the crowded corridors and into the great open inner court. Ambassadors of many lands were there; tall ebon men with flashing eyes and teeth; dwarfed swarthy men, with dull eyes and lowering brows, very much like the Fomorians, blond-haired and blue-eyed giants conversed with hawk-faced, hook-nosed lords whose shining hair and beards lay curled upon their fantastically embroidered robes.

As the brothers made their way through the crowded court, the conversations, held in a score of languages and signs, died as the three proud-featured men passed. The brothers had not the appearance of either bards or poets. Standing as tall or indeed taller than most of the assembly, the bulging muscles of their uncovered arms and legs proclaimed them warriors; their gait - swift and sure, yet almost silent - told of their confidence and their gaze proclaimed them lords.

Tuas leaned across and spoke to his chamberlain. 'These are not poets; where do they hail from, and what are their names?'

'They say they are the sons of Tureen, a lord of the Tuatha De Danann, in the land of Banba, which is the furthest island of this continent. In that country sire, all the poets and lords are warriors. It is a rough and violent land and many of their lays are dirges and their sagas dark and gloomy, full of death and destruction and over it all hangs the dark harpie-like shadow of the Morrigan, the goddess of Death.'

Tuas nodded. 'It will be interesting to see what they bring with them, these warrior-bards of a barbarous land.'

The brothers bowed to the King of Greece, and Brian stepped forward.

'My lord, we have come from the furthest part of this

20

continent, drawn by the reputation of both you and your court. The reputation of Tuas, Scholar-King of Greece has spread even to Banba's misty shores.'

Tuas inclined his head, secretly pleased that his reputation as a scholar had spread so far. 'You bring some examples of your work with you?' he asked.

Brian nodded and began one of the High Sagas of the Tuatha De Danann, which told of an episode in the history of the People of the Goddess and the ancient Fir Bolg. His voice rang out strong and clear in the silent hall and though there were many there that did not understand his tongue, they could appreciate the mastery with which Brian recounted the tale.

Iuchar and Urchar followed him, recounting the tale of the sons of Fearchar who loved the maiden Nerba and who fought and killed each other for her. And though their voices were almost matched, still that slight difference between them, as they sang both parts, made the ancient saga come alive.

And then the three sons of Tureen sang a marching song of the Formorians and sang it with such gusto that some of the assembly joined in the chant.

The sun, which had been at the king's back, had moved across the skies whilst they sang and declaimed and now hung low in the heavens bathing the king in warm amber light. Slowly it sank and the hall drifted into shadow. The sconces were lit, illuminating the corners with wavering light and the pungent odour of herbs.

As the last notes of the march faded into the creeping night, Tuas raised his head. 'Are all the bards and poets of your isle as good as you?' he asked.

'Why lord,' laughed Brian, his voice still strong and clear even after a day's chanting and singing, 'in our land we are accounted poor bards, and our voices lack the clarity and strength of the professional poets.'

Tuas shook his head, his grey-shot hair glittering in the torchlight. 'But you must be rewarded.' He turned to his chamberlain. 'Let three skinfuls of gold be measured and given to the sons of Tureen.' He turned back. 'Go, claim your reward.'

As they left, the assembly stamped their feet, acclaiming their performance. The brothers followed the chamberlain, a tall grey warrior with the scars of many battles upon his arms and face, down a long and straight corridor behind the throne.

At intervals they passed guards, their tall plumed helmets brushing the ceiling, their short swords and tall, broad-bladed spears naked in their hands. At the end of the corridor behind a huge iron-studded door lay the treasury of Tuas. The chamberlain led them through room after room piled high with treasures from all parts of the known world: gold, silver, orchilurum, copper, bronze, iron and a dark blue nameless metal lay piled haphazardly. Gemstones, diamonds, rubies, sapphires, topaz and a dark green stone which reminded Brian of the fields of Bamba were strewn about the floors. And on the walls were swords and shields, spears and knives, helms and greaves, which the chamberlain told them contained various magical powers. Shimmering tapestries hung on the dark walls, the colours shifting and changing in the light of the torches. In the last room was a massive set of scales and pegged to the wall the stretched skin of a pig. The head of the animal had been mounted upon the opposite wall. Its tusks were almost as long as Brian's forearm and as thick as his wrists. The skin was bigger than that of the largest horse.

The chamberlain pointed to the skin. 'Perseus, who slew the gorgon, is said to have slain that beast.'

'By Danu and the Dagda,' exclaimed Iuchar, 'I have never seen anything like it.' He paused and added, 'But it bears a faint resemblance ...'

'To the clan of Cian, Cu and Ceithne,' finished Urchar.

The chamberlain removed the skin from the wall and ordered one of the two guards to fill it with gold. Brian ran his calloused hand down the length of the skin admiring its flawless beauty. Abruptly he grabbed it, pulling it from the guard's grasp. The chamberlain shouted and reached for his

22

sword, but his cry ended abruptly as Iuchar struck him across the head with the flat of his sword.

But the alarm had been raised and the corridor echoed to the pounding of booted feet.

Iuchar and Urchar stood in the door whilst their brother engaged the two guards already in the room. They were taller than Brian, but encumbered by their breastplates and helms, whilst he was clad only in a short-sleeved jerkin and woollen leggings. However, he was also unarmoured. Behind him, metal rang on metal as his brothers engaged more guards.

He tripped the first warrior as he lumbered by, sending him sprawling across the massive scales. The second guard lunged and the point of his blade opened a shallow wound along Brian's forearm.

Brian sidestepped – and then he stumbled on some of the gold that littered the floor. With a roar of satisfaction the Greek held his sword high and prepared to bring it down in a decapitating stroke.

And then he stiffened as Urchar's sword struck him across the base of his neck.

Iuchar and Urchar were bleeding from a score or more of shallow wounds and cuts and Urchar sported a dark, angry bruise on his chin, where the shaft of a thrown spear had struck him. The Greeks had withdrawn to the end of the corridor and seemed to be regrouping.

'I don't like to say this brother,' said Iuchar.

'But we're trapped,' finished his twin.

There was only one way out of the gold room and that was along the corridor, a corridor that was now filled with most of the palace guards. Abruptly the massed warriors at the end of the hall parted and a figure, tiny in comparison with the rest, appeared. It was Tuas the king.

'There is no escape,' he called. 'Come forth now, and at least you will die like warriors and not like trapped animals.'

'He has a point,' murmured Urchar.

'So what do we do brother?' asker Iuchar.

Brian finished folding the pigskin and then tied it about

23

his waist, leaving his hands free. 'You must follow my lead,' he said. 'Sheath your swords so the Greeks can see them. And you luchar, fetch me the chamberlain's sword whilst you each take one of the guards' swords. Now hold them flat against the back of your leg . . . and try not to stab yourselves in the shin when you walk,' he added with a grin.

The sons of Tureen walked down the long corridor to join the king and his warriors, their swords visible and in their sheaths, but hidden along the back of their legs were the weapons of the slain guards.

Tuas shook his head as they neared. 'It pains me to order such fine poets and bards slain; but why, why did you attack my chamberlain and guards. Was it gold? You only had to ask and it was yours. Why?'

'It was the pigskin, my lord and we did not think you would grant us that.'

Tuas shook his head. 'It has always bred sorrow. For a magical healing treasure, it has always brought bloodshed with it.' He sighed, and continued, 'But you have broken my laws and thus you must die, but at least you will die by the hand of a king.' He held out his long slim hand - a poet's hand, a dreamer's hand - and a warrior placed his sword in it. 'Come forward.'

Brian bowed and stepped closer to the king. In one fluid movement he brought his sword up and impaled the king upon the point.

For a moment confusion reigned, but that was all the time the sons of Tureen needed. Striking forth left and right they cut a bloody swath through the massed warriors until they reached the throne room. Many of the ambassadors were still present, puzzled at the sounds of battle that echoed from behind the throne, when suddenly three wild-eyed and bloody warriors appeared and fled through the halls like daemons of the pit. Even hardened warriors shrank back from them - for they had the stink of death about them.

The brothers raced down empty corridors, followed by the slow booming of a great bell. The walls were deserted and the gates unguarded; they fled through the dark streets, still hot after the day's sun, but every living soul ran from them, terrified at their appearance. By the time they reached the harbour, the word had spread and the brothers found the wharfs empty save for the huge rats.

Iuchar ordered the craft to put to sea, whilst Brian covered Urchar with the pigskin. The skin glowed with a soft bronze-gold light and Urchar felt a million ants walking over his skin. But it healed his wounds, leaving the flesh unscarred and unmarked. Brian treated Iuchar, and then allowed his brothers to lay the skin over him. He felt it drawing away his fatigue, wiping the wounds clean from his flesh.

But the pigskin could not remove the wounds of his mind and it could never wipe clean the shocked accusation that had burned in Tuas' eyes as Brian killed him; a look of betrayal. It was a look he would never forget.

'It's flat,' said Iuchar, picking up a handful of sand and letting the golden grains trickle through his fingers.

'It's Persia,' said Urchar, 'what do you expect?'

The three brothers tramped up the smooth beach, the fine sand billowing in their wake. It had taken the *Watersprite* two days to reach this lonely bay on the deserted shores of Persia. Two days in which the sea had foamed white before their ship's bow as it sliced through the waves with ever increasing speed; two days in which they had been forced to cling to the mast lest they be swept overboard by the stiffening winds.

'I'm hot,' said Iuchar petulantly.

'And thirsty,' added his twin.

'By Babd and Morrigan!' Brian exploded, 'Will you two shut up.' He swore as he sank into a soft patch of sand.

Iuchar looked at his brother and nodded silently. Brian had been withdrawn and moody since they had stolen the pigskin from Tuas and he seemed to have assumed the burden for the king's death.

The three brothers clambered up the first of the rolling

dunes and stood, staring out over the gently undulating landscape. In the distance a range of low purple mountains shimmered behind a haze, making them seem unreal and artificial. A tiny thread of road, bone-white in the harsh sunlight cut across the dunes towards the speck of a city that nestled amidst a sudden explosion of greenery.

Brian wiped the back of his hand across his forehead and squinted into the impossibly blue sky; there was not a cloud in sight - he wondered if it ever rained in this land. He pointed towards the distant city.

'Our destination.'

The sons of Tureen estimated it would take them three days hard marching to reach the city; six days later they still hadn't reached it. Distances were deceptive and although in the mornings the city walls seemed but a day's journey away; by evening they had always dwindled and seemed as distant as ever. What little food and water they had ran out after three days, but they were warriors and used to marching on little or no rations. And they reckoned they would soon reach the city.

They were wrong.

The heat baked them dry and the sun boiled them. The breeze blowing in from the desert was straight from the pit. Their flesh blistered, their tongues swelled and their lips cracked and by the seventh day, they were close to death. They knew they would not survive another night in the open without food or shelter.

But they were the sons of Tureen, princes of the Tuatha De Danann and warriors of Banba; they would struggle on - to the end.

They spent that last night huddled together in the lee of a dune, shivering in the chill desert air.

And had Brian tears to weep, he would have shed them.

Brian groaned and tried to move his arm. He had lain on it through the night, and it was numb. He winced with the agony of returning circulation. He eased his back from the hard-packed sand - sand that had been so soft and comfortable the night before, but which had now assumed

26

the consistency of rock. He lay there, surprised that he had lived through the night, dreading to open his eyes and look into the merciless sun which the Persians worshipped as a god. And then he suddenly realised there was no sun on his face, although he was facing into the east. Cautiously, he attempted to ease open his tired eyes, but they betrayed him and he blinked. His sudden shout brought both his brothers awake, their weapons in their hands, and their backs to the sand dune.

Before them were a score of mounted warriors.

The two groups faced each other silently. The warriors were clad in loose white robes, although armour glinted underneath, and were mounted upon tall, fine-boned white steeds. Conical metal helmets covered their skulls and a flap of cloth was drawn across the lower halves of their faces. They carried long barbed spears, and short curved swords were thrust into their belts alongside flame-edged daggers.

The sons of Tureen were exhausted and clad in rags and the flesh of their hands was so cracked and blistered that they could barely hold their swords.

One of the riders walked his horse forward until he was almost touching Brian. 'You will ride with us,' he hissed in a flat monotone.

The palace of the Persian king was impressive – far more impressive than the rather simple beauty of the Greek theatre, or the rough stone forts of Banba. Deeply incised reliefs decorated the smooth stone walls, depicting the gods and heroes of the Persian pantheon. Beautifully worked carpets covered the polished floors and woven wall hangings of brilliant and metallic decorated the walls.

The brothers were housed in a suite of rooms overlooking a small enclosed garden. Tiny fountains sprayed perfumed water high into the air where it shimmered in miniature rainbows and the air was heavy with the scents of a thousand colourful blossoms.

27

Once again, they had presented themselves as wandering poets drawn to the Persian court by rumours of the great generosity of the king and his reputation as a patron of the arts.

And now, several days since their rescue from the desert, bathed, well-fed and clad in comfortable robes, they awaited an audience with the king.

Iuchar sat on the balcony, putting an edge on his sword with a whetstone, watching the movement in the courtyard below. The Persians had been reluctant to allow them to keep their weapons, but Brian had pointed out that a man could not truly call himself a warrior unless he was armed and he also hinted that the sword was a powerful religious symbol in their own land.

'There are guards below,' said Iuchar.

Brian nodded. 'They have been gathering since dawn; I think the king must be coming.'

'Or else they are coming for us,' added Urchar. 'Do you think they suspect?' he asked Brian.

'They may. If their court magicians are any good – and I'm told they can work wonders with fire, and that the stars are an open book to them – and if the magicians of the Orient have warned their brethren of the theft of the Apples, or those of Greece of the death of Tuas and the loss of the pigskin, then it is entirely possible that they know.'

'So we might be walking into a trap?'

'We might,' agreed Brian.

'Well, I think it's too late now,' said Iuchar. 'A squad of the palace guard have just mounted the stairs on their way up here.' He stood and slid his sword into its sheath, checked his dagger and slipped them both under his robe.

The door opened and a warrior with the sunwheel crest on his breastplate entered. 'You will accompany me; I am to lead you to his majesty,' he said. And then he added with just the slightest sneer, 'He wishes you to recite for him.'

They were led down into the gardens and through an ornate gate into the private garden of Pezaer, King of the Persians. He was seated on a huge crystal throne before a gilded fountain and surrounded on either side by his concubines and guards.

Brian bowed to the king. 'Sire, we are honoured.'

Pezaer, a huge corpulent man, with signs of dissipation upon his broad fleshy face, looked bored and barely inclined his head. 'You are poets: recite.'

Brian glanced at his brothers, warning them to say nothing and stay alert. Something was wrong. He breathed deeply and began a long epic about the early days of Banba, in the time before man.

The king ignored Brian and continued to whisper with a young boy sitting at his feet. The painted youth giggled and simpered through Brian's performance and watched the De Danann prince through indolent eyes.

'Stop!' Pezaer suddenly screamed. 'Stop this farce. Take them!' He stood and waved at his guards. 'I know what you have come for,' he snarled at Brian, spittle foaming at the corners of his mouth. 'Look!'

A guard handed the king a spear. It was almost as tall as the monarch, with a staff of dull green metal. The head was broad and flat with a hollow point.

Brian slipped his sword from beneath his robe and heard his brother's weapons slide free. The king jabbed at Brian, who blocked the thrust with his sword. But when the head of the spear touched Brian's sword, it exploded in a shower of metal droplets. The head of the spear glowed white-hot and hissed and spat like an angry cat. Brian backed away from the king nursing a numbed arm and shoulder and brushed stinging flecks of metal from his cheeks and forehead.

Pezaer lunged again and the point of the spear, hissing like a serpent, passed over Brian's head, crisping his hair.

The sons of Tureen backed away from the king and his guards. But the latter seemed to be hanging back, letting the king make the kill. Brian looked into the monarch's fevered eyes and drawn lips and he knew the reason why: here was a man who delighted in inflicting pain and killing.

Brian ducked another wild blow and, with a trembling

29

hand, pulled off his cloak and held it loosely in one hand.

Iuchar and Urchar stopped suddenly. Warriors had come in through the small garden gate and were now behind them; they were surrounded.

'You are trapped, barbarians – and you will feed the firespear, the Weapon of Mithra.' Pezaer touched the point of the spear against the branch of an ornamental tree. The spear crackled and the branch abruptly blazed into light grey ash. 'There is no escape.'

The king spun the spear about his head, until the point glowed white-hot and hissed angrily. The very air about the monarch tingled and crackled with suppressed power and the taste was metallic in Brian's mouth. Abruptly, the king lunged. Brian fell to one side, bringing the cloak up and wrapping it about the spearhead. The thick cloth burst into flames which shot upwards and into the king's face. Pezaer screamed as his oiled beard caught fire and enveloped his head in a ball of fire. Dropping the spear, he clawed at his face, his screams of agony rending the peace of the garden.

Brian dived for the spear, catching it well down its length, away from the head which had already crisped and seared the hard earth. A guard pushed the king aside and stabbed at the Banban warrior with his sword. With a desperate effort, Brian threw himself to one side, the edge of the sword scraping down his arm and brought the spear up, impaling the guard in an explosion of bubbling metal and seared flesh.

Iuchar and Urchar attacked the guards, hacking a bloody path through to the gate. The Persians fell back, confused and demoralised at the death of their king and the loss of the Spear of Mithra.

Brian swung the weapon back and forth, weaving an intricate pattern of flaming death. Whatever the spear touched, metal, stone or flesh, it immediately burst into flames or ran in slow bubbling streams.

The sons of Tureen ran down the long leafy walks, leaving a trail of destruction in their wake. Trees and shrubs lay in charred ruins and crisped cinders. They cut down the guards and entered the palace, making their way down the corridors towards the stables. Behind them, doors of beaten gold and worked bronze were rendered into bubbling pits of metal; antique wall-hangings crisped and fell in wreaths of oily smoke and even the very stones glowed red and then white hot with the touch of the spear.

Once they reached the stables utter confusion reigned. Pages ran to and fro trying unsuccessfully to quieten the horses maddened by the stench of burning and the heavy smoke. Iuchar pulled three horses from their stalls and slipped their ornate harnesses over them whilst Brian and Urchar kept watch. They mounted the skittish beasts and trotted through the stables towards the main gate.

As they neared they could see the flurry of activity around the winches that opened and closed the huge gates. As one the brothers dug in their heels and galloped towards the rapidly closing exit. They had barely a few lengths to go before the guards spotted the three madly charging barbarians on the snow-white mounts of the king. One screamed a warning and attempted to pull Iuchar from his saddle as he galloped past. But Brian touched him with the spear, engulfing him in a ball of flame.

Iuchar and Urchar came off their horses at one moment and attempted to pull back the great brass-shod bar that had been rammed home across the closed gates.

'We'll never do it,' Iuchar panted, leaning his full weight against the bar.

'Back off,' ordered Brian, and rammed the Spear of Mithra against the bar. The wood exploded into a hail of firey cinders and the metal bubbled and spat. But the fire was almost immediately extinguished and although the bar was broken through, the door was only badly burned. Brian slid off his mount, tossed the reins to his brothers and ordered them to keep the massing Persians at bay. Then, standing firmly before the huge door, and shielding his eyes as best he could, he rammed the spear again and again against the solid wood.

The weapon hummed and hissed like a living creature

31

with a soul that exulted in destruction. The hardwood – imported from the east – burned with a thunderous roar, sending billows of thick smoke up into the hard metallic sky. Flakes of ash clung to Brian's face and settled on the smouldering remnants of his clothing.

Brian fell back as the heat became unbearable, spitting ash and blood. He dragged himself up onto his mount and called to his brothers, warning them to be ready.

Fire had almost completely enveloped the hardwood gates, climbing crazily from the blackened pit near the centre where Brian had struck it with the spear. The fire swiftly consumed the wood around the massive hinges until even they ran molten down the ruined gates. With a ponderous roar, the great gates collapsed down in a hail of smoke and fire – until it lay, the height of a tall man, across the opening.

'Go!' Brian screamed and kicked his heels in. The crazed beast lunged towards the flaming obstruction, until it seemed as if it were about to crash directly into it. But at the last possible moment, Brian urged it up – up and over. With a powerful surge the animal took flight over the barrier and out into the hot sands. Brian glanced back in time to see his brothers come sailing through the fire and smoke on their wild-eyed steeds.

The sons of Tureen paused as they crested the first of the dunes. A thick pall of smoke hung over the city and they could see countless tongues of fire licking high into the skies.

'It seems death is our gift to the peoples of the world,' whispered Urchar.

'Death and destruction,' agreed his brother.

Brian held the quiescent spear up to the light. 'Are we evil?' he asked, 'Or is it the artifacts we use?' He shrugged and, without waiting for an answer, turned his mount and headed for the shore, and the *Watersprite*.

The grizzled legionnaire eyed the three men standing

before him appreciatively. 'Ah, now here is something a lot better.' He knew professional soldiers when he saw them, having been one himself for almost twenty years before settling down and taking a commission in the army of King Doabre.

'Come to sign up, eh? Well, we can always use good men – all we are getting now are beardless boys and farmers and none of them can hold a sword.' He spat with feeling. 'Mercenaries!' He spat again and sighed. 'Just give your names and countries of origin. Although,' he added with a laugh, 'I doubt if either will be real.'

Brian stepped forward and leaned over the low table until he was face to face with the legionaire. 'We are the sons of Tureen. Brian,' he tapped his chest, 'Iuchar and Urchar,' he indicated each in turn. 'And though we may choose to hire our swords, we are not so free with our honour. Our names are real, as is our homeland. We are men of Banba.'

The legionnaire swallowed hard and nodded at the open-mouthed scribe to record the names and country. 'I cannot promise you much; food and drink and sometimes a dry place to sleep. But I can certainly promise you plenty of fighting. Doabre, the king, wishes to extend his borders – which is going to be difficult considering we're on an island, but before he tries that, he has to secure his own land, especially the mountains which hide bands of rebels. He must hold all Sigar before he looks across the seas.' He shrugged, and then stood and pointed down into the hollow where the camp sprawled. 'There is food down there if you want it, but no strong drink – we fight tomorrow. Get some rest if you can, you're going to need it.'

The sons of Tureen stayed with the mismatched mercenary army of Doabre of Sigar whilst the moon waxed and waned twice. The campaigns in the hills were bloody and sickening, little more than the massacre of unarmed peasants. There was one pitched battle in the foothills in which the sons of Tureen acquitted themselves with honour and held a bridge whilst the army retreated.

And because of that action, their courage in battle and

33

their proficiency with weapons, they rose through the ranks and quickly became part of Doabre's personal bodyguard.

As the second month drew to a close, Brian drew his brothers aside and suggested that if they discovered nothing about the horses or chariot in the next few days, then they might consider kidnapping the king and 'persuading' him to reveal their location.

Neither the horses nor chariot were kept in the camp, for they had searched it thoroughly, nor was there any mention of the talisman in the king's letters or books.

However, on the last day of the month, Doabre's spies finally succeeded in locating the rebel stronghold. They were camped on a small island off the southern coast of Sigar. The island, which had formerly housed a strange religious order of which nothing now remained save a massive ruin, was connected to the coast by a thin strip of land which was uncovered only at low tide. And even then the way was treacherous with shifting sands and patches that might swallow a man instantly.

For ten days, Doabre laid siege to the island, sending out squad after squad at low tide in an attempt to take the island fortress. But all the attacks failed and none of the mercenaries returned alive. The boats that were sent out were equally unsuccessful, for the currents were fast and unpredictable about the island and the craft were dashed to pieces on the rocks.

In desperation Doabre called his commanders together after the failure of his last attack in which he had lost almost a third of his remaining army. The mercenaries were sullen and dispirited, angry at the king's waste of good men. Some advised starving the rebels out, but Doabre was too impatient for that and, moreover, the island was capable of supporting a small community. A massed sea and land assault was suggested – but it seemed unlikely it would meet with much success. The only other alternative was to wait for the low spring tide – but that was almost half a year away.

'Can no-one here tell me what to do?' Doabre screamed,

his corpulent body quivering with rage, tears of frustration standing in his eyes.

'What we need,' said Brian lightly, yet watching the king all the time, 'is someone who can walk on water.'

The mercenaries laughed – until they saw the king's face. It was the face of a delighted child. 'Of course, of course,' he shouted. 'The chariot; yes we can do it.'

'I don't understand,' said Brian.

'"Someone who can walk on water",' Doabre repeated. 'Or rather, something – something such as a chariot crafted by the Other Folk and drawn by steeds that are half of this world and half of the Other World: steeds that can pull the chariot as easily across water as they can across land.' He sat back, his small black eyes glowing.

'My lord, do you possess such animals?' asked Brian carefully.

'I do, I do. They were gifts from my father and he had them from his father and so on, back through the generations. They were given to a distant ancestor of mine by one of the early gods.' He rose from the chair suddenly, sending it crashing backwards. 'Come, I will call them.' He almost ran from the tent, followed by a confused and sceptical group of warriors.

Doabre made his way through the scattered camp, down through a crack in the cliffs until he reached the shore. And there in the sheltered cove he raised both hands, palms upwards towards the skies and cried aloud in an alien tongue – and in that moment he no longer seemed a fat old man, but rather a godlike, primeval figure calling upon his subjects.

For a long time nothing happened, and just as the group was beginning to move restlessly, a tiny speck appeared on the horizon. The king pointed. 'Look, it comes.'

The chariot approached with amazing speed, driven by a tall, crimson haired youth, whose skin was bone-white, giving his head a skull-like appearance. But he handled the unnaturally thin and skittish animals with great care, and the utmost ease, bringing them to a gentle stop before the king.

35

Close up, the chariot was a masterpiece of elven art. Carved into the silvered wood were countless tiny pictures and glyphs that seemed to writhe and shiver with every movement of the chariot. The wheels were larger than normal and had only four spokes apiece. A covering of dark metal banded the wheels and set into the hub were slots where knives might be fitted in battle.

'Show them what they can do,' ordered Doabre. 'Bring it back and forth on the beach and into the water.'

Silently the charioteer wheeled the horses and brought the chariot around in a lightning fast turn, sending soft sand showering upwards.

As the chariot manoeuvred up and down the beach and out and over the waves, Brian drew his brothers aside. 'This is probably the only chance we'll have of stealing the chariot – and unfortunately I can think of only one way ...'

'That is?' prompted Iuchar.

'We are going to have to kill the charioteer.'

'Babd and Morrigan,' Urchar spat, 'are we warriors or butchers?'

'Well, if we must kill the charioteer, then we will kill Doabre also – without him, this army will fall apart, the mercenaries will return home and there will be a little less killing.' Iuchar looked at Brian and Urchar. 'Agreed?'

Silently, they both nodded.

The brothers swiftly moved out to a point on the beach where the chariot must pass as it swung in from the sea. They loosened their weapons and waited.

The elven charioteer brought the horses around in a tight circle, until the metal wheels actually cut the surface of the water, sending it showering upwards in a rainbow hued spray and then raced for the shore, demonstrating the speed and stamina of the half-elven mounts.

As the chariot neared, Urchar climbed up the cliff face and clung there out of sight – waiting. When the horses' hooves bit into the soft sand, Brian stepped forward and waved his hands. Swiftly, the chariot slowed, the horses changing from a gallop to a quick trot and then a walk with no apparent effort. Brian could see that they were unlathered and unwinded by their mad dash. The charioteer looked at him enquiringly and Brian pointed to the group standing in the distance.

And Urchar leaped.

He came down with his knee in the charioteer's back. There was a single sickening snap, and the elven youth went limp. Urchar searched the body for signs of life and, finding none, pushed the body from the chariot. Iuchar took the reins and attempted to learn the feel of the horses whilst Brian stood by their high-boned, almost skeletal heads, soothing them – and also to shield them from the king and his commanders further down the beach.

'Let's go,' said Iuchar, confident of the chariot and the horses' responses. Brian jumped aboard and drew his sword, holding it down by his side and Urchar drew his and stood at the other side of the chariot.

Carefully, Iuchar urged the half-elven steeds into a walk, a trot, and then a full gallop.

Doabre didn't realise until it was too late that the chariot careening madly towards him was not driven by its elven master. His eyes, weakened through excesses and old age, could just about make out the fast approaching shape. But as it neared and he squinted against the glare of the sand, he suddenly knew something was wrong ...

And then the chariot was upon him. He saw the glittering edge of a weapon come out of the mists that clouded his sight, and heard the keening blood-cry of a sword, and then ...

The head didn't stop rolling until it reached the waves.

The mercenary commanders fell back, stunned at the sudden assassination of their paymaster. But no-one made any attempt to attack the brothers – theirs were swords for hire, and their contract had just been abruptly terminated. They gathered on the beach, standing above the headless, bleeding body of Doabre, late king of Sigar, and watched the chariot disappear around the island.

*

'Hah, that was easy,' Urchar exulted from the bow of the *Watersprite*.

'Killing is never easy,' muttered Brian.

'But by killing the king, we saved greater loss of life,' argued Iuchar.

'And what does that make us? What are we to do then? Are we to wander through these barbarous lands, killing all whom we decide – *we* decide – are causing suffering and death. What are we then, the handmaidens of the Morrigan?'

'But we only had to kill two that time,' said Urchar. 'We killed many more to obtain the other Treasures, and ... Look.' He stood suddenly and pointed. 'The Golden Pillars.'

'I wonder how much we will have to pay for the seven pigs?' murmured Iuchar.

'Whatever we pay, the price will be too high,' added Brian.

Swiftly, the *Watersprite* swept in towards the twin isles of the Golden Pillars. Dusk was falling, but the last rays of the setting sun still touched the tips of the two mountains, striking fire from the gilded shrines to the Elder Gods.

And all along the shores of both isles were tiny points of light – torches. The sons of Tureen were expected and the islanders were gathered and waiting.

Brian ordered the *Watersprite* into the shore and, wearily, he and his brothers gathered up their weapons and prepared for battle.

The elven craft eased its way gently into the natural harbour. The people of the cliffs and beaches were silent, watching the enchanted craft work its way through the treacherous shoals and reefs. With a delicacy that made it seem as if a master helmsman were at the tiller, the craft barely touched the wooden pilings of the dock.

A single figure stepped out of the crowd and walked towards the craft bobbing on the dark oily water. He was a tall, grey-haired and bearded man, leaning on a thick staff. He raised a gnarled hand.

'Aesal of the Golden Pillars gives greeting to the sons of Tureen and honours their quest.'

The brothers' astonishment quickly turned to amazement as seven dusky maidens stepped out of the crowd, each one leading a tiny pig on a silver lead.

'My lord ...' began Brian.

Aesal shook his head. 'Do not thank me, but by the same token, do not think I fear you. I am an old man – death holds no fears for me, but I would not see you rend my tiny kingdom and slay my subjects. Take them, they are yours. We never had cause to use them. And now,' he said, changing the subject, 'you will honour us by breaking your journey and eating with us? We have, you see, prepared for your coming. Indeed, the whole continent is afire with tales of the barbarian princes who seem intent on capturing the elven artifacts of every nation and putting the ruler to the sword.'

'My lord,' Brian protested, 'I know it must seem that way, but that is not the truth. Let me explain ...'

'But not here, not here. Come.'

The sons of Tureen spent the night with the king of the Golden Pillars, feasting and taking their ease for the first time in many months and Brian explained how their quest had come about and the circumstances that had led to the killing of the three princesses of the Orient and the kings of Greece, Persia and Sigar.

Aesal ordered one of his scribes to set down the facts so that the sons of Tureen might be remembered in future ages with honour rather than with fear and loathing.

As the first grey fingers of dawn touched the eastern sky, the king asked Brian where their destination lay and what treasure they now sought.

'We are seeking a pup,' he said, 'but a dog that will grow into a beast that even the lion, the fabled king of all the animals, will obey. And to find this dog, we must journey to the land of ...'

'Of Irouad,' finished the king, staring deep into his goblet.

'You know of it?' Brian asked.

'My only daughter is the wife of Irud, the King of Irouad,' said Aesal sadly. 'But he is a hard-headed and strong-willed man; I doubt he will surrender the dog to you.'

39

'But surely he must, knowing that we will take the animal or die trying – and before we die we will slay many of Irud's warriors, and perhaps even the king himself.'

'He will not surrender the dog, unless ... unless I go and try to reason with him. He might listen to me: you must take me with you.'

Brian nodded. 'We will. We would prefer to be given the animal, but if we must fight for it, then we will do so ...'

Aesal grasped Brian's forearm and held it tightly. 'You must let me try to talk to him. If he will listen to me, then you can avert the bloodshed you detest.'

'If he will listen,' whispered Brian. 'If.'

The *Watersprite* rocked on the gentle swell outside Irouad's harbour. Across the entrance were anchored two huge warships and the cliffs above the harbour were dark with men and machines of war.

The three brothers stood in the bow of their craft and watched the small boat returning with Aesal. The young oarsman was obviously frightened, but trying to put up a brave front before the foreign daemons who slew kings and princes as if they were common beggars.

Aesal climbed aboard wearily and shook his head. 'He will not listen; he does not want to listen. He even admitted that the dog meant nothing to him, but he also said that he would not allow savages to frighten him.' The king shrugged. 'I also think he wants the honour of having been the monarch who slew the sons of Tureen.'

'He will not slay us,' whispered Urchar, gazing far out over the sea, 'we will not be slain by mortal men ...' His voice faded and was lost in the lapping of the waves. Brian and Iuchar shivered, for their brother was fey and sometimes had glimpses of the future, a gift he inherited from his late mother.

'What are you going to do?' Aesal wondered.

'There is little we can do at present,' said Brian. 'The harbour is blocked and the cliffs are manned. Squads of archers and slingers are camping on the beaches and the watchfires have been burning since they first sighted us.' He paused, and squinted into the horizon. 'But I think a storm is brewing and night will soon be coming on. Perhaps we will be able to do something then.'

'I think we'll have to do it quickly then,' said Iuchar, pointing off to the starboard side, where tiny specks dotted the horizon. 'Ships: Irud has called upon reinforcements and they will soon have us trapped.'

Brian gazed thoughtfully at the shore. 'Tonight then.'

The storm rolled in late in the afternoon, bringing with it flurries of ice-cold rain, the distant rumble of thunder and sudden flashes of lightning. By late evening, visibility had decreased and the shoreline was only a distant smudge sprinkled with the tiny flickering spots of watchfires.

The *Watersprite* drifted silently towards the shore, running contrary to both the wind and tide, until it rocked gently half a length from the rough beach. The sons of Tureen, clad only in loincloths, their swords wrapped in oiled sheaths, slipped easily into the chill water and swam for the shore.

They made their way past the first two lines of sentries, until they reached the perimeter of the camp. But here there were too many guards and warriors moving about and the light of countless campfires and hissing torches turned the whole area into a rough semblance of day. And here, cunning, rather than stealth, must take them through.

They slew three patrolling guards without a sound and quickly divested them of their clothing and armour. Then, moving quickly and confidently, they made their way through the camp towards Irud's huge and ornate tent in the centre of the camp.

'Halt; state your business with the King of Kings.' The young guard stared insolently at the three warriors clad in crude and ill-fitting garments. His companion grinned and leaned on the haft of his hooked spear.

41

'Well,' said Brian, in a barbarous accent. 'The King of Kings wishes to see us ... I think.'

. The guard laughed crudely and winked at his companion. 'And who might you be, that the Lord Irud wishes to see so badly?' He poked Brian in the chest with the butt of his spear.

'We,' said Brian, slowly and distinctly, all trace of accent now gone, 'are the sons of Tureen!' The guard reeled backwards as Brian struck him across the head and went crashing over into the tent. His companion doubled over as Iuchar kicked him in the pit of his stomach and pushed him on top of the unconscious guard.

Brian, Iuchar and Urchar slashed their way through the rich fabric and into the tent. They found themselves facing a very surprised and dishevelled young man. Behind him, a wide-eyed young woman cowered on the floor, the thick bed furs held tightly against her heaving breasts.

'Who ... What is the meaning of this?' Irud demanded.

'You must be Irud, King of Kings,' said Iuchar.

'And Lord of Irouad,' added Urchar.

'We are the sons of Tureen,' said Brian. 'I think you should get dressed.'

Getting the king out of the camp proved surprisingly easy. With Iuchar walking in front, Urchar behind and Brian by his side with a knife nestling against his ribs, they marched Irud through the rows of tents. Warriors bowed as their lord walked past and looked curiously at the three strange bodyguards, but no one made a move to question or hinder them.

Once they had passed beyond the confines of the tent, Urchar gagged the king to prevent him crying out and then half-carried, half-dragged him towards the shore. Irud's eyes opened wide and a strangled scream escaped as Iuchar and Urchar picked him up and tossed him bodily into the chill sea.

'Swim,' Brian ordered.

*

The morning broke bright and clear with a stiff breeze blowing in off the horizon. The craft they had spotted the previous night were much closer now and Brian estimated they would reach the *Watersprite* by mid-morning. He went aft to where Aesal was talking with his son-in-law.

'There is no dishonour in giving these men what they want,' he was insisting. 'I have given them the seven pigs. They have wrested by force the treasures of other kings, even if it meant slaying them. They have captured you and brought you through your camp and yet they might have slain you ... but they did not. Irud, I beg you, give them what they want – give them the pup, I do not want to see my daughter widowed so soon.'

'We must have the dog,' said Brian quietly. 'Do not force us to take it – or your life.'

Irud sat silently, staring towards the shore and then he sighed. 'I do not think you are mortal men. You must be gods, the sons of gods – or daemons – and mortal men, such as I, cannot resist the will of gods.' He turned away.

'You can have the dog. And now,' he turned and looked at Brian, 'what will you do with me?'

'Why, we will put you ashore.'

'I will have the animal sent to you,' he said bitterly. 'And then, go. Go!'

'We will.'

Water dripped in the darkness, but Lugh and his uncles, Cu and Ceithne, ignored it and concentrated on the bowl of ancient silver that lay on the low table before them. The light from the huge fire crackling in the hearth cast a ruddy glow on their faces as they bent over and stared intently at the oily liquid that nestled in the bowl. Gradually, the shadowy figures that had been illuminated in its depths faded and Lugh sat back with a sigh and wiped the sweat from his brow.

'So, they have the pup, the fifth treasure,' he mused.

'I didn't think they would get this far,' said Ceithne.

'They have not finished yet,' said Cu, moving over to the fire and warming his hands before the flames. 'They still have to find the cooking spit and give three shouts on Midcain Hill - and I do not think Midcain and his sons will allow that.'

'Nor I,' agreed Lugh. 'But we need those treasures and we need them now. The Fomorians are massing for another attack - and those treasures might just tip the odds in our favour. We must have them!'

'How?' Cu wondered.

Lugh remained silent for a while and then he stood and paced the hall. He stopped by the fire and stared deep into its depths, tiny fire-images forming and fading before his eyes, smoking shadow-wraiths rising up and vanishing: all part of the fire's magic.

'Sorcery; we must use sorcery.' He turned to his uncles. 'A simple spell, or rather, a double spell. The first part to induce forgetfulness about the cooking spit and the shout and the second part to bring on an intense longing for home.'

'Can you do it yourself,' asked Ceithne, 'or must you bring in a Druid?'

'I can do it myself.'

And a thousand leagues away, off the coast of Irouad, the sons of Tureen directed the *Watersprite* to return home to Banba, joyful that their quest was now complete.

The stone flags of Maecadre, the Great Hall of Tara, rang with the steps of the sons of Tureen. The crowded hall was silent, the atmosphere tense and expectant as Brian, Iuchar and Urchar stood before Nuada, King of the Tuatha De Danann.

'Our quest is complete, we have returned,' said Brian.

'We are pleased to see that you have returned safely; we have heard some whispers of your exploits - you have made

44

the very name of Banba one to be feared across the continent.'

'It was not what we intended.'

'You have the treasures?' asked Lugh, coming up behind the brothers.

'We have,' said Iuchar, turning to face him.

'I have seen some of the treasures outside ... but only some,' said Lugh, and then he added. 'I do not think you have completed your quest.'

'Beware,' whispered Brian in an icy tone, 'lest I stain Maecadre's stones with the blood of a De Danann prince.'

Urchar placed his hand on his older brother's arm. 'We have the three apples from the Garden of the Hesperides, the golden pigskin from the Land of the Greeks, the spear of Mithra from the Land of the Persians, the chariot and half-elven horses from the Isle of Sigar, the seven magical pigs gifted to us by Aesal of the Golden Pillars and the pup, presented to us by Irud, King of Irouad.' He paused, his brow furrowed briefly, but then he smiled. 'That is all, our quest is complete.'

And Lugh laughed, his laughter harsh and mocking.

'No, that is not all! You have forgotten the cooking spit of the women of Fioncure Isle, nor have you shouted thrice upon Midcain Hill. So, you are oath-breakers and liars as well as murderers.'

Nuada's shout silenced the sons of Tureen. 'Tell me,' he said to them, 'did you truly believe that the capture of the dog was the last part of your quest?'

'My Lord, that is so. Although ...' Brian paused, and Urchar continued. 'I felt - indeed, we all felt - that there might be something else, but we did not know what that might be, all we knew that we had to get back to Banba.'

The king nodded. 'I know you to be men of honour, I know you would not break your oath to complete the quest - at least of your own accord.' Abruptly the king stood, and called for Diancecht, his sorcerer-physician.

'Did you not say to me, not two nights past, that you felt sorcery afoot.'

The ancient Druid nodded. 'I tasted it on the air, sharp and acrid, with no trace of good in it – only malice.'

'Would it be difficult to cast a spell of forgetfulness coupled with a spell of longing for home?' Nuada wondered.

'No Lord, it is a relatively simple spell.'

'I thought so. Would Lugh be able to cast it?' he asked suddenly.

'He trained with me for a short time during his youth. Yes, he could do it.'

Nuada turned to Lugh. 'Did you cast such a spell, and before you answer, remember that you are in the Hall of Maecadre – do not lie to me.'

Lugh was silent, conscious of the eyes of all the lords of Banba upon him. And then he nodded briefly. 'We need those treasures in the coming battle,' he said defensively.

'You have dishonoured your name and that of your family,' said the king, his voice cold and hard, his eyes blazing. 'Your presence offends me – leave my sight!'

Lugh turned away and as he reached the door, he looked back at the king and the sons of Tureen. 'But they must complete the quest,' he insisted maliciously. 'They must.'

'We will,' said Brian quietly, 'we are not without honour.' He turned and bowed to Nuada and then, followed by his brothers, walked from Tara's Great Hall.

The isle was not listed on any mariner's maps or charts and although they haunted the seaport taverns they could find no-one who had even seen it. Oh, many had heard of the fabled Isle of Women, inhabited by the fairest of all the elven women, all maidens, but nevertheless skilled in all the arts of love.

'It sounds like a sailor's dream,' Iuchar remarked when he heard the story.

His twin nodded. 'A sailor long at sea, imagining fishes to be maids and weed to be monsters. Is it any wonder that he would create an island populated with the most beautiful maids awaiting him – and just beyond the horizon?'

'But it must be there,' Brian snapped, bending over a

cracked and rune-incised chart. 'It must be there.' He tapped the chart again in the space between the irregular mass that was Alba and the oblong that was Banba.

'Could it be confused with Mona?' asked Iuchar, pointing to the isle between the two.

'I've never met any beautiful maids on Mona,' Urchar grinned, 'only dry and bitter Druids.'

'Well then, we'll go to Mona,' said Brian.

'But I've just said that there are only Druids there ...'

'If the isle is inhabited by elven maids and is not listed on any of these charts, then surely only the Druids can help us.'

'But why?' wondered Urchar.

'Because the isle must lie beyond the world of men, in the Shadowland!'

The Druids however, could not help them and the only mention of the isle was in an ancient fragment of verse:

> 'The Isle of Fioncure
> Rests not on Land
> Nor on Sea
> But in the Place Between'

The moon waxed and waned fully three times whilst the brothers cruised the chill waters between Banba and Alba, searching for the island. And with winter fast approaching, they knew they would soon have to abandon their quest and wait half a year whilst the seasons changed.

But one morning, with the sun pale and wan on the horizon and storm clouds massing in the west, a huge white bird came and settled on the *Watersprite*'s snarling figurehead. The sons of Tureen had never seen anything like it in all their travels. Its wingspan was twice that of even the largest bird and its flat and hard eyes burned with a strange intelligence.

It stayed motionless on the figurehead for most of the morning and then abruptly it took flight, veering away towards the east. Immediately, Brian ordered the *Watersprite* to follow. The bird continued east well into the afternoon, its huge, powerful wings carrying it effortlessly against the stiffening wind. And then towards evening it stopped and waited until the *Watersprite* was almost directly below it. Brian halted their craft. The bird circled overhead for a while and then, with a hoarse squawk, it dived into the sea – and did not reappear.

'I think,' said Brian slowly, 'we may have found the location of the Isle of Fioncure which …' he paused, and then finished, 'which is between the land and the sea!'

The brothers leaned over the side and stared down into the ebon, foam-lashed depths. 'So who goes down?' asked Urchar.

'I do,' said Brian and then waved his brothers to silence when they protested. 'I have been trained in the arcane arts, whilst only Urchar's foresight has been developed and Iuchar's ghostsight. Neither of you have either the ability or stamina to venture down.'

Reluctantly, the twins agreed and watched in silence as Brian prepared to descend in search of Fioncure.

He stood in the bow of the ship and held both his hands high, as if in prayer or offering and then he cried aloud in the tongue that was ancient before even the Nemedians came to Banba's shores. Hesitant blue tendrils of writhing fox-fire ran along his fingertips and gathered in the palms of his hands. Swiftly, he spun the blue fire together in a crackling web and then pulled his hands apart, stretching it. Deftly, he wove it until it resembled a rough sphere and then he cried aloud and the sphere solidified. It now looked like a rough diamond, cut and faceted, blue-veined and shining, with an open circle at one end.

They then collected long strands of seaweed and wove them into a complicated cross-hatched pattern. Brian stood whilst Iuchar and Urchar wound the weed around his arms and legs and finally set the crystal helmet on his head. With a whispered prayer to the Dagda and Danu, Brian slipped over the side and disappeared in a welter of bubbles into the darkness.

As he fell he spread his arms, feeling the seaweed inflate and help keep him upright. He whispered a word through gritted teeth and touched the helmet. Abruptly, the blue veins in the crystal flared into incandescence, illuminating the blackness all around him. He dropped his arms to his side and continued falling.

Unreal shapes darted before him and once a huge twisting figure slid past with fluid ease, its immensity terrifying him. Shifting tangles of slimy weed clutched at him like the fingers of drowned mariners and he fell through whole shoals of tiny fish, like a god through the world of men.

He had been falling for some time when he became aware of a growing illumination. He touched the crystal helmet and the ghostlight faded, leaving him alone in the growing twilight. He spread his arms and floated, staring down into the depths.

At first, he could see nothing and then gradually, as if seen through shifting smoke, a shape materialised, a shape Brian struggled to make out, until he realised he was looking down onto a mountain.

A mountain and the Isle of Fioncure.

Brian fell into Fioncure's clear morning, descending like a god from the heavens. He was aware when he passed the tip of the mountain that the water pressure and the bone-numbing chill were gone – but still he drifted down . . . and down.

The grass beneath his feet was cool and dry. Carefully, he removed the crystal helmet and breathed deeply of the fragrant air, savouring its sweetness. He walked uphill where, hidden by a low copse of trees, a thin thread of smoke spiralled upwards. He paused by one of the trees. It was small and delicate, with a soft spongy bark which yielded to his touch and broad flat leaves which quivered constantly.

The women of Fioncure were waiting for him as he rounded the copse. They were seated on the soft ground in a large open circle, weaving. They spun delicate tendrils of gossamer thread, weaving it into a faery tracery of captured light, but, try as he might, Brian could not see where the finished tapestry went. Certainly it did not gather about their feet as it should, nor was it piled anywhere.

As one, the women turned towards him and smiled. 'Greetings, Brian MacTureen. Welcome to the Isle of Fioncure where the Fate of Man is spun.'

Brian bowed and faced the woman who sat in the centre of the group near a low fire, turning a long spit which held a roasted carcass. 'My Lady, the sons of Tureen send you greeting.' And then he paused and added, 'But I fear my mission will make a mockery of any greeting we may exchange.'

The elven maid raised her long, slim hand. 'You need not continue; we wove your fate long ages past. Your striving, your joys and sorrows, your quest, your coming here, aye, and even your deaths were all foretold here.' She touched a long silken thread and then she stood in one fluid movement. She wrapped a dark cloth about the cooking spit and lifted it off the fire. With a long fork she picked the joint of meat off the spit and then handed the long shaft of metal to Brian.

'Take the spit and, with our blessings, take it as a reward for your endeavour. Now go,' she said suddenly, and resumed her seat, the joint of meat still held on the fork.

As Brian turned to go, she called to him. 'Are you hungry, would you care to join us?'

Slowly Brian shook his head, mindful of the warnings neither to eat nor drink with the elven folk. 'I am not hungry,' he lied.

The maid nodded. 'Perhaps it is just as well,' and then she added, almost wistfully, 'your quest has fed us well,' and sank her delicate, sharp teeth into bubbling flesh.

Brian retched, and then turned and ran from the presence of the women of Fioncure.

'So we are only puppets, playthings of the gods,' Urchar spat.

Brian finished sipping the hot broth Iuchar had prepared for him. 'So it would seem. The maid gave me to understand

50

that our fate had been spun and sealed long ago.'

'Have we no choice then?' argued Urchar. 'Must we now carry out this quest, are we tied to it, like animals to the seasons?'

'We are honour bound,' whispered Brian. 'We have little choice, little choice.'

Midcain Hill overlooked the cold waters of the Northern Seas, deep in the land of the Fomorians. A bleak and barren volcanic rock, pitted with crevasses marking the passing of the great ice flows during the harder winters, it rose, dark and forbidding on the sharp morning air.

And at the foot of the hill was an ancient dolmen and beside the dolmen stood a man.

The brothers rested on the stony beach. They had come armed and armoured, for the Hill of Midcain was said to be guarded by four warriors under a geas to allow no voice to be raised in joy or anger upon its slopes.

Brian loosened his sword in its scabbard and gripped his spear. 'I will talk with him; perhaps if I explain, he might allow us ...' he trailed off, realising how implausible it sounded.

The warrior stirred as Brian approached. He was a giant of a man, standing almost as tall as the dolmen, and topping Brian by a head. He leaned upon a huge double-headed battle-axe and glared at Brian through small dark eyes.

'Come no further,' he growled, his voice harsh and rasping, like an animal's. 'Speak your name, and state your reason for trespassing upon my mountain.'

'I am Brian, son of Tureen; yonder are my brothers, Iuchar and Urchar, and whilst we did not realise that this was your mountain, we have come to fulfil a quest.'

The giant moved, bringing the axe up in one easy movement, as if it weighed no more than a dagger. 'Ah, the sons of Tureen. I have waited for you.' He paused and spat at Brian's feet. 'The killers of my boyhood companion, Cian.' He spun the axe in one hand. 'I am Midcain of the Hill, and my sons and I are under a geas to keep this sacred place silent. But,' and he smiled with yellowed, broken teeth, 'I

51

will gladly break the holy silence with your screams.'

He lunged – and the battle-axe bit deeply into the ground at Brian's feet. Had he not thrown himself back, it would have split him in two. He blocked the next blow with the haft of his spear. The axe swung in low and then Midcain changed direction, striking upwards at Brian's head; the blade skimmed his face, lifting his hair as it passed. Brian jabbed at Midcain's stomach with the butt of his spear, doubling him up, and then reversed the spear and struck him across the nape of his broad neck as he fell. But the blow struck the giant across his mailed shoulders and the haft snapped. Midcain fell to one side, recovered quickly and struck upwards from a crouching position, almost disembowelling Brian.

The son of Tureen fell backwards, coming to his feet in a roll with his sword in his hand and his dagger resting lightly in his left hand. Midcain wove his axe to and fro, the broad blade catching the wan morning sunlight in a glittering, blinding display. The two warriors circled each other, cautiously jabbing, testing each other's strengths and weaknesses. Abruptly, Midcain struck, bringing the axe across in a huge scything sweep. Brian stepped back as the axe whispered past and then leaped inside the blow. His knife found Midcain's throat, whilst his sword sliced at the giant's wrist, almost severing it. Brian's hand was suddenly covered in thick, reeking blood, the knife felt slick in his fingers. Midcain's eyes bulged, he stiffened and then went limp as his life fluid pumped away.

On the hilltop, three figures rose and began to run down, the sunlight catching their armour and weapons.

Iuchar and Urchar joined their brother and Urchar's gaze was troubled. 'Our death approaches,' he whispered.

Brian cleaned his knife on a tuft of rough grass and watched the three sons of Midcain leaping from rock to rock, nearing them. 'Their anger will cloud their judgement and reflexes. They have just lost their father, that will demoralise them, and,' he laughed grimly, 'they have just run down a long hill. We have the advantage, let us make sure we keep it.' He stood as the three dark warriors slid to a halt before him and looked at their father's bloody corpse.

'You have killed him,' one accused Brian.

'In a fair fight.'

'We know you; you are Brian, Iuchar and Urchar, the sons of Tureen of Banba.'

'We are.'

'We are Corc, Conn and Aedh, the sons of Midcain of the Hill,' said the taller of the three warriors. 'You have added the death of our father to your other crimes.' He slid his sword free. 'And you must die.'

The sons of Midcain attacked them with an almost animal-like ferocity. They fought well into the morning and the sun rose over them and began to sink behind the hill in the early afternoon. Both sides had given and received wounds – wounds which would have slain a mortal man. But neither the sons of Tureen nor those of Midcain were truly mortal, for they were of the Tuatha De Danann and thus more akin to gods, and of the Fir Bolg and thus closer to daemons.

But towards the end, Urchar received a long shallow cut across one arm and another, deeper cut in his thigh. He fell back, desperately defending himself from Corc when his foot slipped on the gravel and he crashed onto his back. The son of Midcain straddled the fallen warrior and brought his sword high – and Urchar struck upwards with the last of his strength, disembowelling him in one blow.

Iuchar found himself up against Conn, who wielded a short sword and axe with terrible dexterity; the two weapons flickering and darting like serpents. Iuchar parried the sword on his knife and struck with his sword, but the blade struck ringingly against the axe-head. He twisted his knife and lunged, simultaneously chopping down with the sword. He scored a long flesh wound in Conn's thigh, but received a thrust through his right shoulder in return. They were almost evenly matched and whilst Conn might have the advantage of height and weight, Iuchar's reach was longer and he was stronger. And at last, his strength began to tell and Conn found himself more and more on the defensive. Both warriors were covered in sweat and bleeding profusely from a score of minor wounds.

Conn rallied the last of his strength and attacked. His sudden surge pushed Iuchar back, but realising that his opponent was on his last reserves of strength, Iuchar was content to let him wear himself down. Then he saw an opening. He lunged – and his sword penetrated Conn's throat; he died instantly – but his axe fell, severing Iuchar's ear and biting deep into his neck and shoulder.

Brian's opponent was Aedh, the eldest son of Midcain. Like his father, he stood a head taller than Brian and he was of a heavier build. He fought with a sword almost as tall as himself, a great broad-bladed weapon of some dark, almost stone-like metal, which struck sparks from Brian's rune-inscribed sword.

He found himself almost immediately on the defensive. Aedh's longer reach and the length of his sword effectively kept him at bay. Grinning triumphantly, Aedh played with Brian, as a cat will a mouse, the flickering black sword drawing a thin line across his forehead, cutting one cheek, and then the other, turning Brian's face into a red mask.

Both warriors could hear the cries of their brothers and the clash of metal on metal about them, but beside that, and the scuffle of feet on bare stone, the hill was silent.

Brian could feel his strength going and he knew he must attack soon, or else Aedh would wear him down and kill him slowly. With a desperate ferocity, he attacked. his sword blurred as he beat off Aedh's attack, darting, probing, testing, and then drawing blood along his opponent's forearm and across his chin. But the son of Midcain countered and the black sword seemed to come alive in his hands. He parried a blow and struck – and Brian felt the hot-ice of metal enter his chest high on his right side. He stood transfixed on the weapon, which exited above his collar-bone and for the first time Aedh laughed. 'You are dead, son of Tureen.'

But the laughter died in his throat as Brian, with the last

ragged remnants of his strength, struck the head from Aedh's shoulders.

For a long time after there was silence on the Hill of Midcain. Dark birds gathered and circled on the cold, sharp air, and then, taking courage from the lack of movement, swooped and settled by the blood-spattered bodies.

Suddenly one moved, and the carrion crows took to the air in ungainly flight. The figure, like a spectre of the battlefield, slowly and painfully raised himself on one arm, whilst the other held his chest where bright, thick, red liquid still glistened. Trying to breathe as little as possible, Brian dragged himself over to the body of his brother, Iuchar.

His face and neck were a welter of blood, for the falling axe had cut deeply into his neck and shoulder muscles. But when Brian touched his neck, he could feel the weak and ragged pulse-beat. Gathering what little remained of his strength and an ancient spell, he poured that strength into his brother.

Iuchar's eyes flickered open and he smiled weakly.

Both Brian and Iuchar dragged the stinking body of Corc off Urchar. When one discounted the amount of blood that was Corc's, Urchar seemed to have escaped unscathed. But there was no response when they attempted to rouse him and when Brian felt his pulse, he found it to be almost non-existent. Iuchar examined his brother's wounds more closely and found that the great artery in his thigh had been severed. He had lost a lot of blood and was very close to death.

Once again Brian summoned what little remained of his strength and, with Iuchar holding him, shared it with his brother, willing him to live.

For what seemed like an eternity nothing happened and then Urchar groaned.

Together, the three brothers staggered and crept and crawled up the Hill of Midcain, leaving a slick trail of blood to mark their passage.

The wind pulled and tugged at their stiff blood-soaked garments as they crested the hill. Supporting one another, they turned and faced back the way they had come, looking down the hill.

'We are Brian, Iuchar and Urchar ...'

'The sons of Tureen ...'

'Our quest is complete.'

Three shouts on the hill.

Ethne touched her father's arm, and pointed out to sea. Tureen shaded his eyes with a gnarled hand and stared out across the water. A small craft was rapidly approaching, running against both the tide and wind: the *Watersprite*.

With its sails billowing in no earthly wind, the enchanted craft rode up onto the beach with a tearing and scraping of hardened timbers.

Brian staggered from the craft. He was a terrifying sight, his clothes and hair matted and stiff with dried blood, his face haggard and drawn, and with the bright fire of fever burning in his eyes. He collapsed into his father's arms, whilst Ethne climbed aboard the *Watersprite* and tried to help her dying brothers.

'Father ... our quest is complete,' Brian managed to whisper through cracked and swollen lips. 'Take the cooking spit to Lugh and beg him for Tuas' pigskin ... only it can save us now ...' He sagged and Tureen gently eased his son to the ground, covering him with his cloak. Then, calling upon what he remembered of the Old Magic, he assumed the shape of a great, greying hawk. Clutching the cooking spit in its rough claws, the hawk took to the skies and headed north, for Tara.

Ethne tended to her brothers whilst her father was away, cleansing their wounds and cooling their fevers. But she knew deep in her heart that unless their father returned with the pigskin, her brothers would die.

Towards evening the great bird came winging out of the northern sky and came to rest by the three sleeping brothers. Ethne ran to her father and embraced him and then she drew back, an icy chill enveloping her, as she saw the tears in his old eyes.

'Did he . . .?'

Tureen shook his head. 'Lugh refused; he said my sons did not wish to save his father and he does not care to save my sons.' He shook his head and wept openly. 'He laughed as he condemned them to death.'

Brian opened his eyes and smiled through his pain and suffering. 'We were dying anyway – our fate was decided a long time ago. But at least we have completed our quest . . . our honour remains unblemished.' He reached out and took his brothers' hands in his. 'Our name will live on . . .' he sighed, closed his eyes and the three sons of Tureen died as they had lived – together.

Tureen cried aloud and fell to his knees before the still bodies. Ethne placed her hands on his shoulders and wept also. And then Tureen shuddered and fell forward across the bodies of his sons – dead of a broken heart.

Ethne stared out to sea, the wind catching in the long folds of her gown. The tears had passed and there was nothing left – nothing save a burning anger. She raised her eyes to the darkening skies and whispered to the wind,

'Although my father and brothers may be dead, the legend of the sons of Tureen is only beginning.'

CHAPTER 2

THE CHILDREN OF LIR
(The Second Sorrow Of Irish Storytelling)

The midwife stood before Lir, a cloth-wrapped bundle held in the crook of either arm. The king started awake, blinking in the early morning sunlight, rubbing the sleep from his eyes with a pale, long-fingered webbed hand. He stood stiffly and descended from the huge emerald, rune-carved throne. With infinite care, he pushed back the edge of the cloth that hid the babe's face.

'Twins again?' His voice – strong and booming, like the crash of the surf on the shore – held a trace of wonder.

The old woman's voice trembled as she spoke. 'My Lord, your queen has borne you two lusty male children.' She held one of the boys to the light and Lir could see the sharp elfin features, the slanting eyes and the green tinged skin. The midwife held up a tiny, perfectly formed hand – with webbed fingers.

For Lir was of the Tuatha De Danann and Lord of the Sea.

The king smiled as he took one of the tiny babes into his arms. 'And Eva, my queen, how is she?'

Abruptly, the midwife began to weep. Lir raised her head with one hand and gazed deep into her eyes, reading the truth that lay therein. 'The birth was not an easy one,' she sobbed, 'and the queen was not strong ...'

The king nodded slowly, his face expressionless, his eyes empty. And Eva's death was a reminder that although the De Danann were close to godhood, the Dark Lord could still claim them.

'Leave me,' he commanded, 'tend our ... my children.'

The midwife bowed and shuffled silently from the great hall.

Lir slumped upon the throne, his long thin fingers absently tracing the angular runes etched deep into the stone. He was cold, cold and ... empty.

He stood and went to stand by the high arched window, and stared out over the fields of ripening corn that lay below his hillfort. Tiny ant-like figures moved through the fields, their faint cries drifting up to him, shouts and commands, laughter and screams. They were untouched by his wife's death: life went on.

He suddenly sensed another presence in the hall and, turning with the sun still dazzling his tear-filled eyes, he cried aloud, for his wife stood before him!

'Father ...?'

'Fionuala!' He gathered his daugher into his arms and stroked her white-gold hair whilst she wept. The memory and image of Eva lived on in her only daughter; the high delicate elfin features, wide slanting blue-green eyes, innocent and all-knowing, girl and woman.

Lir and Fionuala stood silently by the window, staring out over the morning. Fionuala touched her father's arm and pointed. 'Look, Aedan is returning.'

A group of youths were running up the long winding path that led to the fort, with one far in the lead, a tall young man with a shock of white-gold hair.

Lir turned to his daughter. 'He does not know yet; will you tell him for me?' He paused and added softly, 'I cannot.'

Fionuala nodded.

'And you have two brothers to look after. See that they are well cared for and find wet-nurses for them: they are your mother's legacy to us.' And as his daughter turned away, the king added, 'Call the larger child, Fiachra, and the smaller, Conn. They were the names your mother had chosen should she bear twin boys.'

Without Eva, Lir found the White Fort cold and deserted.

He found it hard to accept that she was dead and would wander the lonely corridors half expecting to hear her laughter behind him or her light footfall on the stair. And then for him, she began to live again. He saw her in every corner, smelled her scent in every room, heard her voice by his side, felt her presence in his bed. At last he could stand it no longer and, taking his children and servants, set out for the palace of Bove, his father-in-law.

Away from the White Fort, Eva's ghost ceased to haunt him and the children of Lir saw their father begin to smile again.

Although the king had planned only a short stay at Bove's palace on the banks of the Sinann, the months slowly passed and he felt no inclination to leave, for he was loath to return to the White Fort with its memories and ghosts.

And there was Aefe.

She was half-sister to Eva, but whereas his late wife had been a creature of the light and day, Aefe was at one with the night.

He had first met her whilst out hunting with Bove. She had come flitting through the dark wood like one of the Sidhe folk, her long dark hair loose and flying behind and a bloody hunting spear in her hand. Behind her had come her servants carrying the spitted body of a boar.

Her wild dark beauty had first attrracted Lir, her easy laughter and skill with weapons. She often joined him on his forays into the surrounding countryside and she never failed to kill. On more than one occasion Lir remarked on her ability to attract the great wolves or deer, bears or cats to her.

And as the months passed, Lir fell more and more under the spell of this strange woman, more at home in the woods than in the dwellings of the De Danann.

They were wedded on Beltave Eve, when the first of the watch fires burned across the hills.

Lir took Aefe back to the White Fort and life quickly returned to the place. Eva's ghost no longer haunted it, and the only echoes in the corridors now were the happy shouts of his children. Aefe was more than a mother to the four and treated them as if they were her own - for she was fully confident that with the passing years she would bear Lir children and then they would rule, rather than Eva's children.

But the years passed and Aefe remained childless and it was whispered that she had trafficked with deamons in her youth and they had rendered her barren. She took counsel with the Druids, and read the stars and entrails of animals. But there were no children in her future.

She took to watching her husband when he was with his children and the love he bore them rankled within her like a festering sore. She imagined he loved them more than he loved her; her jealousy turned to fear and her fear turned to an all-consuming hatred.

One morning in late autumn, Aefe rose early and crept from the chilly bedchamber. The corridor was deserted, although faint in the distance she could hear the first stirrings of the servants. She stole down the dim corridor until she came to Fionuala's room. She stood outside, listening. There was no sound within, so silently she undid the latch and entered.

Fionuala lay asleep on the furs beneath the window, her childlike features relaxed, her white-gold hair spread like a banner about her head. Looking at her, Aefe was suddenly reminded of her half-sister: this was why Lir loved his children so. They were a constant reminder of his dead wife. She fingered the bronze dagger beneath her cloak. She could strike now - it would be so easy and Lir would be hers.

But Fionuala and her brothers were of the Tuatha De Danann and their blood would cry out for revenge. She could not - must not - slay them. As she stood over the bed, the naked dagger gleaming ruddy in the first shafts of sunlight, a flock of birds rose wheeling and diving from the lake below the fort. In that instant a plan was born. Silently she turned and slipped from the room.

And Fionuala's blue-green eyes snapped open.

*

61

'Father, must you go?'

Lir kissed his daughter and brushed a strand of hair from her forehead. 'Yes Fionuala, you know I must; this boar must be slain before it kills again. I shouldn't be gone long.'

'Father ...' began Fionuala.

Lir paused by his chariot. 'Yes daughter, what is troubling you?'

She glanced over at her stepmother who stood deep in conversation with her ladies-in-waiting. At that moment her three brothers joined her.

'Nothing father. I ...' She gathered her two younger brothers in her arms and Aedan stood by her side. 'We will miss you,' and she added gently. 'We love you.'

As Lir wheeled his chariot out of the high gate, he called one of his young knights, a charioteer named Daire, whose father was of the De Danann but whose mother was of the race of Man.

'My Lord?'

'Daire, you are close to my daughter; how has she been of late?'

'Quiet, my Lord. But if she is troubled she will not admit it.'

'She is proud - like her mother.' He turned and looked back at his four children and then at their stepmother in the background. 'Stay with them Daire, I will feel happier if you do.' He shrugged. 'There was a curious air of finality about our parting. It may be nothing ... but my wife has been acting strangely of late. Stay, be my eyes and ears here whilst I am gone.'

Daire saluted. 'Trust me, my Lord.'

The king smiled. 'I do.'

'Fionuala, where is father going?' asked Conn as the last of the horses and chariots disappeared down the long road.

'He has gone south into the marshes; there is a wild boar there which has killed both men and beasts and destroyed crops. Father must kill it.'

'He will,' said Conn, full of boyish enthusiasm. 'I hope he brings me back the tusks.'

'You got the tusks last time, this lot are mine,' said his twin, Fiachra. He turned and lowered his voice. 'Look, Aefe is calling us.'

The queen stood on the bottom step, below the great bronze doors. Her gown of crimson shimmered in the early morning light, its colour matching that of her lips and long nails. Her raven hair had been piled high atop her head and held in place with a pair of ruby-tipped pins which sparkled like tiny drops of blood. As the four approached, one of her ladies brought the queen her riding cloak and placed it about her shoulders.

'Come children, this day has promise, let us not waste it. I have had provisions prepared; let us ride north and we can break our fast by Derravaragh Lake. What do you say? We have not ridden together for a long time,' she added.

'Mother, I do not think ...' began Fionuala anxiously, but the two younger boys were already running towards the stables. Aedan looked curiously at his sister and then he turned and followed his brothers.

Aefe came and stood beside Fionuala. 'Why do you not like me, child?'

'You are my stepmother, I ... I love you.'

Aefe gripped Fionuala's shoulder with a long nailed hand that brought a gasp of pain from the girl. 'Do not lie to me,' she spat. 'You -and your brothers - you all hate me.' She stared deep into Fionuala's blue-green eyes. 'No, do not try and deny it. You are trying to take Lir away from me.' She tightened her grip on the girl's shoulder. 'But you never will,' she promised. 'Never.' She whirled away in a flurry of crimson, her threat lingering on the suddenly chilled air.

'You are going riding, my Lord?' asked Daire as Aedan saddled his roan.

'Aye, Aefe wants to ride out to Derravaragh; hitch up her chariot, will you? Hurry up,' he called to his brothers, as they struggled to saddle their ponies.

Daire hitched two jet-black geldings into an ornate

chariot, and then for some obscure reason slipped his long knife into his belt.

With Fiachra and Conn astride their shaggy ponies and Aedan mounted upon Nathair, Daire brought the chariot around into the courtyard. Aefe was standing by the gate, waiting for them, a woven wicker basket of provisions on the ground beside her. As they approached, Fionuala ran up, having changed into a riding outfit of leather leggings and jerkin.

'Aedan, where is my horse?'

Her twin frowned. 'I thought you would ride with Ae ... Mother.'

'Of course she will ride with me.' Aefe smiled coldly and, placing a thin hand on Fionuala's shoulder, urged her into the chariot.

They rode down from the high gate along the route that Lir and his warriors had just taken. Aefe led them through the meadows and away from the road, along the banks of the stream that fed into Derravaragh Lake. The queen was in a good mood, singing in her high clear voice, an air that stilled the birds on the trees. Aedan joined in occasionally, but his voice was breaking, and he left it to his brothers to carry the tune in their sweet unbroken voices.

Only Fionuala did not join them.

The queen took the reins from Daire and drove the chariot herself, exulting in the strength and power of the horses, the rush of the wind through her hair as she unbound it and the thrill of impending triumph.

And Daire, standing beside Fionuala, caught the bright glisten of tears in her eyes, as she turned and looked back at the fast disappearing White Fort.

Aefe brought them along the banks of the Derravaragh, the waters cold and dark after the sparkling rainbow colours of the stream. She halted the lathered horses by a large outcropping of rock that stretched out over the lake. The morning sun had burned the mists off the lake and now the waters lay flat and unbroken, almost metallic, to the far distant shore.

Aefe dismounted and went to stand atop the rock overlooking the lake.

Daire helped Fionuala from the chariot, whilst the brothers dismounted and stood by the waters edge.

Aefe pushed a loose stone into the water with her foot. It fell with a dull splash, the ripples growing into the distance. 'Children, would you not like to swim?'

Conn shivered. 'Too cold.'

'Nonsense,' chided the queen. 'Why, if you wish to ride with your father's warriors, you must be able to endure far colder water than this.' She turned to Daire. 'Is that not so, charioteer?'

'We are often forced to bathe in freezing water,' he agreed cautiously. 'But we prefer running water,' he added. 'It is purer and cleaner.'

Conn clambered up the hanging rock and standing by the edge, stared down onto the lake. 'It looks evil,' he whispered, 'who knows that serpents may live in it.' He wandered closer to the edge. 'It shines like mouldy copper.'

'Be careful Conn,' Fionuala called.

Aefe stepped forward, her hand outstretched to grab the boy, but her foot slipped on a patch of weed and she fell heavily against him. With a shrill scream, Conn toppled into the dark water.

Aedan launched himself from the shore, striking out strongly for the thrashing boy, Fionuala immediately following him.

The shock of the chill water was like a blow, instantly robbing her hands and feet of all sensation. The water stung her fair skin and tasted acrid in her throat. Her body responded automatically; the tiny gill-like slits behind her ears opening, extracting the oxygen from the water, and the inner eyelid sliding down protecting her eyes. Deftly she unhooked her cloak and kicked off her boots, and then, with her arms by her side, slid through the water like an eel. She could hear the frantic booming of her younger brother as he struggled before her, and the steadier beat of Aedan approaching. She opened her eyes wide, but the water was dark with silt and peat and she could only grope in the darkness for her brother. Her questing fingers closed on sodden cloth ...

Abruptly the water boiled and exploded and a weight struck her across the back, pushing her down ... down ... down.

Blind panic made her strike out; her fists struck something soft and yielding. She grasped it convulsively and pushed upwards for the surface. And when she had brushed the water from her eyes and the inner eyelid had retracted, she found she was holding her brother Fiachra.

'She pushed me,' he gasped.

Aefe capered on the rock above them like a wild thing. Her long black hair and crimson riding cloak streamed out behind her in a breeze that did not ruffle the water.

'Sorcery,' shouted Aedan, as he attempted to keep Conn's head above water.

The queen raised both hands above her head. She was clutching a stave ... a stave the children of Lir suddenly recognised as their father's Rod of Power.

It was a short length of silver wood, cut from the forests of Tir fo Thuinn, the Land Beneath the Waves. Ogham runes were incised along its length, angular, gold-filled lines set with tiny stones. Thin tendrils of fox-fire writhed along the wand, striking sparks from the stones, turning the gold molten. Blue fire throbbed and pulsed as she waved it to and fro and the ogham runes seemed to hang trembling on the suddenly darkened sky.

Aefe began to chant in the Old Tongue, a language that predated the Tuatha De Danann, or the Fomorians, and was even older than the Nemedians; the tongue of the Partholonians. She screamed aloud, but her voice was lost, torn and shredded on the ghostwind. But her words had effect.

The water suddenly blazed about the children of Lir, a chilling blue-white fire which blinded without burning. Fionuala lost sight of Aedan and Conn and even Fiachra seemed thin and insubstantial in her arms. The light

66

dazzled her eyes, bringing tears and causing red-black spots to dance wildly on her retina. Sensation returned to her limbs in a rush and she almost screamed in agony, and then almost as quickly it went again, until she lost all sensation. The world lurched; the dark sky and burning water losing definition and depth whilst the colours shook and vibrated.

And above it all the voice of Aefe chanted in the Old Tongue, calling forth her familiars to bear witness and carry word to their masters of the sacrifice she was sending them. Dark shapes gathered behind her, bestial and hideous, but with frighteningly human eyes. With a final flourish, Aefe completed her incantation and reverted to the tongue of the People of the Goddess.

> 'And Earth shall not hold thee,
> Fire shall ye fear,
> Water be thy element,
> And that of Air.'

And as the blinding light died off the lake, Daire, cowering in the reeds on the bank, saw that the four children were gone ... and in their place floated four snow-white swans!

'This is your punishment,' Aefe screamed. 'You tried to take Lir from me, but now I have taken you from yourselves.'

And the largest of the swans replied. 'No, queen; you may take our forms, but you cannot take our spirits and whilst that remains, we remain.' The voice was Fionuala's.

'How long must we remain in this form?' she asked then.

Aefe etched a glowing rune into the silent air with the tip of the wand. 'I have set the spell for thrice three hundred years,' she gloated. 'You will spend the first three hundred here upon Derravaragh, the second in the Straits of Moyle which lies between Banba and Alba, and the final three hundred in the wild seas about Inish Glora, in the Western Ocean.'

'Father will save us,' shouted one of the smaller swans, Fiachra.

Aefe boiled the water about the swans, sending them fluttering on untried wings into the air. Exhausted they fell back. 'Your father has not the power,' she laughed. 'He will need this wand to undo the spell, none other will suffice, and if he is without the wand …?' With a shrill cry Aefe tossed the Rod of Power high into the air.

There was a stench of something rotten, of death and decay and a monstrous shadow passed over the dark waters of the lake. A giant black raven hovered over the queen for a moment and then it turned and disappeared south, the wand clutched in its talons.

'Is there no escape?' whispered Conn.

'Not until the day when the bell of the New God rings across the waters of evening and the man of the north shall take in marriage the woman of the south. Only then will the spell have run its course, only then will the enchantment be lifted.'

'I pity you,' said Aedan suddenly, 'for you have yet to face our father's wrath.'

Aefe gathered her cloak about her. 'Your father will have no-one left, he will not harm me, for he needs me: I am all he has.' And then she added. 'He will never know anyway; you were swimming in the lake, and you drowned,' she shrugged.

Fionuala laughed gently. 'We are the children of Lir, the Lord of the Sea; we cannot drown.'

Aefe frowned. 'I will think of something.' And then she turned and leaped down from the rock, heading back towards the chariot. She paused by the horses, looking for Daire. Abruptly she laughed and said softly, almost to herself. 'No mortal man could have witnessed the transformation and retained his sanity.' The queen climbed into the chariot and pulled them about, heading back for the White Fort.

Daire had remained hiding in the reeds until Aefe had disappeared over the brow of the hill. When he rose and stood knee deep in the chill water, the four swans drifted over to him and the largest laid its head on his arm.

68

And though the body was that of a swan's, the eyes and voice were those of Fionuala.

'Daire, you stayed.' There was surprise and affection in her voice.

'Your father asked me to keep an eye on you,' he said gruffly, 'much good I did.'

'No Daire, there was nothing you could do; why you are lucky to be still sane. The spell should have blasted the mind of any mortal man.'

'I am partly of the People of the Goddess,' said the charioteer. 'That saved me.' He looked at Fionuala. 'What must I do now?'

'You must reach our father, for you are our only link with him. And Daire ... be careful.'

'Aefe thinks me mad and running wild through the woods,' he said. 'She will do nothing against me.'

'She might accuse you of killing us,' said Aedan, drifting close to his sister.

The charioteer nodded. 'She might; and if I were to be found later, hopelessly insane, then no-one could doubt her story that I killed you. I will be careful. I'll ride directly south and attempt to overtake your father before he goes into the marshes and then I'll bring him directly here where he will have the evidence of his own eyes.'

'Take my horse,' suggested Aedan, 'he will find the king, and remember, avoid the White Fort at all costs.'

Daire agreed, his voice curiously muffled and then he turned away and ran stumbling from the lakeside, before they could see the tears that ran from his eyes.

The charioteer rode south as fast as the roan would carry him. He gave the White Fort a wide berth, but even from a distance he could see it was the scene of great activity. Armed men patrolled the heavily wooded countryside and guarded all the wells and pools of fresh water. It was then Daire discovered how the horse had earned its name, Nathair - Serpent - for it slid through the thickest undergrowth and even the most impenetrable woodland to avoid the patrols. The charioteer spent much of his time lying flat across the animal's back, lest he be torn from the saddle by branches.

It was late in the afternoon, four days after the transformation of the children, when Daire came upon Lir's camp.

It was situated on a small knoll in a clearing in the forest. Beyond the camp, the first sodden outcrops of the marsh trickled off into one of the countless streams that ran through the trees. A great fire blazed in the centre of the camp and Daire could see Lir's tall form stride in and out of the firelight, appearing and disappearing like a woodsprite. A snatch of song drifted across the clearing to the charioteer and the smell of roasting meat hung upon the heavy air.

He had ridden halfway across the clearing towards the camp when a sentry stepped out from the undergrowth and placed the tip of a spear in his back.

'No further. Your name and business.'

Daire turned in the saddle. 'Conal, it's me. I must see the king.'

The sentry relaxed his guard. 'You're a long way from home, is something wrong ...' he paused and stepped closer to the horse. 'Isn't that Nathair, Aedan's mount?' he asked suspiciously.

Daire nodded. 'I must see the king,' he repeated, his voice trembling with exhaustion.

'Go then; Lir is by the fire. Call out to Starn and Gamal by the stream and they'll let you pass. What's wrong?' he asked as the charioteer spurred his mount away. But he received no answer.

Lir knew something was terribly wrong as soon as he saw the foam-flecked horse bearing the slumped rider push its way towards the firelight. A sudden silence fell on the assembled warriors.

'My Lord,' gasped Daire, rising from the saddle, 'treachery ... sorcery ...' and he fell from the roan in a dead faint.

When he came to some time later, Lir was bending over him, pressing a flask of bitter-sweet liquid to his chapped lips. He coughed and struggled to rise, but the king pushed him back with surprising strength. Lir's large colourless eyes glittered strangely and his inner eyelid flickered once or twice across his retina, like a snake's. The dancing firelight lent his skin an even deeper greenish hue and gave his high, thin, elfin features a sinister, evil cast.

'Speak,' he commanded. 'What has happened?'

'My Lord,' began Daire slowly, 'your queen has, by foul sorcery and by calling upon the Elder Gods, changed your children into the likeness of swans upon Lake Derravaragh,' he finished in a rush.

Lir moaned as if in pain. His warriors drew back in horror, some making the sign of the fist or horns, whilst others clutched talismen or amulets. For sorcery could only be fought by a darker sorcery and whereas they would gladly give their lives in combat, the very whisper of sorcery filled them with a mind-numbing fear.

'But how?' wondered the king, 'she has not the power.'

'She used your wand,' said Daire, 'and then, when she had set the spell, she tossed the wand high into the air and a raven of enormous proportions and carrying with it the stink of death, carried it off.'

'One of the Morrigan's pets,' Lir murmured. He stood abruptly, towering over his men. 'Break camp, we ride at once for Derravaragh.'

The camp immediately dissolved into a whirling chaos of shouting men and skittish animals. Chariots were hitched, horses saddled and tents struck – and all within the length of time it took Daire to snatch a hurried meal and quench his thirst. The sky was ablaze with stars when they moved out. They galloped all through the night and rested briefly with the coming of the morn. By noon they had set out again.

The chariots thundered down the High Roads, flanked on either side by horsemen and those they passed on the road kept to their homes and bolted the doors, making ready their weapons, for they feared that the Fomorians had come south again and Lir went to do battle with them.

A day later, as the sun rose over the dark waters of the lake, Lir and his company reached Derravaragh. The king waved his men back and went alone to the lakeside where, far off in the distance, four snow-white swans could be seen making their way swiftly towards the shore. As they neared it, they uttered strangely human cries of joy and sorrow which Lir recognised as the voices of his children. The four swans crowded about the weeping king, pressing their long slim heads against his rough hands, and they too wept.

Lir spoke with his children there by the lakeside on that cold, bright winter morning and when he did rejoin his men about midday, he seemed resigned to their fate. Leaving half his men by the lakeside to tend to their needs and protect them, he rode for the White Fort – and vengeance.

Bove had arrived at the White Fort in Lir's absence. He had been met by his daughter, her face ashen, her eyes swollen with tears. She had told him that whilst Lir hunted boar in the marshes, the four children had gone missing, kidnapped and presumably slain by a charioteer named Daire.

And as the Lord of the Sea rode through the main gate, Bove was making ready to ride out in search of Lir, the children and the missing charioteer. A sudden silence fell on the courtyard as the king dismounted. He had lost weight, his eyes were sunken, lost in his haggard face.

Aefe, standing by her father's side, suddenly caught sight of Daire. 'There he is.' She pointed accusingly. 'He has kidnapped our children.'

She went to Lir and embraced him. 'You have captured him, my husband; but how? How did you know?' she wondered.

With a sudden savage moment, Lir struck her and she fell sprawling at the feet of the Red King. 'Witch,' he spat. 'I have spoken with my children: the children you so treacherously changed into the likeness of swans. You have betrayed me.' He slowly drew his rune-inscribed sword from its sheath.

Bove stepped between the king and Aefe. A stray shaft of

afternoon sunlight touched his fiery red hair and beard, touching it with gold. 'Wait Lir, I must hear more of this tale before you strike. I was told your children had been kidnapped by a charioteer named Daire, who was now running wild through the woods. We were about to ride in search of him.' He gestured at Daire. 'Yet here he is with you and clearly he is not a prisoner, but you accuse my daughter of sorcery against your children, my grand-children ...'

'He lies,' screamed Aefe, scrambling to her feet, one hand pressed against her split lip, which leaked a pale ichor.

Lir shook his head sadly. 'I do not lie.'

'I wouldn't have the power to do as you have said.' She grinned in triumph. 'You have been caught in your own lies!'

The king shrugged and then he presented his sword to Bove. 'Test her on my blade.'

The Red King took the proffered weapon and held it up. Silver light suddenly blazed upon the length of the blade, sharp and bright.

'Place your hand upon the sword,' he commanded Aefe. Silently she shook her head. 'Do it!' he snapped.

Reluctantly the queen touched the shining blade.

'Now,' began Bove, 'you are oath-bound to answer me truthfully; lie and the blade will show it.' He paused and looked deep into his daughter's eyes, but he found no comfort there. 'Do not lie,' he whispered softly. And then, raising his voice so that all might hear, he asked, 'Have you used sorcery against the children of Lir? Have you changed them into the likeness of swans?'

The silence hung heavily over the courtyard. Aefe remained silent, her eyes fastened on the blade, her fingers stuck to the shining metal.

'Answer!'

She started at the sound of her father's voice, and slowly she shook her head. 'No ... No, I have not.'

Instantly a crimson stain spread down the shining silver length of the sword, until its radiance was lost beneath a blood-red covering. An angry murmur ran about the courtyard, quickly swelling to a roar.

'She lies!'

Bove sighed resignedly, as if the answer did not surprise him. 'You have betrayed your husband, you have betrayed your adopted children ... and you have betrayed me. Why?' he asked, his voice heavy with confusion and pain.

'Because I loved him,' said Aefe. 'Because I loved him so much I did not want him to share that love with anyone, and because he loved his children more than he loved me.'

'No, no it was never like that. They were my children – but you, you were my wife.'

'Well now, you do not have to share your love,' Aefe sneered. 'I am all you have left.'

Lir shook his head. 'No; you are nothing to me now.' He turned away, and stared into the evening sky.

Bove lowered the sword. 'The High Law will permit only one sentence.'

'But you cannot slay me,' cried Aefe triumphantly. 'I am of the De Danann!'

Her father nodded. 'That is true, we cannot slay you. But we can do to you what you have done to the four children: rob you of your natural form, and then cast you out.'

Aefe shrank back as Bove handed Lir his sword and then called for his Rod of Power. The king turned suddenly and touched his wife with the tip of his sword. 'You are still oath-bound; what form would you fear most, what form would you deem fitting punishment for yourself?'

Aefe clasped her hands across her mouth, trying to prevent herself from answering, trying to prevent pronouncing her own judgement. Her throat worked, and the answer was torn from her mouth. 'A deamon of the air.'

Lir sheathed his sword. 'Thus shall it be.'

Bove agreed and, raising his wand high in the air, called aloud for the Old Gods. The hushed courtyard felt the eerie trickle of power from the wand. Abruptly it blazed with a brilliant blue-white fire that shed light but gave off no heat. A globe of pulsating foxfire gathered at the tip of the wand, growing larger and larger, until it waxed like a full harvest moon. Slowly it detached itself from the wand and drifted down over the queen. The globe of light shivered and darkened and then swiftly dispersed in a shower of glittering dust motes.

And where once a young woman had crouched, now a hideous winged serpent clawed the earth with hooked talons. But its eyes were those of Aefe. With a terrifying screech, the deamon took to the air and disappeared south in a rush of leathery wings.

The years passed. Lir moved his household and court to the banks of the Derravaragh to be close to his children. He sought Druids and Mages from all parts of the known world and offered them vast rewards should they succeed in lifting the spell - but every attempt failed and at last Lir grew resigned to his children's fate. He had bards and minstrels, sages and teachers from the length and breath of Banba brought to instruct the four and the new court at Derravaragh quickly established itself as a centre of learning and culture. The other De Danann lords came to the lakeside also, but they came for a different reason: to hear the children of Lir sing.

Their music was not of this world, it was hauntingly eldritch. It could soothe the most violent warriors and calm the crazed beasts, it could lighten the heaviest hearts or break the hardest. And in the evenings, as the sun dipped behind the far distant mountains and shed its last light across the dark waters of the lake, the children would sing. And the crowded lakeside would grow silent, listening to the ancient lays and ballads of the De Danann, or the softer, sadder songs composed by the four.

And their fame spread.

But the years passed.

One morning late in the year, with the bite of winter already in the air, Fionuala awoke from a troubled sleep and called her brothers together.

'The first part of our sentence is done; we have spent three hundred years upon this lake and now we must make our way to the Straits of Moyle.'

They made their way out of the mists which still clung to the waters for the shore, where they knew their father would be waiting - as he had waited every morning since he had first come to the lake. He was standing on the banks of the lake in full armour, the burnished metal mirroring the waters and the distorted shapes of the swans.

Fionuala looked at him, her eyes heavy with unshed tears, conscious that she would never see him again. Although the children had not aged and Lir was of the Tuatha De Danann - and thus more akin to god than man - Fionuala noticed for the first time the lines about his eyes and the silver in his hair. He embraced each of his children in turn, his hands trembling and his jaw clenched, but he couldn't hide the tears in his eyes.

They parted swiftly and the swans took to the air, their large wings ruffling the waters of the lake, sending tendrils of mist darting and writhing like serpents. They circled once over the palace and the lonely figure standing on the shore, and then they turned and set out for the north and the Straits of Moyle.

The Straits of Moyle was a long open stretch of sea between Banba and Alba. It was a chill, desolate place, with the dark cliffs of Banba on one side and the distant blur of Alba's many islands on the horizon. Often small iceflows from the northern seas would make their ways south into the Strait and even in the height of summer, the water was always chill.

In winter it was bitter.

Storms were frequent upon the wild waters and few ships braved the Strait. In winter even the hardy seabirds were forced to move to a less inhospitable spot.

The children of Lir arrived in time for one of the worst

storms in recorded history upon the sea of Moyle.

The day had dawned dull and overcast with a chill wind sweeping in from the north. Low dark clouds had massed on the horizon and frequently a flash of lightning would ripple through the skies, touching the crests of the heaving waves with silver. By noon it was almost pitch black and the four swans could barely make out each other. Above the howling of the wind, Fionuala ordered them to keep together if possible, but if they were separated, then they were to make their way to Carricknarone – the tiny chunk of windswept rock they had landed on the day before.

The storm rolled in swiftly and the sea rose in welcome. Towering waves crashed and rose again, huge fists hammering at the shivering birds. Ice-flecked gales tore across the turbulent waves, stinging and blinding. Levin bolts ripped through the roiling heavens, their bone-white light etching the swans in stark relief onto the blackness of the storm tossed seas.

Time lost all meaning, day drifted imperceptibly into night and back into day again. The storm lasted three days and soon the Strait was littered with lumps of ice washed down from the northern iceflows, trees and parts of buildings ripped from the land, and bodies ... many torn and shattered bodies, some still clad in the tattered tartans of Alba.

The four swans were separated early in the storm, for it was impossible to keep together in the wild seas.

The sun rose in a clear sky and the sea was calm and gentle when Fionuala reached Carricknarone Rock. She was bitterly cold and badly bruised from the battering she had received from the waves. She struggled up onto the rock and slumped there – waiting. But as the morning drew on and there was still no sign of her brothers, she began to fear that they had been slain and she mourned their passing, singing a piteous lament that carried across the chill waves. And the morning grew very quiet.

And then, from her position high atop the rock, she saw a tiny white speck far out over the waves. A new note entered her song, one of joy, one of welcome, drawing the swan on. It was Fiachra. He struggled up battered and bruised, his slim head drooping in weariness.

'Fionuala,' he gasped, 'it was your singing that led me here. I feared you lost ... I thought ... I thought I was alone.'

Fionuala embraced her brother and, nestling close to him, covered him with her wing. Fiachra, trembling and weary, soon fell into a fitful doze and his last conscious memory was of his sister's voice ringing out sharp and clear on the late morning air.

When he awoke, he found that Aedan, his elder brother had arrived, also drawn by Fionuala's song.

But of Conn, the youngest, there was no sign.

They spent a cold and anxious night upon the rock awaiting their brother. Fionuala, her voice hoarse and raw, could sing no more and she stared desperately at the surrounding waves, willing her brother to appear. Aedan and Fiachra sang together, both for their own comfort and in an effort to call Conn - if he still lived - to the rock.

The following morning dawned bright and cold, with low clouds whipping across the distant horizon and the morning so clear they could see the far shores of Bamba. Fionuala awoke abruptly, stiff and aching and scanned the seas about her. Her shrill cry brought her brothers suddenly awake.

For in the distance, weaving slowly towards them, was their brother, Conn.

Aedan and Fiachra swam out to the small figure and helped him back to the rock. The storm had tossed him far and he was cut and bruised after being dashed against the cliffs of Banba and his left wing was twisted and broken. Fionuala wept when she saw his injuries, but with Aedan's help, she cleansed the wounds as best she could and set the wing.

And then they slept in peace, united at last; Aedan beneath Fionuala's right wing, Fiachra beneath her left, and Conn tucked under her breast.

The years they spent upon the Straits of Moyle were the

hardest they had to endure whilst under enchantment. Often it was so cold that the flesh of their feet stuck to the cruel rock; they were often hungry and always cold.

But the long cold years passed and one day, as the first of the autumnal storms gathered, Fionuala called her brothers together. 'Our time here has ended and now we enter the last part of our sentence. We must fly west and a little south to the Western Ocean and Inish Glora.'

The four swans took to the air, their powerful wings lifting them higher and higher, until they could see both the shores of Banba and Alba and in the far off distance the shadow that was the Isle of Mona. They flew westwards across the green and wooded fields of Banba, which a later race would call Eriu.

It seemed little changed in the three hundred years since they had left it. There were new roads and new forts, but these were insignificant when compared with the vast forests and lush pasturelands. Suddenly Conn, who was flying a little below the others called, 'I want to see home.' He wheeled south in a long slow arc, ignoring Fionuala's frantic cries. They were forced to follow him down, skimming low over the land and here the differences were more apparent. The open fields were now fenced and many of the great trees had been felled and used for kindling. Huge open pits were cut into the soft earth and vast quantities of stone had been removed to build the small, but growing, towns. And when they reached the spot where their home should be, they found nothing but a grass-covered mound and even Lake Derravaragh seemed somehow smaller and not the vast expanse of water they had known.

For the Age of Gods and Heroes had passed and that of Man was at hand and the children of Lir had lived beyond their time.

In many respects the seas about Inish Glora - a barren windswept island - were much like those of the Straits of Moyle. The wind sweeping in from the grey Western Ocean was always chill, bringing with it sleet and snow and they spent many nights flapping their wings in an attempt to stop freezing to death. And death began to have a strange attraction. It would have been easy, so easy, to surrender to the sea and the cold and sink down into its warm embrace, thereby gaining release.

But they could not – for they were the last of the Tuatha De Danann and proud.

One day, whilst flying over the island, Fiachra spotted a tiny inshore lake. It was sheltered somewhat from the wild seas, but was still part of the Western Ocean and thus it did not break their geas to move there.

In the evenings, as the sun was setting in a bloody death across the waves, shedding its baleful light across the heavens, they would sing. Their voices were high and pure, untainted and unbroken by their great age and flocks of birds flying homewards would often swoop down to listen to them, settling upon the still waters of the little lake, or upon the stunted trees and bushes that bordered the banks.

In time the island became known as the Bird Isle.

Now, towards the end of their enchantment, an old man came to the deserted isle. He was small and dark and his hair and beard were long and silver, but he walked without a stoop or the aid of a stick. The children recognised his type, for even in their youth, there had been hermits, men so devoted to their gods that they would cut themselves off from all others, spending their time in prayer and contemplation. And the children of Lir wondered what gods this hermit worshipped; surely not the Dagda and Danu, the gods of their people.

The hermit set about building a rude hut by the lakeside, a makeshift affair of reeds and mud and upon the hut he erected a tall length of wood, with a shorter crosspiece halfway up it.

He spent many days in prayer and fasting either outside the hut facing the curious crosslike affair or else by the lakeside. He took an almost childlike delight in the presence of the swans and he spoke to them, as a man will when he is alone, talking of his plans to build a monastery upon the island, a place of peace and solitude. When he had it, he gave them bread, although he could ill afford it for his diet consisted of roots and boiled fish.

As the year turned, men came to the island, bringing with them many slabs of dressed stone and polished wood, and in a relatively short space of time they had constructed a sturdy beehive-shaped hut and now the device they raised over the roof was of metal and not wood. They also built a smaller stand outside the hut, its roof slanting to either side covering a small upended cup.

When the builders left, the peace on the island seemed even more profound. But that evening the terrified children of Lir heard for the first time the liquid notes of a bell drifting across the still waters of the lake.

Fionuala suddenly remembered her stepmother's mocking words, uttered so long ago on the day she had set the spell. ' "... the day when the bell of the New God rings across the waters of evening ..." '

That night, as the moon cut a silver swathe across the black waters, the hermit stood by the lakeside, gazing serenely into its ebon depths. A tiny splash disturbed the silence of the night. He looked up as the four snow-white swans appeared from the rushes that bordered the lake. He smiled and raised a hand in welcome. He had once thought it strange that such beautiful creatures should want to live in such a desolate place, but when he sometimes despaired, he thought of the swans and took comfort from their presence – it was as if they were a sign, a sign telling him to continue, to carry on.

'Greetings hermit.'

The old man reeled back in shock, one hand clutching for an amulet that hung about his scrawny neck. He stared at the four ghost-like birds in horror. One of them had spoken!

'I am sorry, I did not mean to startle you.' The voice was soft and gentle, that of a young woman. And it came from the largest of the swans.

The hermit swallowed hard and squeezed his eyes shut.

Perhaps he was going mad ... lack of proper food ... little sleep ...

.'No,' said one of the smaller swans, this time with the voice of a young man, 'you do not imagine us, we are real.'

The hermit took hold of himself and, straightening up, raised his hand and etched a strange symbol in the air before him. 'In the Name of God the Father and of His Son, that is of the One and of the Ghost, that is also of the One, if ye be spirits of evil or deamons of the pit, I command ye depart.' He paused, but the swans remained.

'What ... Who are you?' he ventured at last.

The large swan with the voice of a young girl, but with the eyes of an old, old woman, answered. 'We are the children of Lir, condemned by a jealous stepmother to spend a thrice-three hundred year enchantment upon the cruel seas about Banba's shores.'

'The children ... the children of Lir,' began the hermit in excitement. 'Yes, I have heard of you, the legends speak of the swan-children.' He fell to his knees by the lakeside and stretched out his gnarled hands to the swans. And one by one they came and placed their heads in his palms and as they did so they introduced themselves:

'I am Fionuala ...'

'... and Aedan, her brother and twin ...'

'My name is Fiachra, and this is my twin ...'

'Conn ...'

'And I am called Kemoch, sometimes called the hermit, but usually called mad.'

'We heard your bell,' said Fionuala, 'and we came, for it was prophesied that the sound of the bell of the New God would mark the nearing of the end of our sentence.'

'Teach us of this New God,' said Aedan.

And there by the lakeside, Kemoch the Hermit, taught the children of Lir, of the New God, of the One called the Christ, and of His followers, and of Patrick, who had brought the faith to Banba, which men now called Erin.

*

About a year later, Decca, a princess of Munster in the south was bethrothed to Lairgen, the king of Connaught, and he, wishing to impress her, said that she might have anything she so desired.

'I have heard,' she said, 'of a lake which lies within your domain . . .' and she paused, for Lairgen had raised his hand.

'No, I know what you are about to ask me, but I beg you, do not request that; do not bring the ancient taint of sorcery into our marriage . . . see what it did to the marriage of Lir and Aefe.'

'What,' cried Decca, her dark eyes flashing in amusement, 'is this fear I see in bold Lairgen's face. What do you fear, my brave warrior,' she asked mockingly, 'an old man and four swans?'

'Someday,' promised the king, 'someday, you will go too far in your demands. Yes, I will get you the swans, though I think you will get little pleasure from the poor creatures.'

The morning was cold and bright with a stiff breeze blowing in off the Western Ocean, when Lairgen at the head of a small company of mounted warriors rode out to Kemoch's little cell and chapel.

The hermit was nowhere to be seen, but from within the tiny chapel came the sound of the most beautiful singing the king had heard. The music itself had life, it was vibrant and pure, etherial. But when Lairgen strode into the building, his armour and weapons jingling and flashing in the sharp sunlight, there was no-one there except the old hermit . . . and the four swans.

'So, the legends are true,' snapped the king. 'The children in swan-shape do exist.' He had only half-believed it. He felt the chill breath of ancient magic blow across the nape of his neck. He wanted nothing to do with this. But . . . but he was committed and if he did not return with the swans, what would Decca say?

Kemoch had arisen and now stood before the king. 'You are in the House of God, sir; remove your helmet and arms,' he cried angrily.

Lairgen pushed the old man roughly aside, and he fell

sprawling on the cruel stones. 'I have come for the swans, hermit, do not stand in my way.' He commanded four of his men to take the birds outside where they had nets ready for them.

The children did not struggle, but once beyond the confines of the church, the warriors stumbled as if beneath a great weight and then were thrown backwards by an invisible hand.

Time stood still.

' "... and the man of the north shall take in marriage the woman of the south ...".'

The air suddenly chilled and rime formed on the feathers of the birds, turning them silver. The silver flowed and ran with a myriad of rainbow colours and the bright sun shattered upon it blindingly, making it impossible to make out the forms of the birds. The warriors covered their eyes, some making the Sign of the Cross, or the older Fist of Thor, or the Horned Sign of Cernounoss; some cried aloud, for there was no shame in fearing sorcery.

The colours froze and the four birds were now enclosed within a glowing silver sphere that dazzled and burned the eyes; a wind howled about the ball, but it was the wind of the Other World, for it did not even ruffle the waters of the lake. Voices cried on the wind, the howling of the damned, the lost and the air was heavy with the pungent odour of cloves and salt.

And abruptly it was gone.

The wind died; the sphere contracted and disappeared. The children were gone and the swans were gone ... but in their place stood four incredibly ancient creatures. They stood taller than the warriors, although their backs were now bent and some of the majestic beauty of the De Danann could still be seen in their skull-like faces. One was barely recognisable as female, whilst the other three were male. The female turned to Lairgen and Kemoch and spoke and her voice was that of a young girl, made all the more obscene coming from those withered lips and toothless gums.

'Behold the children of Lir.'

Lairgen suddenly broke from the spell that had held him rooted to the spot and ran for his horse, his warriors stumbling and falling in an effort to mount up.

The four ancients and Kemoch watched them flee. 'We really should thank them,' said one, which the hermit knew was Fiachra, from his voice.

'They have freed us,' agreed Fionuala. 'A woman's greed, and a man's lust.' And then she turned to Kemoch. 'Our time grows short. You have taught us of the Christ and His works and now we wish you to baptise us into the Faith before we die - for our gods are long since dead and no man should go godless to his death. And when we die, I wish you to bury us in the old way, that is, standing up. And you will put Aedan on my right side, Fiachra on my left and place Conn before me, for that is how I sheltered them upon the sea of Moyle and off Glora.'

Kemoch nodded silently, not trusting himself to speak.

And he buried them there by the Lake of Birds in the manner that Fionuala had requested and he placed a stone above their grave. Upon it were the words:

'The Children of Lir: Betrayed; Enchanted; Saved.'

CHAPTER 3

DEIRDRE AND THE SONS OF USNACH
(The Third Sorrow Of Irish Storytelling)

Deirdre and Naise stood on the cliffs, listening to the crash of the waves on the shore and the mewling cries of the sea birds. A stiff breeze was whipping in off the chill Western Ocean, bringing with it the promise of rain. Deirdre snuggled closer to Naise, shivering slightly. Gently, he caressed her red-gold hair and kissed the top of her head.

'Are you cold, my love?'

She shook her head. 'A ... feeling.' She pointed out over the foam-topped waves, to where three lone birds winged westwards into the sinking sun. 'I had a dream last night. A dream about three birds.' She turned and faced Naise, looking up at him from wide green eyes that glistened with unshed tears. 'Naise, I'm frightened.'

Naise kissed her lightly. 'There is no need to be; nothing can happen to you – not whilst Ardan, Anle and myself still live.'

Deirdre ran her long fingers through his blue-black hair, feeling it flow like raw silk in her hands. 'I do not fear for myself. The three birds I dreamt of last night – they were three great ravens and although they had the touch of death about them, they were not Morrigan's pets.' She closed her eyes and her voice became distant and sad. 'They came out of the south and west and alighted on the palisade of our fort.'

Unconsciously, Naise glanced back along the cliffs to the ruined fort which clung to its edges.

'And then, one of our men offered the ravens a piece of meat from a golden platter. The birds would not touch it,

86

but only opened their beaks and left three glistening drops of amber honey on the plate. And then blood seemed to seep from the meat and soil the honey and the ravens each took a sip of the bright blood and took flight . . .' her voice faded and was lost on the breeze.

Naise shivered suddenly and then forced a laugh. 'It is probably nothing. You are tired, exhausted. We have been running for a long time – but now we can rest.'

'But can we?' she whispered.

He pointed to the fort. 'Ardan and Anle are supervising the rebuilding of the main section and the outer wall. Once that's fortified, no-one, neither Banban king nor Alban warlord will be able to take you from me.'

Deirdre sighed. 'I wish that could be so ... but I cannot believe it. You know Conor wants me; has wanted me, since the day – the very hour – of my birth.'

Naise laughed. 'Ever since the Druid prophesied that you would be the most beautiful woman in all Banba.'

'He also prophesied that I would cause the downfall of kings and the death of princes,' she added bitterly. 'Some of the other lords present wanted me slain then and I sometimes think it might have been for the best.'

Naise held her tightly. 'No, never say that.'

'But because of me, Conor has exiled you from Banba and put a price on your head; because of me you are now a mercenary; because of me, you and your brothers have been forced to sell your swords to a succession of petty Alban warlords – and because of me, we have had to flee each time.' She raised a tear-streaked face to the skies. 'Why could I not have been born ugly?' she cried.

'But you were not. You were born beautiful and I love you.'

'Do you?' she asked gently.

'With all my heart,' he smiled. 'I've loved you since I first set eyes on you outside that woodsman's hut where Conor had hidden you away.'

Deirdre smiled fondly. 'I remember. My guardian had brought in a hart he had slain and it was beautiful, even in death. Some of its blood had stained the snow beneath its breast and there was a night-black raven perched on the hard ground beside its head. I remember turning to Lavarcham, my teacher and guardian, and telling her I would wed no man but the one with the colour of the hart's blood in his cheeks, the colour of the snow in his skin, and,' Deirdre touched Naise's hair, 'the colour of the raven in his hair.' She laughed gently. 'And she brought me you, Naise MacUsnach, and I brought you only trouble.'

'No, no,' Naise corrected her. 'You brought me love,' and he kissed her with a passion that matched the foaming of the waves against the wild, windswept cliffs of Western Alba.

The sun sank into the sea in a welter of crimson and gold. Dark storm clouds were massing in the north and the breeze had stiffened and moaned about the draughty hall. A huge fire roared and spat in the rebuilt hearth, bathing the large room in a gently wavering light.

Deirdre and Naise sat huddled together by the fire, basking in its heat and light, whilst Ardan and Anle sat hunched over a chessboard. In the shadows, a harper gently strummed his instrument, matching its haunting melody to the rising and falling of the wind. The few servants who had accompanied Deirdre and the sons of Usnach into exile moved about quietly, removing the remains of the spartan evening meal.

The door scraped open roughly and the captain of the guard crossed the worn flags, his boot heels clicking ominously in the sudden silence.

He stopped before Deirdre and Naise and bowed. 'My lord, my lady. There is a craft approaching the loch, running contrary to both tide and wind, coming from the direction of Banba. It's hard to tell in this light, but there seems to be at least three men in it.' He paused and added, 'But no crew.'

*

The three sons of Usnach stood on the cliffs above the inlet and watched the small craft slip in almost silently towards the shore. The sail had dropped and no sound of oars disturbed the water, but still the craft came on. Anle pointed to the thin lines of blue fire that hovered about the figurehead.

'Sorcery,' he spat, with a warrior's disdain of magic.

Ardan touched his older brother on the elbow. 'Our men are in position. We can sink that craft now – and all in it.'

Naise was about to agree and then something ... something stayed his hand and he held off giving the order. Deirdre joined them on the windswept cliffs and watched the craft beach itself with a scrape of hardened timbers.

In the twilight, they could see a single figure disembark and move up the deserted beach. Abruptly, a single flame shot upwards, illuminating the warrior and the craft in a brilliant circle of light. A battle cry echoed off the cliffs above the pounding of the waves.

'Banban!' Ardan and Anle said together, recognising the shout.

'No, I think it's Alban,' corrected Deirdre.

The shout came again.

'It's Banban,' Ardan insisted.

'No, no, it's Alban,' Deirdre repeated, with a touch of desperation in her voice.

The flame on the beach suddenly roared higher and the cry came again, only this time, sharper and clearer.

Naise took Deirdre in his arms. 'That's the cry of Fergus, son of Roy, one of Conor's Champions,' he said gently.

Silently, Deirdre began to weep.

Naise said quietly to Ardan. 'Have him escorted to the fort.'

Fergus MacRoy was standing with his back to the fire when Naise and Deirdre finally entered the hall. The flame-haired warrior bowed mockingly, his wide eyes glinting in amusement.

'My lady, you are as beautiful as rumour paints you.'

Deirdre bowed. 'Your reputation goes before you, Fergus MacRoy,' she said coldly, and took a seat away from the fire, in the shadows.

Fergus indicated the two younger men standing to his left. 'My son's,' he said proudly. 'Illan, called the Fair, because he takes after his mother, and Buinne the Red, sometimes called the Ruthless Red – because he takes after me,' he winked.

'Fergus, why have you come here?' Naise asked suddenly, seating himself by the chessboard and absently toying with a knight.

Fergus hooked his foot around a stool and pulled it over to the fire. He shivered. 'The night is cold and the chill of sorcery is still in my bones.' He nodded in the direction of the shore. 'Catbad, the Druid, called forth some wind elementals to propel our craft across the waves; we could hear the lost souls whispering and chanting all about us. Sometimes the voices became almost distinguishable and we would hear names, always names on the wind, as if the elementals sought to retain their identity.' He downed a goblet of local ale. 'Ah, doesn't compare with the home-brewed stuff. But now ...' he set his goblet aside and leaned forward, his elbows on his knees, and stared intently at Naise and Deirdre.

'Conor wants you back!'

'And has done for a long time,' said Naise.

'But now he is prepared to pardon you!'

For a few moments the hall was so silent they could hear the flames eating away at the dried wood and then Deirdre snapped, 'It's a trick.'

'No trick, my lady, you have the word of Fergus MacRoy on that,' he tapped his chest.

'Why the sudden change of mind?' Naise wondered, toppling the black knight.

Fergus shrugged. 'Who can say? Conor is an old man now, Deirdre no longer seems so important and ...' he smiled apologetically at the shadowy figure in the background, '... he has other mistresses.' His voice changed then and he added, 'And he cannot afford to deplete the fighting force of

Banba at the present. Next to the Three Champions, Conall the Victorious, Cucuhulain the Hound and myself, there are no greater warriors in Bamba than the sons of Usnach.'

Ardan stepped out of the shadows, the firelight painting his thin features in sharp angles and planes. 'Can we trust Conor though?' He caught the glint in Fergus' eye, and added hastily, 'It's not that I do not trust you; the word of Fergus MacRoy is legendary, but I would trust Conor only as far as I could spit in a strong wind.'

Fergus nodded. 'I am sorry to say that I must agree with you - but he has given me assurances that you will not be harmed, and,' he added slowly, 'you have *my* assurances that you will not be harmed.'

'That is good enough for me,' said Ardan, looking at Naise.

'And me,' said Anle.

Naise toyed with a white queen, looking intently at its finely carved features. 'Fergus, Conor had pursued us the length and breadth of Banba and had even sent raiding parties into Alba after us. He hired local chiefs to attack us on the roads and sent spies to Lurgan, the High King, telling him of Deirdre's beauty, inflaming his passions, until we were forced to cut our way to freedom through his warriors - warriors who had only that day been our comrades in arms.'

'I can understand your distrust,' said Fergus. 'But he has changed,' he added earnestly, 'he wants you back. Trust me.'

Naise turned to his brothers. 'What do we do?'

'Let us go home,' said Ardan.

'I agree,' said Anle.

'It would be nice to see the green fields of Banba once more,' mused Naise. Turning to Deirdre, he asked. 'What would you have us do, my love?'

'If you return to Banba, you are going to your deaths,' she said ominously. 'Remember my dream? The three drops of honey brought by the ravens are the promises Fergus brings you now - and the three drops of blood signify your deaths. There is nothing for you in Banba except betrayal, treachery and death.'

Fergus surged to his feet, sending the stool crashing

backwards into the fire; Illan and Buinne were at his side immediately. The sons of Usnach closed protectively around Deirdre.

'My lady, you insult me!'

'If I have offended you, then I apologise,' she said. 'I meant to cast no slur upon your honour – but I do not trust Conor and you are a fool if you do. You may be one of his Champions, but he is not above lying to you when the need arises.'

'He would not,' Fergus said immediately, but his voice held a trace of doubt. Abruptly, he pulled his sword free from its sheath, the firelight running like amber liquid down its length. He held the sword out from him, the point tilting up towards the age-blackened rafters. He quietly commanded his sons to place their hands upon the shining blade.

'I swear by this sword, my lady, to protect you from all harm. It will strike in your defence and shield you from all blows. If any man passes insult on you, it will be taken as an insult to me – and avenged, for your enemies are now my enemies ... and my sons'.'

Deirdre stepped from the shadows into the light. The effect was startling; it was as if the goddess Danu had taken corporal form and life. She smiled at Fergus and his sons. 'My lord, I could ask for nothing more; you have calmed my doubts and fears and if Naise wishes to return to Banba, I will gladly accompany him.'

The mists hung low over the chill waters of Loch Etive as Deirdre and the sons of Usnach set out with Fergus and his sons for Banba. The craft was still under enchantment and steered itself at Fergus' command, slipping silently from the mouth of the loch and into the Firth of Lorne. As they passed out into the chill waters of the Western Ocean, the sun burst through the mists, turning the sea into a blinding metallic bowl.

Naise made his way back through the swaying boat to

where Deirdre sat in the stern, staring back at the rapidly disappearing shore of Alba.

'What troubles you, my love?'

She turned and looked at him and Naise was shocked to find her eyes full of tears. He gathered her into his arms and held her gently until her sobs subsided and she lay still.

At last she stirred and looked back at the sinking cliffs, her eyes full of longing. 'We will return some day,' said Naise.

'No. No, we are going to our deaths,' she said, with a note of resignation in her voice.

The morning wore on and presently the misty outline of the cliffs of Banba appeared on the horizon. Naise led Deirdre to the bow and pointed across the waves, and began to speak. But she laid her hand across his arm, her long nails digging into the hard flesh. 'Listen,' she whispered.

'I hear nothing ...' he said after a moment.

And then they all heard it. The haunting, melodious cries echoed across the oily waves, cutting through the air like a knife through flesh. The sound was heavy with pain and anguish – and an incredible loneliness.

It was the song of the cursed children of Lir, as they endured their second term of banishment upon the Sea of Moyle.

'It is a portent of death,' said Deirdre.

It was close to midday when the craft beached on the rough sands of the northern coast. The sun had burned away the last vestiges of the morning mist and the air was heavy and warm, thick with the smell of the sea and the mewling cries of the gulls.

Ardan leaped ashore and breathed deeply of the heady air. 'You can almost taste it,' he shouted.

Naise helped Deirdre ashore, carrying her through the foaming shallows to the drier upper reaches of the rocky beach.

'We're home,' he said simply.

93

And a party of horsemen moved out of a cave in the cliff.

Naise shouted a warning, his sword rasping from its sheath. Ardan and Anle raced across the beach to their brother, followed by Fergus and his sons.

The horses moved skittishly in the shadows, their metal shod hooves ringing hollowly against the cliff-face.

'Come forth and face us,' Fergus called, hefting his huge broadsword.

A single rider broke from the group and urged his horse forward, letting it pick its way through the boulders down onto the beach.

He reined his mount to a halt before Fergus. 'Identify yourselves,' he called, his voice harsh and cold – and knowing.

Fergus stepped forward. 'I am Fergus, son of Roy, one of the Three Champions of Conor and this party is under my personal protection.'

The rider leaned forward over his horses' head. 'Identify them.'

'Your manners leave much to be desired,' Fergus said softly. 'Take care, lest I teach you some. These are my sons, Illan and Buinne,' he continued. 'And this is Naise, Ardan and Anle ...'

'The sons of Usnach,' finished the rider, 'and this,' he said, looking intently at Deirdre, 'must be the beauteous and treacherous Deirdre, daughter of Fedlimid, the Bard.' The rider spat at Deirdre's feet. 'Whore!'

Before anyone had time to react, Fergus struck the horse across the throat, causing it to rear up, throwing its rider onto the stones. Dragging him to his feet, Fergus struck him savagely across the face with the hilt of his sword, opening a long gash from temple to chin. The warrior moaned and went limp. Fergus hefted the body and hurled it before the rapidly advancing horsemen. A horse reared as the body tumbled in its path, crashing sidelong into another, sending them both screaming to the ground.

And then Fergus was amongst them, swinging the huge sword as if it weighed no more than a dagger. With brutal precision, he butchered the warriors, slew two wounded animals and gathered together the six remaining horses. When his bloody work was complete, he leaned upon his sword and grinned crookedly at Deirdre. 'Thus end all who insult you. You see, I keep my word.'

Deirdre bowed and smiled thinly. 'It is a deed that Cucuhulain himself would have been proud of.'

Buinne the Red moved amongst the butchered bodies. Nothing moved save the wind idly plucking at scraps of torn cloth. Some had been shorn almost in two by Fergus' longsword, whilst others lacked heads or limbs.

'Do you want the heads, father?' Buinne called.

Fergus, collecting the reins of the horses, spat in the direction of the corpses. 'I would rather collect the heads of wolves than such scum.'

They had ridden the stolen mounts up the rocky beach and had almost reached the gap in the cliffs, when more riders came pouring out of the caves.

'It's a trap,' Anle shouted, dragging his sword free, but Ardan grabbed his arm and held it. 'Wait,' he cautioned.

The warriors quickly surrounded them, the sunlight turning the armour gold and bronze and striking fire from their shields. Their swords were sheathed and their spears held upright. An older man rode forward and saluted Fergus.

'I am Borrack, sent by Conor to greet you on your return to our land and to extend the hospitality of my Fort to you.'

Fergus bowed. 'I thank you, Borrack, for your invitation, but I fear we must refuse, we cannot delay ...'

'What! You are refusing my hospitality; I did not think that was possible for you.' Borrack leaned forward in the saddle and smiled slyly.

Fergus ignored him and rode back to Deirdre and Naise. 'You heard? He has invited us to his Fort - it would mean losing a night and possibly a morning. We cannot afford the time.' He jerked his head back in the direction of the still-steaming bodies. 'You saw what our reception is likely to be. The price upon your heads is too high and too tempting for most people.'

'I think we'd better hurry on,' Naise said softly. 'At least when Conor acknowledges our presence and takes the price off our heads, we'll not be subject to such abuse and I'll breathe a lot easier.'

'Can we not just refuse Borrack's invitation?' asked Deirdre.

'My lady, in my youth I refused a traveller hospitality; but he was a Druid and in return he placed a geas upon me never to refuse the hospitality of another. I must accept.'

'I see Conor's hand in this,' Deirdre murmured.

Fergus looked uncomfortable. 'It's possible, it's possible; he could be attempting to divide the party. Look,' he said, reaching a decision. 'I will go with Borrack - I have to - but Illan and Buinne will stay with you. And you must ride with all speed for Emain Macha. Once there, Conor would not dare harm you.'

'But until we get there?'

'Until you get there ...' Fergus paused and added ruefully, 'You are fair game for any wandering mercenaries, outlaws or even slaves, tempted by the huge reward.'

'Is there nothing we can do?' asked Deirdre.

'Nothing, except run for Emain Macha, Conor's capital.'

Borrack led the small group surrounded by his guards up through a sharp cleft in the cliffs, their horses' hooves echoing off the dark stone. Once they were up off the beach, the ground levelled out into a broad plain dotted with a few stands of stunted trees and in the distance the rising walls of Dun Borrack crowned with a thin spiral of smoke. They followed a worn beaten track that led from the shore in the direction of the Dun until they came to a slow meandering stream.

'We must part company here,' said Naise suddenly, as the company milled about the small ford.

'You are very welcome,' said Borrack, but without much enthusiasm.

'No ... No, I do not think so; we must go on.' Naise wheeled his mount and, followed by Deirdre, his brothers and the sons of Fergus, set out for Emain Macha in the south and west.

'I'll follow on as soon as I can,' Fergus called and then he turned to Borrack and lowered his voice. 'If I find that you are holding me here on Conor's orders so that he can try and slay them . . .' He let the threat hang for a moment, and then added, 'I will add your head to my collection.'

Borrack looked after the sons of Usnach and Fergus, with the slight figure of Deirdre in their midst and smiled weakly.

They camped late in the afternoon by a stream in a forest glade. The day had turned chill and overcast and there was rain on the wind. They sat in silence around a small smokeless camp fire, listening to the wind rustle the leaves and moan through the branches.

'You do not have to stay with us,' Deirdre said suddenly to the sons of Fergus.

Illan smiled briefly. 'My lady, we do – our father bound us to you.'

'You are likely riding to your deaths, do you know that?'

'It will be an honourable death, at least,' smiled the fair-haired youth.

'And our father will avenge us,' added Buinne.

'Why was your father chosen from the Champions to come for us?' asked Ardan.

Illan broke a twig across his knee and tossed it on the fire. 'Conor called together the Three Champions and told them of his decision to pardon you. And then he asked them – a rhetorical question, he said – what would they do if you were . . . slain?' The youth paused.

'And?' Ardan prompted.

'So, Conall said he would slay anyone who laid a hand on you, be they beggar or king. Cucuhulain said he would slay even Conor himself, should he attempt to break his word and slay you. But our father said that he would slay anyone who so much as offered you insult – except the king, to whom he owed his first loyalty.'

'Do you think Conor will betray us?' asked Anle.

Buinne grinned broadly. 'He will undoubtedly try – and we will probably have to kill a score or so of his men to discourage them. It promises to be great sport.'

'Killing is not sport,' said Deirdre coldly. 'Men are not animals.'

'When men are without honour, my lady, then they are little better than animals.'

And in the silence that followed they heard the baying of war hounds in the distance.

They fled into the gathering night, the harsh cries of the dogs spurring them on. As they rode out of the forest they could see the golden spots of torchlight moving through the trees in the distance. They crested a rise and halted their lathered mounts. The forest was behind them and in almost total darkness, save for the torches and one spot, where the last rays of the sinking sun brought a stand of trees to vibrant life. And through this band of light rode a large body of mounted warriors, their armour and weapons molten, and, running before them, a pack of huge wolfhounds.

Naise stood in the saddle and stared at the war-party. 'I don't recognise them – they are carrying no standard or totem. They could be bandits, mercenaries ...'

'Or Conor's men,' said Buinne, joining him. 'Probably mercenaries in his employ. He has hired some companies of Alban and Monan fighting men and even some from across the seas; tall, blond haired, cold-eyed giants.'

'Do we fight or run?' Naise wondered aloud.

'We run and choose our own battleground.'

The warhounds pursued them through the night, gaining relentlessly. Naise ordered them to pace their mounts, walking them as much as possible, but towards morning it was obvious that they could not continue. And even Deirdre, accustomed as she was to hard riding, was reeling in the saddle, her face pale and drawn with exhaustion. As the first grey tinge of the approaching dawn lightened the eastern sky, Naise called a halt.

'We can't go on like this much longer. The dogs will have caught up with us by sunrise and even if we push our mounts to the limit, we wouldn't reach Emain Macha until noon. We'll have to stand and fight.'

'But not here,' said Buinne. He pointed south and east. 'There is an old fort there; if we reach it before the hounds get us, we'll have something at our backs.'

They reached the tumbled ruins just as the first of the massive hounds caught up with them. A huge wolfhound leaped at Anle's throat, sending him crashing from his exhausted mount. He felt its warm breath against his face and the scalding splash of saliva across his throat. He frantically scrabbled for his knife, but his arm lay trapped beneath him and his other shoulder was numb and useless from the fall. The beast growled deep in its throat and opened its mouth.

He closed his eyes.

Abruptly, the weight was gone and he opened his eyes in time to see Buinne lift the hound above his head and dash it against the stones - the sudden snap sounding sharp and clear on the morning air. Buinne reached down for Anle and then his dark eyes widened in shock and horror as the son of Usnach stabbed at him with his sword. The glittering steel slipped under his arm, almost brushing his ribs and Buinne heard a liquid grunt behind him. A weight fell against his back and a long dagger fell from a mercenary's lifeless fingers.

Naise pushed Deirdre into one of the small rooms which had withstood the ravages of time and weather and then stood in the doorway, beating off the slavering hounds and savage mercenaries, until they piled before him in a gory wall. Ardan and Illan led the mounted warriors through the ruins, splitting them up, and then attacking, until the worn stones echoed to the savage screams and childlike cries of men and beasts.

Illan was struck to the ground and Ardan stood over him, until Buinne and Anle joined him. The shattered corpses of a score of warriors and the hewn remains of an equal number of hounds told of his battle.

A single blast of a hunting horn broke through the sounds

of the battle. The mercenaries retreated, picking their way through the ruins, harried by the sons of Usnach and Fergus, leaving their dead and wounded on the bloody stones and with the few remaining hounds limping in their wake.

Ardan held Illan as he stumbled. The youth was dazed and a thin trickle of blood ran down his face from a shallow wound in his scalp.

Naise and Deirdre joined them and she, with a strip of cloth torn from the hem of her dress and water from a canteen, cleansed and dressed Illan's wound.

Naise and Buinne meanwhile, moved through the dead, seeking a token or banner - anything that might show their allegiance. They found a wounded mercenary, one of the northern folk, with corn-yellow hair and ice-blue eyes, lying apart from the others. He had been wounded high in the chest on the left side, the blow having sheared through the thick leather and metal rings to bite deep into his flesh.

Buinne turned him over with his foot. 'Now here's one that still lives - but not for long, by the looks of him.'

Naise squatted down beside the northerner. 'Who hired you?'

The mercenary grinned, his lips pulling back over his teeth in a ghastly shadow of a smile. 'I knew we couldn't take you, not even with the dogs,' he gasped. 'He has betrayed you ...'

'Who?' Naise asked. 'Who?' he cried - although he already knew the answer.

Buinne touched his shoulder. 'Leave him, he has gone to his gods.'

Naise's face was cold and hard when he rejoined the others and Deirdre shivered at the brooding fire in his dark eyes.

'Where to?' Illan adjusted the rough bandage on his head. 'Do we go to Cucuhulain?'

Naise shook his head. 'We ride for Emain Macha with all speed. Once there, Conor must acknowledge us pardoned and then he dare not move against us.'

It was late in the evening when they crested the rise above Conor's capital and found themselves looking down on the stone walls of Emain Macha. The sun was sinking behind the rough walls, touching them with crimson and gold - it looked as if blood had been spilt on bronze, and Naise recalled with a shiver Deirdre's dream of the ravens with their gift of honey and blood.

As they neared Emain Macha, they could see the sudden flurry of activity and the flash of sunlight on weapons and then the huge gates opened and a long line of warriors marched out.

Anle squinted against the sinking sun. 'They are the Knights of the Red Branch, the élite.'

Naise grinned bleakly. 'We have little to fear from them, they are honourable men. I doubt they would attack us even if Conor himself ordered it.'

The warriors lined up along both sides of the dusty road and some touched their hearts and bowed as Naise and the veiled Deirdre passed.

Once inside the gate, the great doors swung shut and were barred for the night. The courtyard came alive with torches, banishing the dusk. Fiacha, Conor's son stepped into the light. 'My father bids you welcome and has set aside the Hall of the Red Branch for your personal use. There is food and drink prepared and he bids you break your fast, rest and refresh yourselves - he will attend you then.'

Deirdre laid her hand on Naise's arm and whispered urgently. 'Let us leave now, because once we enter the Hall, we will not come out alive.'

Naise gripped her hand and squeezed tightly. 'He dare not touch us now.'

Conor flung the goblet into the raging fire. The volatile liquor exploded into blue-green flames. 'I will have her,' he screamed, his eyes bulging and the cords in his neck standing out. 'She is mine by right and I will have her.'

'You cannot father, you have promised them your pardon,' Fiacha protested.

Conor looked at his son with contempt. 'If you intend to rule this land when I am gone, you must learn to abide by no other laws save your own – and a king makes his own laws, changing them when it suits his purpose. Tell me what she looked like,' he asked suddenly, changing the subject.

'She ... I do not know, she went veiled and cloaked.'

'Her voice then, describe it.'

'She spoke only once and then it was in a whisper to Naise.'

'I must know whether she still retains her beauty,' the king muttered.

'And if she does not?' Fiacha wondered.

'Then Naise can keep her,' Conor snapped. 'But if not ...' his voice chilled and his laugh was ugly.

Fiacha shivered.

Conor poured himself another drink, a quiet smile playing at the corner of his lips. He turned to his son. 'Find me Lavarcham, Deirdre's old teacher and nurse; perhaps she can help us.'

Naise moved his queen. 'Check,' he said quietly.

Deirdre smiled and moved her king, the light from the large fire turning the crystal pieces to amber. Ardan and Illan walked out of the shadows at the back of the huge hall murmuring softly together. Anle sat before the fire honing his sword with slow persistance, whilst Buivva hovered about the barred door. The food and drink which had been prepared for them lay untouched and although they were almost exhausted they were too excited to attempt sleep.

Suddenly Buivva spoke from beside the door. 'Someone approaches.'

Deirdre was abruptly aware that everything seemed to be coming together – it was almost as if she were part of a play, a drama which had been prepared a long time ago. 'Lavarcham,' she whispered softly to herself, as Buivva opened the door and admitted a cloaked and hooded figure.'

'It's Lavarcham,' he said.

Deirdre embraced her old teacher and nurse, tears flowing down her face. The old woman stroked her wild red hair, soothing her as if she were a child.

'I'm frightened,' she whispered softly, 'not for myself, but for the sons of Usnach and Fergus.'

Lavarcham eased herself into a chair by the fire. She was frail and birdlike, her hair snow-white, almost feather-like in its texture. But there was nothing soft about her eyes; they were hard and sharp and glittered with almost eight decades of experience. 'You must listen to me carefully,' she said, and like her eyes, her voice was vibrant and alive. 'Conor wants Deirdre and he is prepared to break every oath and principle of kingship to get her. And if he takes her by force, he will plunge this land into almost three hundred years of warfare and strife. But he only wants Deirdre if she still retains her beauty,' and the old woman smiled, 'which she does.'

'Is that why he sent you here?' asked Illan.

'I was sent to see if Deirdre was still as beautiful as she was when he last saw her. I will go back and tell the king that she does not, but I don't think that will be enough, I'm sure he will want to see for himself. So, you must bar the windows and guard the door - at least until the morning. Cucuhulain is on his way and Fergus is approaching also, they should be here by then and they will not let Conor refuse to fulfil his promise.' She stood suddenly. 'I must go, but remember, be on your guard, Conor is treacherous.'

The king raged when he heard that Deirdre's incredible beauty was lost and that she was now haggard and drawn, wasted by the years of rough living, fleeing Conor's wrath. But there was something about Lavarcham's story, something intangible, some note which rang false - or perhaps the king just did not want to believe it. But he sent one of his personal bodyguards to the hall of the Red Branch with instructions to check the old woman's story. The guard found the long wooden building in almost total darkness; chinks of flickering light showed through the cracks in the shutters and all the doors were barred. He pressed his ear against the smooth wood, but he could hear no sound from within. He walked around the building. There was a tiny open window set high up in the south wall and so, taking off his boots, he began to climb the polished timbers.

Within, Deirdre and Naise sat side by side crouched over the chessboard, vainly attempting to while away the few remaining hours to morning. Anle and Ardan and the sons of Fergus prowled restlessly about the hall, awaiting the attack which they knew would almost certainly come.

The guard gripped the sill and pulled himself up level with the window. He found he was looking down into the hall almost on top of Deirdre and Naise.

And his breath caught in his throat as Deirdre moved into the light.

He had always imagined that the stories of her beauty were greatly exaggerated, mere poet's fancies and bard's tales, but she was even more beautiful than they painted her. She turned to say something to someone out of his range of vision and the flickering light touched her face, bathing it in gold, turning her eyes to points of amber light. She stood and as he moved to follow her, the hilt of his dagger clinked against the edge of the windowsill. He saw Naise's lined and weary face look and the cold dark flash of his eyes. He saw him pluck a chessman from the board before him and throw ...

The queen struck the guard in the eye. With a hideous scream, he clawed at his face and fell backwards onto the ground with a sickening crunch. He lay screaming on the rough stones, his legs twisted at an unnatural angle, blood trickling from his lips.

A score of guards ran up and one knelt by his side. 'Tell ... tell the king ... that she ... she is beautiful,' he gasped and then he pleaded, 'kill me.'

*

Conor's anger when he heard of Lavarcham's treachery was awesome to behold, but the old woman was gone, having fled back to the mountains of her birth. And the flame of his anger raged higher when the Knights of the Red Branch refused to surround the Hall, for they were honourable men and wanted no part of the king's proposed treachery and betrayal. And, in the end, Conor was forced to use his mercenaries to surround the hall.

Buivva's sword rasped as it slid from its sheath, the sound shockingly loud in the silence. 'They are coming.'

Deirdre, with the sons of Usnach and Fergus, peered from the slits in the shutters, watching the armed and armoured warriors quietly taking up position around the hall. At last Conor appeared. He stood before the main door and folded his arms across his broad chest. 'I will receive you now, you may come forth.'

'Let us wait until morning, king; the morning sun will bring many things,' Naise called.

'Obey me; come forth now!'

'Dawn is fast approaching,' said Ardan. 'We can afford to wait.'

'But Conor will not,' said Buivva. 'I will go out and engage his men in single combat, they are honour bound to stand before me singly and perhaps Cucuhulain or my father will arrive early.' He slid the bar across the door and slipped out into what remained of the night. Illan quickly dropped the bar back into place.

Buivva faced Conor and his warriors outside the door. The king smiled, but only with his lips – his eyes remained hard and chill. 'So, you have come to join us; someone knows where his duty lies.'

Buivva shook his head. 'You are mistaken, lord, I have come out to challenge your warriors to single combat.'

'Fool!' Conor spat at Buivva's feet. 'Why not fall on your sword now and have done with it. What are you about to die for? What are the sons of Usnach to you? Does Deirdre mean anything to you?'

105

'I am honour bound to protect them,' he said simply.

'Have they honour? Had the sons of Usnach honour when they stole my bride and then fled my court? Naise, Ardan and Anle had sworn oaths of fealty to me, they were Knights of the Red Branch and honour bound to protect their king and their country. And what did they do? They abandoned one and deserted the other.

'How can you protect them knowing of their crimes? By doing so it makes you worse than them. It makes you a traitor, it makes you dishonourable, it makes you a coward ...'

Buivva's face burned red in the flickering light of the torches and when he spoke his voice was low and trembling. 'Your kingship protects you Conor, but have a care lest I forget that kingship ...'

'And what will you do?' Conor sneered. 'Kill me? You can try, but at least these men –' he gestured at the shadowy figures surrounding the hall, '– at least they are men of honour; they have sworn to protect me and they will not desert me.' He paused and added, 'As you did.'

'Never!'

The king looked surprised. 'Then what are you doing now, eh? You are protecting traitors, killers, thieves – so what does that make you?' Conor shrugged and turned away.

'Wait.' Buivva let his sword fall to his side. 'Tell me what to do,' he pleaded. 'My father has ordered me to protect them with my life and you ordered him to bring them home – and yet, now you tell me it is dishonourable to protect them. What is right?' he cried.

Conor smiled indulgently. 'Your first duty is to your father, of course, but his first duty is to me and even he, Buivva, cannot always be right. And I fear he has been sadly misled by the sons of Usnach.'

'I am uncertain ...'

'You honour your father,' Connor persisted, 'and he honours me – am I not then like your father? And answer me this: where does your duty lie – with the traitorous sons of Usnach or towards your king?'

'Towards my king,' Buivva said slowly. Sheathing his sword, he walked the short distance across the pool of light into the shadows by Conor's side.

'You will be well rewarded,' assured the king.

'I do not want your reward – only spare my brother.'

'I will do what I can.'

Inside the hall, Illan hung his head in shame and wept bitterly. Deirdre laid her hand on his arm. 'Do not curse or grieve for him; he has been tricked by Conor. He is not the first, nor will he be the last.'

But Illan refused to be comforted and, taking his sword and gear, went out to do battle with Conor's mercenaries. 'I will not listen to you,' he shouted as he came out the door, 'so do not waste your time trying to beguile me with your lying tongue – but come closer lord and I will cut it out for you.'

The king shrugged resignedly and, breaking all the codes of honour, sent three of his men against the single warrior. With almost mechanical ease Illan cut them down, parrying their blows with his spear and thrusting with his sword. Conor ordered another trio of warriors against the son of Fergus. But Illan had been trained by one of the greatest warriors in Banba – his own father – and could not be taken by common mercenaries.

Conor called his son to him. Fiacha was taller than his father, though with the same small mouth and tiny eyes. He was well built and his long reach and dazzling skill made him an almost unbeatable swordsman. The king armed him with his own weapons – a long, double-edged sword forged from starstone and a large circular shield which wailed with the voice of a banshee when its bearer was in danger of death.

Fiacha strode confidently into the circle of light cast by the torches, his arms and armour glittering golden in the warm light. Illan watched him carefully. The prince felt certain of victory, both his long reach and now the unusual length of the sword assured him of victory. But the weapons were new to him and the shield weighed heavily on his arm, whereas Illan was fighting with his own weapons and unencumbered by a shield.

Fiacha attacked suddenly, without the courtesy of a challenge. His sword darted out, feinted to the right and then came back in a long slash, which would have opened Illan from side to side had it connected. But the prince's eyes had betrayed him; Illan stepped back from the blow, caught Fiacha's sword on his spear and beat it to the ground.

Illan attacked, the point of his sword scoring a long wound along Fiacha's forearm and another below his neck - but although both were painful, neither were serious. The prince was more wary now, he brought the shield across his body and waited. Illan probed with the point of his spear, testing the metal of the shield. It rang with a dull, heavy clang and the surface of the metal was unmarked.

Fiacha suddenly brought his sword up and over his body, driving it downwards in a vicious arc, whilst at the same time pushing forward with his shield. The heavy metal hit Illan on the left side, numbing his shoulder and arm and his sword dropped from nerveless fingers. He barely deflected the sword with his spear, batting it to one side. He continued the spear's circular motion, striking Fiacha across the side of his head with the butt. The prince stumbled back, dazed and sick with the pain. Illan brought the spear in low, cracking it across his shins and then bringing the butt up again, striking Fiacha under the chin. The prince's jaw closed with an audible snap and his eyes rolled in his head as he slumped to the ground. Illan brought the spear around for the killing stroke ...

And the shield moaned.

It was a long strident tone that plucked at the nerves and set the teeth on edge. It hung trembling on the cool pre-dawn air - a terrifying otherworldly death knell.

And then out of the shadows came a warrior, the torchlight running like blood along his drawn sword and gleaming armour. It touched his broad face with amber and shaded his red beard and his long trailing red plait to rust. He was Conall, called the Victorious, one of the Three

Champions of Conor. He had been drinking in his rooms in the main building, his thoughts dark and angry, a slow hatred of Conor building, when he heard the moaning of the warning shield.

His king was in danger.

The discontented thoughts disappeared as almost three decades of unwavering loyalty to the monarch took over. Grabbing his sword, he raced for the Hall of the Red Branch. He pushed his way through the mercenaries. The moaning grew louder, more urgent, bone-chilling, mind-numbing.

Bursting into the circle of light, he saw a figure standing over a fallen warrior. The man on the ground wore the royal insignia, and Conall recognised the long black sword. The warrior standing above the fallen king raised his spear and prepared to strike ...

Conall lunged - his sword passed through Illan's body and emerged from his chest. He stood swaying, the sword still protruding from just above his heart as Fiacha pushed himself to his feet, a broad grin on his face.

Conall staggered back aghast and then Conor stepped out of the shadows. 'You have done well, my Champion, now slay him.'

Conall turned and looked at Illan. All traces of pain and fatigue had faded from the youth's face, as if the cares of this world were fading as quickly as his life.

'You have tricked me,' Conall screamed. 'This was my friend.' He held Illan as his legs began to buckle.

'He was a traitor,' said Fiacha casually. He struck at the dying warrior with his sword, but Conall caught the blade in his mailed fist and wrenched it from the prince's grasp. The Champion deftly flipped the weapon and, with a single blow, struck Fiacha's head from his body. He spat on the decapitated body.

Illan sank slowly to the ground, despite Conall's supporting arm. 'Find ... Cucuhulain or ... my father ... tell ... tell him,' he gasped. 'And ... beware Conor's treachery.'

And Conall wept as Illan, his life-long friend died in his

arms. He gathered up the body and walked away from the Hall of the Red Branch. Conor stared after him, fingering his sword, refusing to look at the headless thing on the blood-clotted ground. And abruptly, he remembered Old Catbad the Druid's warning the day the child Deirdre had been born: 'She will bring with her death and destruction. She will divide the kingdom, and set brother against brother, she will cause the downfall of kings and the death of princes.' And Conor shivered.

Thrice, during what little remained of the night, the king's mercenaries attempted to fire the building. But its builders had constructed well and the hardwood only scorched and refused to burn. The fire arrows sputtered out harmlessly against the sloping roof and the thrown spears snapped against the walls. Conor refused to let the mercenaries storm the building. There was too little time left and he could not allow the sons of Usnach to be slaughtered within the Hall of the Red Branch, lest the Knights themselves turn on him.

The first grey tinge of dawn touched the eastern sky and the king knew that either Cucuhulain or Fergus would arrive soon. And in desperation he sent for Catbad, the Druid.

Within the hall, Deirdre and the sons of Usnach awaited the coming dawn. Conor could not afford to anger all three of his Champions, not now, not whilst Maeve was gathering her armies in Connaught. As it was, his reputation was tarnished almost beyond redemption. He had lost Conall and surely he had lost Fergus now as well, and Cucuhulain, who placed honour above all other things would leave him also. All that was left for the king now was the capture of sons of Usnach and the taking of Deirdre.

'You will work an enchantment – drive them out,' said Conor to the aged Druid when he arrived.

'I will not.'

'You will do as I say old man, or ...' Conor let the threat hang.

The Druid laughed gently. 'You will what? For all your

blustering, you are nothing more than a coward and a dishonourable coward, at that. I will work no enchantment to drive them out.' Catbad gathered his long robes about him and left. When he was gone, a young man in the pale blue robes of a student approached the king.

'My lord, I could not help but overhear what you were discussing with my master.'

The king eyed the young man disdainfully. 'Yes, and what can you do?'

'I am not unaccomplished in the arcane arts ...'

Conor nodded slowly. 'I see. Can you drive them out?' He nodded in the direction of the hall.

'It would be a little difficult, but it could be done,' the young man hesitated, and the king recognised the look in his eyes.

'You would not find me ungenerous,' he said. 'Catbad is an old man now and today he has refused my command; I will soon need a new court Druid.'

The young man nodded and smiled quietly. He stepped away from king and raised his long alder wand high. The first rays of the sun touched its tip with fire as he chanted aloud in the Old Tongue - a tongue which men said was older than the land itself.

In the hall it was still dark. Naise and Deirdre huddled together by the dying embers of the fire, whilst Ardan and Anle stood by the shuttered windows, staring out from the cracks into the morning.

'There is a Druid outside,' said Anle.

And fire blossomed in the hall.

It hung in the centre of the long room, a glowing, pulsating ball of intense white light. Naise grabbed a pitcher of water and threw it at the fireball. The clay pitcher exploded with the heat and the water steamed furiously as it touched the outer fringes of the fireball. The heat was incredible. The wooden table and chairs began to smoulder and char and Ardan yelped as the metal of his breastplate grew too hot to touch.

And slowly the ball began to grow.

'We must get out,' said Ardan, 'before we bake.'

The sons of Usnach doused themselves and Deirdre with water and stood by the door. They formed a fighting wedge, Ardan to the left, Anle to the right, Naise leading and Deirdre behind him and between the brothers. As quietly as possible, Naise lifted the bar from the door. But before they went out into the morning, Naise looked back at the rapidly expanding ball of fire and spoke the Name of the Dagda, the Father of All.

The fireball suddenly shrank in upon itself with an icy blast and as they erupted from the hall, their weapons ready, the first thing they saw was the Druid wrapped in writhing blue flames which consumed him before their eyes.

Conor ordered his mercenaries against the trio. But the sons of Usnach beat them off, taking only minor cuts themselves. The king retreated deeper and deeper into the body of his men as the three warriors cut a bloody path through his guard. But then the archers appeared.

The sons of Usnach gathered shields from their fallen foes and sheltered behind them as the arrows rained about them. And still they advanced.

A runner approached the king, one of the guards from the battlements. He had seen a cloud of dust in the west – Cucuhulain was approaching.

Conor stepped out from his men and ordered the archers to cease firing and called the others off. He held out both hands to Deirdre and the sons of Usnach. 'I offer you peace,' he said.

Naise laughed. 'Peace; you call this peace?'

'It was an impulsive act; anger momentarily clouded my judgement.'

'You are a liar,' said Naise. 'A traitorous, cowardly liar.'

Conor smiled, showing his teeth like a cornered animal. 'Can we not settle our differences?'

Naise looked around him at the dead and dying. 'I doubt if our differences can ever be settled – except in blood.'

'And there has been enough shed this day,' said the king piously. 'Let there be an end to it.'

Naise nodded his head. 'Aye, let there be an end to it. I grow weary of this fighting, the stench of blood disgusts me.' He looked over his shoulder at his brothers and Deirdre. 'Do we trust him?'

Ardan and Anle laughed. 'Trust him; never.'

'But in this case,' Naise persisted, 'can we trust him now?'

'I think he has little choice,' said Anle.

'Do not trust him,' said Deirdre quietly. 'There is treachery in his eyes.'

'Come, come, let us be friends – or if not friends, then let us not be enemies,' Conor amended.

'That is impossible,' said Naise sadly. 'There are too many years, too many bodies, too much blood between us.' He raised his head and looked into the morning sunrise.

'Look, a new day is dawning, let it mark a new beginning between us also.' He sheathed his sword with a snap.

Reluctantly his brothers followed suit and Deirdre's murmured protest went unnoticed.

Conor came forward, his arms outstretched, his face creased in a smile. He held Naise by the arms. 'I have waited a long time for this moment,' he said gently. 'SEIZE THEM!'

Thus were the sons of Usnach taken through treachery.

'Who will slay these traitors for me?' the king called. No-one moved. To slay bound warriors was the act of a coward.

'Is there no-one man enough to slay them – or must I do it myself?'

'You know you cannot do it yourself,' said Naise, still standing tall and straight despite the bonds which cut into his wrists. 'You know that if you kill us, either Cucuhulain or Fergus will have your head.'

A tall, blond-haired, blue-eyed youth came out of the crowd. 'Let me kill them; I do not fear your Champions, king.'

'Then you are a fool,' laughed Ardan.

The youth pulled his sword from its sheath. 'Which one shall I kill first?' he asked Conor.

'You must kill me first,' said Naise.

'No, me,' said Ardan and Anle together.

'If you slay them, then you must slay me also,' screamed Deirdre, held in the grip of two warriors.

'One of you must die first,' said Conor reasonably. 'Come, who is man enough to die first?'

'I have never been called a coward,' said Naise. 'I have fought deamons and beasts and men, without flinching - but I cannot bear to see my brothers slain, or to see Deirdre's face broken in sorrow.'

The youth raised his sword and prepared to strike Naise.

'No, you cannot,' said Ardan. 'We were always one in life, let us die together.'

'That is impossible.'

'Take our sword, "The Retaliator",' said Naise. 'It was a gift to us from the Lord of the Sea, but we have never had cause to use it.'

The sword was found amongst their belongings in the hall, a long, single-edged weapon, almost three times the length of a normal sword. It glittered blue-green in the morning sunlight.

Naise, Ardan and Anle knelt on the ground together. Their executioner raised the overlong sword and Naise looked across at the weeping figure of Deirdre. 'I love you,' he whispered.

The sword fell.

Thus ends the tale of the sons of Usnach. But for Conor, it was only the beginning of the end of his kingdom. When Fergus returned and found one of his sons slain and the other's treachery, and learning of Conor's own treachery, he gathered together his men and marched south and west for Connaught and took service with Maeve. Some time later, Connaught attacked Ulster, and it was Cucuhulain the Hound who held the army of Maeve, commanded by Fergus, at bay, but when he fell, Ulster was overrun, and Emain Macha was no more.

But beyond the hill that was once the capital of the north there is a little grove of trees surrounding a sparkling pool. And it is said that the pool sprung from the tears shed by Deirdre for Naise and his brothers. The trees are said to grow from the spot where the three sons of Usnach are buried and across the pool is a single tree, a willow, its branches drooping in sorrow into the pool – and it grows from the spot where they buried Deirdre, for she slew herself before Conor could claim her.

CHAPTER 4

MIDIR AND ETAIN

'The harlot has stolen Midir away from me,' said Fuanach, Queen of the De Danann, the People of the Goddess.

'His heart is certainly hers,' agreed the Druid cautiously, 'but what do you want me to do about it?'

Fuanach paced the stone cell impatiently, measuring its length and breadth in angry steps. Dusk was falling and the tiny fire in the rough grate bathed the little chamber in wan amber light; smoke coiled about the blackened stones, stinging the queen's hard eyes and burning her throat.

'You must kill her!'

Tarlaim the Druid shook his head. 'You know that is impossible, she is of the De Danann, I have neither the ability nor the power to kill her.' He stirred the coals of the mean fire with his brass shod staff. 'However,' he added, 'we could dispose of her ...'

Fuanach gripped the Druid's thin shoulders and gazed into his sightless eyes. 'How?'

Tarlaim ran a calloused hand down the queen's raven hair, seemingly lost in thought. Abruptly he gripped it and pulled hard; tears started into her eyes, but she bit her lip and made no sound. 'By turning her into what she is not ...'

'A transformation?' asked Fuanach between clenched teeth.

'A transformation,' agreed the Druid. 'And what would you have her: bird ... beast ... insect ...?'

Fuanach pulled away and knelt, staring into the glowing embers. 'Can she be killed in her new shape?' she wondered.

'Certainly, but not by any deliberate action of yours. But

were she to succumb to hunger, thirst or exhaustion – then she would die.'

The queen nodded silently, her ice-grey eyes glittering strangely and then she laughed. And Tarlaim – who had traded his eyes with the deamons of the pit in return for arcane knowledge – shivered with the sound of that pitiless laughter.

'Then turn her into a butterfly, Druid: it should suit her character, something beautiful, but shallow and fragile – something easily broken. Then call up a wind, the like of which has never before blown across Banba's shores, and let it carry Etain to the ends of the land.'

'That can be done,' agreed the Druid.

'Why do you wait?' asked Fuanach, when he made no move to set the spell. 'Do it now!'

'And payment?' wondered Tarlaim mildly.

Slowly Fuanach rose from before the fire and, taking the Druid's hard hands, placed them on the gold clasp high upon her shoulder. His breathing quickened as he fumbled with the pin, and then it was undone and her heavy gown fell in shimmering folds about her feet. Savagely Fuanach kissed him ...

Night crept slowly over Bre Leth, the fort of Midir, King of the De Danann. But the stars that shone over the sidhe were not those that glittered in the heavens above the world of Man. And whilst the De Danann might inhabit the world of Man, they were still separated from it, living in a realm of their own, a Shadowland, where death held no domain and sickness was unheard of.

The tiny sliver of the new moon rose low in the sky, touching the few clouds with silver, whilst overhead, the alien stars trembled hard and sharp on the thick velvet cloth of heaven.

Midir and Etain stood on the battlements and watched the skies. The king encircled Etain's shoulders with one arm whilst pointing out constellations with his free hand.

'See, there is the Evenstar and there below is her maid-servant, Etive, and that triple cluster to the right are her bodyguards, Conn, Corann and Conan.'

'And that one, my lord?' asked Etain, nestling close to her lover and pointing to a group of stars.

'That is the Cup of Heaven; see there is the bowl, the stem, there the base. It is a horn of plenty, or riches and ...' he bent and kissed the top of Etain's corn-yellow hair, '... of love.'

They stood awhile longer, staring silently into the night, content in each other's company. Suddenly Etain shivered. 'It has grown chill.'

Midir slipped the cloak from his shoulders and drew it about Etain. 'Let us retire now, my love,' he said.

Shivering, she agreed.

By the time they reached Etain's bedchamber, she was shaking so badly she could hardly stand. Midir placed his hand on her brow, but she was not feverish. Lifting her in his strong arms, the king carried his mistress to her bed, and wrapped the thick furs about her.

'I will fetch a physician, this is not natural,' he said.

As soon as Midir left her, the shivering stopped. And suddenly the room was like a furnace. Scrambling from the smothering furs, Etain went and stood in the window, her face turned to the light breeze trickling through. But she still burned and her light garments weighed upon her like a warrior's mail. He hands trembled and her fingers were numb and unresponsive as they struggled to undo the straps and pins. A pin pierced her thumb as she frantically pushed her gown and shift to the floor. She felt the cool breeze flow across her hot skin like balm. Throwing her head back, she closed her eyes and luxuriated in its cool embrace.

Gradually she became aware of a tingling in her hands and feet, a tingling that spread rapidly until it engulfed her as if she were sinking into a pit of sand.

She opened her eyes, but the room swayed and lurched as if she were standing on the deck of a storm tossed ship. Tiny points of coloured light exploded before her eyes, leaving trembling afterimages of blackness. The room vanished behind a coloured gauze curtain of shifting light. She was blind.

Etain opened her mouth to scream, but she could make no sound - her body was no longer hers, it was separate, unreal, a stranger's. She became aware of a dull pounding, like that of the surf on the shore, a pounding that embraced and then engulfed her, until she felt as if her entire being might shatter.

Abruptly, it ceased.

Sight had returned, but only a flat, two-dimensional, colourless vision. Hearing had also returned, but now she heard with her entire body.

Body?

Sorcery!

The truth hit her with an almost physical blow. A shape-change; someone had wrought a transformation upon her. And she did not even have to wonder whom: Fuanach. But what shape had her body been warped into? Clumsily, she directed her body to a pitcher of water which lay beside her bed. The room glided past underneath - *underneath?* - and curved off at the edges, making progress erratic and difficult. Reaching the pitcher of water, she forced herself to stop - although she was constantly pulled and tugged in countless directions by intangible, but irresistible forces. Etain directed her gaze downward.

And had she a mouth to scream, she would have done so. For reflected in the water was the image of a butterfly.

Midir raced down the corridor followed by his physician and two warriors. He was conscious of a heavy foreboding nestling at the base of his skull. Etain's sudden sickness reeked of sorcery - but who would wish to harm such a beautiful and innocent maid?

Fuanach!

If she were behind this, the king swore, he would have her head and the heads of those who had helped her. Reaching the door of Etain's bed-chamber, he paused. There were noises within. Drawing his sword he pushed the old physician back and called his warriors forward. Weapons at the ready they pushed open the door and launched themselves into the room ...

... Into chaos ...

It was as if they had stepped out into a winter gale. An icy wind tore at them, buffeting them in all directions, threatening to strip the flesh from their bones, numbing and burning at the one time. The bed furs flapped like angry birds, and the window coverings of heavy cloth were ripped off and flung in their faces.

Midir braced himself against the doorframe and pushed himself into the centre of the room, seeking Etain. The low bed had been stripped bare, and nothing but the leather straps and polished wooden frame remained. As he fought his way to it, the entire frame slowly overturned and came tumbling towards him. He felt someone grip his leg and jerk him forward, and he crashed to the floor beside his warriors. The heavy frame rose on the gale and shattered against the wall over their heads, showering them with thick splinters.

Jars and small bowls flew about the room like angry wasps, breaking against the walls, smearing the stones with expensive oils and ungents. One of Etain's bone combs raked against the king's face, drawing blood and narrowly missing his eye.

Midir scrambled backwards out of the room, his warriors crowding him in their eagerness to quit the enchanted place. Behind them the room dissolved into a maelstrom of destruction.

'Sorcery,' screamed Midir. 'Sorcery. Seal the fort, let no-one leave.' He pushed away the physician, who was dabbing at the cut on his face with a cloth. 'Leave it; you will have blood soon enough to wipe.' He turned to his guards. 'Bring Fuanach to the main hall and all her servants and slaves, aye, and her pet Druid also. Heat the irons and have chains prepared – I will have the truth; I will have my Etain!'

*

The gale gripped Etain in a constricting fist, tightening and squeezing, battering her with incredible force. She could not resist it, she could only allow herself to be propelled at the will of the storm. And as she was flung into the night, her last thoughts were of Midir, her love.

For seven years the gale that had torn through Bre Leth whipped across the fields of Banba, sometimes at such a great height that the only evidence of its passing were the rapidly shifting clouds. But often the gale would tear along at ground level, destroying entire forests in its fury, flattening crops, laying waste entire communities and devastating the hill forts where they were exposed to the full fury of the sorcerous wind. Many died in the Land of Men, and even the People of the Goddess, the De Danann, were hard put to defend themselves from the elemental fury of the storm. They could not reverse the spell, for they did not know how it had been set – and Tarlaim could not tell them, for Midir's guards had found him with his throat slit.

Midir had taken Fuanach and had her questioned under torture, but she had revealed nothing and because she was of the De Danann, he could not order her slain.

The king called together the greatest of the Druids from Alba and Mona and from the Land Across the Water, where men went daubed in blue and the Druids there worshipped in great stone circles and ancient places of power. But even these were unable to wrest from the queen the location of Etain. And in desperation they tried to raise the shade of Tarlaim, but he had been damned and thrice damned in life and now paid the price in death and his shade wandered beyond the Fields of Life, in that place it is not wise to visit.

And in revenge, Midir ordered the assembled Druids to work an enchantment upon the queen and turn her into a lizard and then they cast her out into the Fields of Man, where she wandered for a thousand years until the coming of the New God and of the Truth-Bringer, the one men would call Patrick.

But Fuanach cursed Midir, saying that 'though he would find Etain after thrice seven years of searching, he would lose her again, after thrice seven days, and their second parting would be the hardest to bear, for it would be Midir himself who would cast her out'.

And then Midir set a regent to rule his land in his stead and taking his harp and chessboard, sword and spear, set out for the Fields of Man to search for his lost love.

Etain wandered for seven years over the fields of Bamba knowing little rest and no ease. Hunger and thirst were with her always and her delicate body always ached. Her greatest fear was that her gauzy wings might break beneath the onslaught of the gale and leave her helpless and broken on the ground below.

One morning as she rested on a stone by a tiny glittering stream, she saw a youth approaching and because she was of the De Danann and able to see beyond the surface of things, she recognised him as Angus, the god of Love and Lord of the Birds.

He stood taller than a mortal man and his hair was of the palest gold, as were his eyebrows and lashes. His tunic was of pure white wool and about his wrists were bracelets of rune-inscribed gold.

Etain took flight and fluttered before the god, wary of the four birds that circled above his head. The god raised his hand and the huge butterfly settled gracefully down onto it, her large wings pulsating gently. Angus looked upon her and, with his sight that saw beyond the corporeal, he made out the form of the maid beneath the enchantment.

And the god recognised her, for the tale of Fuanach's jealousy and revenge had quickly spread.

'You are Etain.' The god's voice was sweet and pure with a strangely bell-like quality. With infinite care he stroked her beautiful wings. 'Come with me,' he whispered, 'perhaps I can help you.' And so he took her to his palace beyond the Shadowland, in the place where time stands still.

The god attempted to remove the enchantment, but even he was unable to reverse the spell totally. However, with the

122

aid of the Goddess Danu, he could lift the enchantment from dusk to dawn, but not fully. For, during the hours of shadow and night, Etain regained the form of a maid, but she still retained the great gauzy wings of the butterfly.

Etain stayed with Angus for some years – although it was impossible to measure the length of time she spent in the god's domain. It seemed distant and dream-like, and although she was physically present, her thoughts were always with Midir.

The god had set apart a small grove in a secluded corner of his kingdom for the maid and had his curious servants furnish it with all manner of comforts and trappings, and ordered them to tend to her needs. And he had a tiny jewelled casket fashioned of the pure white gold from the eastern hills of Banba and had it inlaid with crystal from the south, green stone from the west and set on a plinth of red stone from the north and there Etain stayed during the days whilst she was trapped in the form of a butterfly.

But her enforced captivity began to tell upon her and she begged Angus to let her go free during the day and stretch her wings flying over the god's vast kingdom. But he refused, for he feared Etain would leave him – and the God of Love had been smitten by his own gift: he had fallen in love with the maid.

One night, just before dawn broke over the god's kingdom, Etain rose from his bed and went to the tiny casket, and with a pin, she undid the clasp so that it would not lock properly, and then, folding her wings back, she returned to Angus' side.

When the god awoke, he found that Etain had undergone her transformation as usual and where once a fair maid had lain, now only a large golden butterfly lay upon the pillow. Gently, he took the creature upon his finger and placed her within the casket, never noticing that it did not lock fully.

When the god returned about mid-morn, he found the tiny gate of the casket open and the butterfly gone. Angus raged and the very heavens trembled with his wrath. He called together his servants and followers and sent them out in search of the butterfly and then he gathered the legions of the skies – for he was Lord of the Birds – and commanded them to find and return his love to him.

But as the months passed they all trickled back with the same tale: Etain was no more, she must be dead.

And Angus, God of Love grieved, for he felt she was dead and surely if she still lived, one of his winged scouts would have found her? The god walked no more over the Fields of Man, and love ceased to exist in Banba. Husbands quarrelled with wives, parents with children, and brother with brother. And at last the goddess Danu was forced to call upon all her powers to heal her son, but it was said that Angus never fully recovered from his loss, and thus love is one of the most fragile of emotions, beautiful and terrible, life-giving ... and deadly.

Etain wandered far in the guise of the butterfly when she stole from the god's palace. She knew Angus would pursue her and so she fled east, ever eastwards into the dawn, without resting or taking food or drink. It was three days after she had fled the god's realm and returned to the Fields of Man before she saw a building in the distance. It was a large hill fort, built on a knoll overlooking a wide, meandering river. Night was falling and the palace was a blaze of lights and on the still air came the sound of harps and pipes and the voices of many making merry.

Etain flew in through a high window and perched on a smoke-blackened beam overlooking the main banqueting hall.

The noise, the heat and the stench were almost overpowering. The hall was filled to capacity with the nobility of Banba in all their barbaric finery. Almost directly below the trembling butterfly were the two guests of honour and their clothing and ornaments proclaimed them king and queen. They sat close together and whispered often and Etain guessed that this must be their wedding feast.

Suddenly the main doors were thrown open to admit the cook and his retinue bearing a whole roasted ox. But the sudden gust of wind upset Etain and she tumbled from her perch. She fell - straight into the upraised goblet of the queen ...

The queen toasted the ox and then, as custom dictated, downed the heady ale in one swallow.

Nine months later, a girl-child was delivered to the queen of Leinster. And she and her husband rejoiced to have been blessed with a child so soon after their marriage. And they named the child Etain, after the mythical De Danann princess.

Now the years passed, and the child Etain grew into womanhood. She was remarkably beautiful and many observed that she resembled neither her father's dark swarthy looks nor her mother's fiery red complexion and hair.

Etain's hair was corn-yellow, soft and fine; it was a halo in the sunlight. Her eyes were wide and tilted and of the purest green - what the country-folk call elven eyes. She stood taller than most of the youths in the palace and her carriage was always regal and proud.

But of her previous life as Etain of the Tuatha De Danann, Etain the maid knew nothing.

Now Eochaid had recently come to the throne at Tara, and had been proclaimed Ard Ri - High King - before a Council of Kings, and to celebrate, he had announced a great feast to be held in Tara's halls and called for the kings and queens of Banba to attend.

But one by one his messengers returned and all bore the same reply: it went against custom to be guested by a man only and thus they would not - could not - attend until Eochaid had found himself a wife. The High King raged and swore he would rule alone at Tara until such time as he chose - and he would not be hurried or pushed into finding himself a wife.

And one day in late summer, when the high king rode in search of the great wolves that still roamed Banba in those times, he ventured east and south into Leinster's domain. He spent the night with the king, feasting and making merry. And there he met Etain, daughter of the king. She was by then a maid of eighteen summers and well past the age of betrothal and the very night Eochaid asked for her hand.

They were married on Samhain Eve.

Midir wandered the length and breadth of Banba searching for Etain. In the guise of a harper or healer, sage or seer, he went from fort to fort, hall to hall, seeking any clue that might lead him to his love.

And at last he began to hear rumours of Eochaid's recent marriage and the incredible beauty of his bride, a bride that bore the name Etain in memory of the legendary De Danann princess – and who bore a startling resemblance to her namesake. Midir made his way to Tara, stopping off in Leinster to confirm the rumours. He heard the tales the country-folk told of Etain's elven beauty and how the birds and beasts flocked about her; and one wise woman even whispered that she thought the princess a goddess reborn in the guise of Man.

And so Midir came to Tara in the guise of a harper. In the evenings and long into the nights he sang the old lays and recounted the tales of gods and men; he sang of the Dagda and Danu, of the Babd: Macha, Neman and Morrigan; he told of the conquests of Banba by the Partholonians, the Fomorians, the Nemedians, the Fir Bolg and the Tuatha De Danann. The great hall would grow silent whilst he sang and if men closed their eyes they could almost see the invaders come and go, the cries of battle, the shouts of victory and screams of death and the rise and fall of kings and heroes. There was magic in his voice and enchantment in his music.

But the harper troubled Etain. When he sang of the

126

Tuatha De Danann, his words seemed to linger and echo in her head, sending disturbing ripples deep into her unconscious. She found she could put names to faces, she could visualise the locations and the antique architecture of the elder race. For her, his stories lived.

Her dreams were troubled; strange lands and even stranger peoples wandered through her nightmares ... and they were all so achingly familiar.

She would awake suddenly from sleep, her screams still echoing about the bedchamber and find Eochaid awake and staring at her with a troubled gaze. But when he questioned his wife, she would tell him nothing save that she had dreamt, and even when he pushed her to describe her dream, a strange reluctance stopped her and she protested she did not truly know.

The High King sent for his physicians, but when they examined the queen they found her to be healthy, although exhausted. Eochaid then summoned his Druids and they laid spells and incantations about the chamber and placed runes and amulets on the queen's bed designed to protect her against sorcery or witchcraft.

But the dreams still persisted and daily Etain grew more wan and pale. Her clear eyes unfocused and gazed into the distance - a distance unfathomable by mortal man. She heard the harper's songs always now, they haunted her, and they drew her - but where?

For Etain had been too long in the Fields of Men, and her previous life was all but lost to her - except in dreams.

'I am beginning to despair, harper,' said Eochaid, leaning over and filling Midir's cup. 'I am losing her.'

Midir nodded and sipped at the strong ale.

The High King and his harper sat alone at the top table. Around them the company sprawled in drunken abandon amidst the dogs and scattered debris of their feast. A single sconce remained alight above them, bathing them in wavering amber light, whilst the rest of the hall drifted off into shadow. Silence reigned over Tara and only the muted footfalls of the distant sentries disturbed the night.

'It is a bad business,' agreed the harper.

The High King downed his drink and quickly refilled the goblet with a trembling hand. 'It is; it is almost as if she were living in another world. But she is mortal!' he suddenly shouted. 'I know her parents, and whilst it is true that she resembles neither of them, she is their child, born of her mother's womb. And I know that she cannot be a changeling, for she was born with that hair and eye colouring.' The High King buried his head in his hands. 'I don't know what to do.'

'There is little you can do - save wait. Perhaps it will wear off, perhaps the Druids' spells will work.'

'But they say that there are no spells or enchantments laid on her. What she sees is all within her own head, she dreams, she dreams.' Eochaid drank again quickly.

'But she is being drawn into that dream,' said Midir, 'and there is nothing you can do about it.'

'I know,' the king whispered, 'I know.' He shrugged. 'Perhaps her mood will change, perhaps she will return to me. We can only wait.'

Midir picked up his harp. 'Will I play for you, my lord?'

'No; I fear I would find little cheer in your music - it allows one time to think and dream and I wish to do neither at the moment. But I will get a servant to bring my chessmen; we will play together.' He paused. 'Ah, I cannot. The board and pieces are in Etain's chamber and tonight she sleeps peacefully and does not toss and turn; I don't wish to disturb her.'

'We will use my board then,' said Midir. 'Clear a space whilst I fetch it.'

Eochaid swept the table clear, knocking the goblets and platters onto the floor and keeping only a flagon of ale and two drinking horns by his side.

The harper returned almost immediately, a large cloth-wrapped bundle tucked under one arm. Placing it down before the king, he carefully unwrapped it. Eochaid gasped in surprise, for Midir's chessboard was carved from a single piece of pure quartz as thick as his thumb. Intricate runes were incised into the margins of the board and a representation of each of the four prime elements were cut into the four corners of the board. Every second square cut into the quartz was sheathed in a thin foil of gold. The chessmen were individually wrapped in velvet and carved from flawless black and white marble. They were worked in marvellously intricate detail, even down to the expressions on the pawn's faces.

'Elven craft,' Midir explained, setting up the pieces.

Eochaid nodded. He had always thought his own board of silver and pale gold the most beautiful in Banba, but this... this was beautiful almost beyond imagining.

'Shall we set a wager, lord?' the harper asked. 'I will perform a single task for you if you win.'

'And I will grant you a single wish if you win,' Eochaid replied.

They played. The dawn broke over Tara and the palace blazed with morning gold, a gold which hardened as noon drew on and then softened to russet as evening came. At last night returned.

Eochaid moved his queen and said, 'Your king is almost lost.'

Midir nodded and toppled his king, the sound of marble on gold hard and sharp in the silence and conceded the game.

'I have never met a player like you,' said the High King. 'You are not what you seem,' he added.

But the harper only smiled enigmatically and began to reset the pieces. Eochaid rose and went to the window and stood staring down over his fields. Midir joined him.

'And now your forfeit,' he pointed down into the shadows. 'My slaves struggle to till that land, but the ground is hard and even with oxen they make little headway. There must be an easier way, a simpler way.' He smiled slowly. 'Tell me how they might till the land more easily.'

Midir laughed gently. 'Why lord, that is easily done.

Instruct your slaves to place the yoke and harness about the oxen's shoulders rather than on its brow. It can then pull with its full weight, rather than with its head only and you will have fewer blinded or crippled beasts also.'

Eochaid nodded slowly. 'I see how it might be done; it is sound advice - you have paid your forfeit. Now go and rest yourself, we will play again at dawn.'

And Eochaid and Midir played again as the first glimmerings of dawn touched the eastern sky and the game lasted all through the day and into the night, only finishing in the late afternoon of the following day.

Once again, the High King won.

And again Eochaid took Midir to the window. The sun was sinking in the west and the High King could almost imagine it dying a bloody death in the vast Western Ocean. Night was drawing in from the east and Tara seemed caught between night and day.

The High King pointed down and then out to the fields beyond Tara. 'It has always been my wish to build a road to the west through there,' he said. 'That is your forfeit: build me that road!'

Midir bowed and left silently; and Eochaid, rising with the dawn the following morning, went and stared out from his window. In the wan light of morning, a road, broad enough for two chariots to pass abreast, cut into the distance. Several hundred years would have to pass before another road like it would be built across the water in Britain by the southern invaders in their strange metal armour.

And so Eochaid and Midir played together a third - and final - time. But before the game commenced, the harper said, 'Let us change the wager this time; I will stake my most valuable possession: this chessboard. What will you wager?'

The High King laughed. 'My most valuable possession is my wife Etain; I will not stake her.'

'A kiss then,' said Midir slowly. 'If I win let me claim a single kiss from your wife.'

And Eochaid reluctantly agreed, although having won

130

two games, he felt confident he would win the third.

They began to play at noon and by evening Eochaid had lost. He stared in amazement as his checkmated king. 'You allowed me to win previously,' he accused the harper.

Midir bowed slightly. 'My lord,' he said ironically, 'you lack my experience.'

And then he stood. 'I claim my prize: a single kiss from your wife.'

'No!'

Midir rounded on the High King. 'What, you are refusing to honour a wager? Would you wish men to remember you as Eochaid Oath-Breaker?'

The High King gripped his goblet of ale and downed it in one swallow and then he squeezed until the metal buckled and crumpled in his fist. 'You must give me time to prepare my wife,' he gasped. 'Return to me when the moon is full – you may claim your prize then.'

Midir nodded and, gathering together his chessmen and board, took his leave with the promise that he would return in one month.

Eochaid stood by the window and watched the harper ride away on his snow-white horse along the new road and he swore the strange harper would never claim that kiss.

The month flew by and each night the moon, waxing now towards fullness, mocked him with its harsh bone-white light. Eochaid ordered the defences about Tara doubled, and then re-doubled, although he could not say what he truly feared. But the very thought of the harper kissing his wife chilled him.

He was certain the harper was not of the race of Man, but was he one of the sidhe folk? It was true that he carried their handicraft, but the elven race often gifted mortals, so that was no indication. The harper could have elven blood; his height and fair colouring, his curiously delicate fingers and slanting eyes were all features of the old race. But there were many who carried a touch of the old blood and with the blond foreigners coming from the east and the swarthy traders from the south, it was by now almost impossible to tell a man's lineage from his looks.

But why had he chosen such a strange prize - and why did Eochaid fear that single kiss? The High King walked the battlements with Firgoil, his Druid, on the eve of the harper's return.

'Why does he frighten me, Firgoil?'

The tall Druid ran his acid-scarred hands through rapidly greying hair. 'Some men have the ability to induce fear in others, just as others have the ability to inspire respect. But I think you fear the harper on a deeper level; I think you fear him because he threatens that which you love most: your wife.'

'But how?' Eochaid wondered. 'How?'

'Then let me ask you this, lord: When did your lady wife begin to fade; when did the nightmares start?'

'A little more than a month ago.'

'And when did the harper first come to your court?'

'Why, a little more than ...' Comprehension dawned in Eochaid's hard grey eyes. 'A little more than a month ago!'

'It is perhaps a little too much to be a coincidence,' said the Druid.

'Do you think he plans to take Etain from me?'

Firgoil leaned on the rough stone battlements and stared out over the fields, now silent and mysterious with the coming of night. 'Lord, do you know the tale of Midir and Etain; it is sometimes sung by the bards and harpers?'

'It is familiar, vaguely so,' said Eochaid.

'Much of it is unimportant here, but this much is significant. Etain the elven - the De Danann - princess is stolen from her lover's fort - and he goes in search of her. Both disappear and are never heard of again ... at least thus far.'

'Druid,' said Eochaid, 'I do not like what you are hinting at.'

'Midir, the De Danann prince,' continued Firgoil, 'was an accomplished harpist ... and an unsurpassed chessplayer, his board and men having been crafted by the greatest of the De Danann smiths.'

'The harper,' groaned Eochaid, 'is Midir. He has come to claim Etain.' He struck the stones with his fist. 'But he is wrong. Etain - my Etain - is human, she is not the lost De Danann princess.'

The Druid shrugged. 'She was born of woman it is true; but the gods are often born of mortal man.'

There was silence on the battlements then, the only sound the chill wind whipping in from the west and when the High King spoke again, the Druid had to struggle to catch his words.

'But he shall not have her; he shall not have her.'

Eochaid put his armies on full alert and had them camp in the fields about the palace. His captains grumbled at what in their opinion was a stupid display - and dangerous also, for some of the lesser kings might construe the gathering as a threat. And the High King ordered his captains to set pickets; they were to let no-one approach Tara without his permission, and no-one, absolutely no-one was to leave until dawn.

In the main hall, Eochaid gathered his personal guard and explained to them that an attempt might be made to abduct his wife. The doors were locked and the high windows covered with heavy cloths; a huge fire roared in the hearth in the centre of the floor, sending sparks spiralling up to the circular opening in the soot-blackened ceiling. The flickering firelight burnished the weapons and armour in warm hues of bronze and gold.

Etain sat before the fire, a heavy woollen cloak thrown over her shoulders. Eochaid sat beside his wife, her thin pale hand clutched in his. Firgoil stood behind the High King nervously tapping his metal-shod staff against the cold flags. Tonight, Etain seemed even more distant than usual, her eyes were half-closed, with only the whites showing and occasionally she would hold a broken conversation with someone only she could see.

The Druid had blessed her with alder, willow and oak, and hung a wreath of apple-blossom around her neck. He had also scratched runes in charcoal over the door and touched the walls with his staff, drawing a protective barrier around the room. And they now sat still and silent awaiting the coming of the dawn, for if Midir had not claimed her by sunrise, then the wager would be forfeit and Etain would be Eochaid's – always!

The night wore on and the sconces burned low throwing the hall into shadow and one by one Eochaid's guards fell asleep, until only the High King and the Druid remained awake with the semi-conscious Etain between them.

'Dawn is almost upon us, lord.'

Eochaid nodded. 'I think we have defeated him.'

'I am not that easily cheated, my lord.'

Eochaid spun around and roared a challenge, his sword in his hand. Firgoil hissed a spell and pointed his staff at the De Danann prince as the first of the guards stumbled sleepily to their feet.

The High King lunged – and Midir was gone. The Druid's staff sparked green fire which hung trembling in the air where the De Danann lord had stood a moment before. He reappeared in the midst of Eochiad's warriors, striking out with two short silver swords, cleaving through armour and flesh without apparent effort. Again Firgoil launched a bolt of green fire – and once again Midir disappeared ... and reappeared by Etain's side.

He kissed her.

Abruptly, her eyes snapped open. For a single moment confusion reigned in their clear depths and then her gaze alighted on the prince.

'Midir!'

And her cry broke Eochaid's heart.

'Etain, my love.' The De Danann prince gripped her about the waist and as one they began to ascend. A warrior raised a spear and brought his arm back, but Eochaid knocked it aside in case he hit Etain and he could only watch helplessly as they passed gracefully through the high window.

Eochaid and Firgoil, followed by the guards raced outside, but all they could see in the still morning air were two snow-white swans which circled once over Tara's proud halls before winging south.

Midir had found and claimed his lost love.

But the tale does not end here, for Fuanach's curse had still to take effect. Eochaid led his army south in the direction the two swans had taken and, led by the Druid, Firgoil, passed beyond the Fields of Men and into the realm of the Tuatha De Danann.

There they laid siege to Bre Leth, and whilst a squad of warriors dug out the foundations of Midir's palace, others roamed the faery countryside, laying waste to all they found.

Death had come to the elven lands.

And Midir, high in his tower, could see only the smoke and flames as the forests burned and hear the screams of the wounded and dying.

Etain came to him and begged the prince to return her to the High King. She loved Midir, but she could not bear to see the land of the goddess devastated in this manner, nor could she allow Midir to blame himself for what was happening. At first the De Danann prince refused, but at last he could bear it no longer and consented, on one condition: that he might be allowed to cast a spell of forgetfulness upon Etain before she returned to Eochaid.

And so Etain returned to the High King, with no memory of her previous life, of her short return to the Lands of Faery, or of her lover, Midir. It was lost to her forever, even in dreams. And although time holds no sway in the Shadowland, once Etain returned to the Land of Men, she was once again made mortal.

And in time she bore Eochaid one child – a daughter – and she too was named Etain. Although she bore her mother's otherworldly beauty, she had her father's wide grey eyes. Etain Once-Elven died at a great age, an old, old woman – but still as beautiful as she had been in her youth when gods and men had vied for her.

CHAPTER 5

CONLA AND THE FAERY MAID

Conn awoke suddenly and lay staring up at the dark bulk of the tree above his head. The sky was lightening towards dawn, but the sun had not yet risen and a misty twilight still lingered. Conn lay wrapped in his sleeping furs, listening to the muted whispers of the nearby guards, wondering what had awakened him.

Perhaps it was the dream. He had dreamt of a voice talking to him out of the shadows, calling him, urging him ... He sat bolt upright; there it was again – and this time he was not dreaming.

It was a woman's voice, sharp and clear on the still morning air.

He rose in one fluid movement, one hand reaching for the broadsword that lay naked by his side. A guard hurried over to him. 'What is it?'

The guard bowed briefly. 'We have been hearing snatches of conversation since first light; yonder.' He pointed through the trees in the direction of the beach. 'But there is no-one there,' he continued, 'no-one except your son Conla, speaking to himself.' The guard paused. 'But a voice replies, lord; there is someone there – and a young woman too, by the sound of her voice.'

By now the entire camp was awake, standing silently, listening. Aodh, the king's champion, joined him, slipping a bone amulet over his head. 'I don't like it.' He jerked his head in the direction of the shore. 'This reeks of sorcery.'

The king agreed and then a stray gust of wind carried

voices on the air. '... And you shall rule in the Land of the Ever Young ...'

They could not make out the young prince's muttered reply, but the soft, gentle voice continued.

'But why content yourself with a petty kingship in this miserable land? And unless you have a mind to slay your father – and I doubt that you could – you must be content to wait many years before assuming the mantle of kingship.'

Conn gripped Aodh's arm and pulled him forward. They moved through the fringes of the forest as silently as possible and down towards the beach. The sound of the sea was clearer now and the woman's lyrical voice rose and fell with the susurration of the waves.

'And what would you rule? A kingdom of savages, where violence is ever-present, and death always threatens, and hunger is your constant companion; is that what you want?'

Conn and Aodh peered through the undergrowth onto the beach. The sun rose like a ball of crimson fire out of the sea, turning the waves to blood and the beach to bronze. It touched the youth standing on the shore, etching him like a sun god. Conla was standing in the shallows, squinting into the sunrise, the wind whipping his cloak across his face. Impatiently he pulled it away, and spoke – seemingly into thin air.

'And you. What of you?'

The voice came from almost directly in front of Conla. 'I will be your wife in the Land of Youth, and we shall rule together ... forever.'

'I am tempted,' whispered the youth. 'I have never before seen one so fair.' His hand rose and touched something. 'You are beautiful.'

Conn whispered urgently to Aodh. 'Return to camp and get Kernann, the Druid. There is sorcery here and that we cannot combat.'

Aodh nodded and slipped back through the undergrowth towards the camp.

'Let me tell you of the Land, that place men call Tir na nOg.' The woman's voice was softer now, more insistent, alluring, compelling, commanding. 'It exists beyond this world, beyond the Shadowland, in a place which is set apart. A different sun shines on the Land, a great amber ball that bathes the Isle in golden light – and it is ever summer there.' The voice faded, as if lost in memory and even Conn could feel deep within himself, the need, the yearning to visit the Land of the Ever Young.

'There is no evil in the Land, nor is there death,' continued the alluring voice. 'There is no sickness, nor is there birth.'

The undergrowth rustled as Aodh led Kernann, the aged Druid forward.

'And the Land is inhabited by a happy people, the elven folk, the last of the Tuatha De Danann, who once ruled this land when it was young. But there are many heroes of this world there also, taken there by the elven folk either as reward for some great service or else . . .' The voice faltered and then continued, softer than before. 'Or else because one of the elven folk loved one of the sons of Man.'

'Stop her,' insisted Conn. 'She seeks to lure my son away.'

The Druid nodded. 'I will do what I can. She is one of the Sidhe-folk, the elven race,' he explained. 'If Conla goes with her, you will never see him again.' He took a short alder wand from his belt and plunged it into the damp soil, drawing power from the earth. The wand pulsed and throbbed and the soil began to flow and twine in arcane patterns.

Conla stretched out his hands, and took a step forward.

Kernann stood suddenly, the wand held high above his head. The alder pulsed with a warm green light, a light reminiscent of life and growth. The Druid sketched a symbol in the damp salty air, a symbol which lingered in a ghostly afterimage. And then Kernann called out in a strange guttural tongue, more animal than human.

Conla stopped abruptly. He raised his hands imploringly and they were immediately touched with thin tendrils of green fire.

Once again Kernann called out and this time a wavering wall of green mist coalesced before the youth, cutting him off from whatever he alone saw. Conla turned and looked at the Druid, Aodh, and his father. His eyes glistened in the morning sunlight. 'Why?' he implored. 'Why?'

And then he turned back and looked out to sea, as if his name had been called, and he raised his hand as if to catch something and then he fell on his knees in the sand and wept.

The Beltane feast came and went as the year moved swiftly towards summer and the moon completed its cycle across the heavens. In all that time, Conla neither ate nor drank.

'I think he has been given one of the elven fruits,' said Kernann, when Conn questioned him. 'If so, then he is already living partly beyond this world, in the Fields of Faery, for as you know, one must never eat nor drink the elven food.'

Conn stalked about his chamber. He felt so impotent; he was losing his son and he could not stop it happening. He could not battle sorcery. Although he was not a coward, he was frightened now. He had fought in many battles and skirmishes – in those days Eriu was threatened from both without and within – and in one day alone, he had defeated fully one hundred warriors in single combat, thus giving him his name, Conn of the One Hundred, but this, this he could not fight. He was forced to sit at his table day after day and watch his son refuse all food, merely staring into the distance with a secret smile upon his lips, as if he alone saw and heard sights and sounds beyond the ken of mortal man.

'Your son is already lost,' said the Druid gently. 'It might be better to let him go to the Land of the Young.'

'Never!' Conn felt the rage building up inside, a battle fury that threatened to overwhelm him. 'He is my son, I will not lose him to some banshee.'

Kernann bowed. 'I will do what I can, my lord; I will do what I can.'

The white-capped waves rolled in and broke lazily, hissing

upon the dark sands like serpents and then broke into a creamy froth that disappeared beneath the sands. Tiny crabs scuttled through the shallows and tiny darting creatures were trapped in sand-locked pools. It was the hour after sunrise, when all colours still seemed wan and undefined and the sea was a blinding mirror of reflected light.

Conla walked down the deserted beach, his head sunk upon his chest, lost in thought. He shook his head to clear it – but the mists and drifting fragments of dreams that were utterly alien to him persisted. On one level, he knew it was because he had eaten the apple the elven princess had thrown him that first time he had met her. He pulled the fruit out of the pouch by his side and held it up to the light. Its skin was warm and sensuous to the touch and it held the light like satin.

He remembered eating it that first evening. Its flesh was moist and succulent and it had numbed his mouth and throat with a thousand tiny needles of fire, but he had finished it. And when he awoke the next morning after a troubled dream-haunted sleep, the apple was whole again. Every morning it was the same: the apple whole and uneaten where the core had lain the night before. He neither hungered nor thirsted after eating the fruit, but he always felt immeasurably distant afterwards. His thoughts were clouded as if he wandered through a dream – and at nights he dreamt of strange and distant lands, of curiously-hued peoples and equally curious beasts. But the dreams were becoming more and more tangible ...

'Conla ... Conla ... Conla ...'

The youth started. She was back. He felt the burden that had rested against the base of his spine since their last meeting leave him – and for the first time in a month he felt complete.

'My Lady ... you have returned.'

She smiled gently, her full red lips parting over startlingly white teeth. Her hair was white-gold, the colour of the sun-touched spray and her skin was as soft as smooth water. She was tall – almost as tall as Conla and her strange head-dress made her seem taller. Her garments shimmered and reflected like metal, always changing, always in motion.

'Come with me, Conla.' She stretched out her hands, the fingers long and incredibly delicate. 'Come with me.'

The youth could feel the decision forming within himself when, from the forest that bordered the beach, his father and Kernann the Druid appeared.

'Conla, my son ...'

The Druid called aloud in the tongue of the Elder Race and the green fire leaped and darted from his wand.

But the elven maid merely laughed. 'Your pretty magics cannot harm me now – for he is almost mine.' She stretched out her hands again and Conla reached for them. On the beach Conn and the Druid could only see him reaching into thin air.

Tiny spots of green fire darted before the youth's eyes and flickered in long traceries of light across the space that separated him from the banshee.

'Your power is spent, Druid,' she called. 'You are a dying breed; soon a new race of magicians will challenge your power and they will cast you and your elemental gods back into the Abyss whence they came.' And the maid gestured, shattering the green fire like so many pieces of broken glass.

'Come Conla.'

And out of the waves rose a longship of white crystal, without sail or oars and its name was cut into the side in red gold.

'Come Conla, we will rule in Tir na nOg for all eternity.'

The youth paused on the beach and then he turned and looked back at his father and the aged Druid, his brow furrowed as if he sought to remember something very important.

'Come Conla,' she persisted, 'your people await.'

Slowly shaking his head, Conla turned back to the sea and climbed into the crystal boat – and he never looked back as it set out for the horizon, rapidly disappearing into the morning sun.

On the beach Conn of the One Hundred wept.

CHAPTER 6

BIRTH OF THE SHANNON

Sinann crouched behind the hedge of wild holly watching the Arch-Mage complete the incantation and put the final touches to the runes incised into the crystal fountain. The Druids stepped back and the Arch-Mage touched the base of the fountain with his long alder wand. Immediately water rose and fell in a graceful arc, fracturing into a million tiny diamonds in the first slanting rays of the morning sun. He then touched each of the seven hazel trees that surrounded the fountain, linking them to it in a protective circle. The leaves on the trees began to tremble violently, the berries pulsed and throbbed with slow persistence and almost before their eyes, the hazelnuts swelled and hardened.

The Arch-Mage bowed reverently. 'Behold the Fruit of Knowledge.' The Druids murmured a refrain as the old man went from tree to tree inspecting the fruit.

'They are all perfect; our task is complete.' He leaned upon his long staff and his hard grey eyes softened as they stared into the morning sun. 'It is the beginning of the end.' With the sun at his back, he turned and walked away from the small grove surrounding the crystal fountain.

'How long will it last?' asked one of the younger men.

'Until man gains the knowledge to breach its defences.' He gestured back towards the grove. 'We have gathered together the entire knowledge of the Tuatha De Danann in those seven trees and in the fruit they bear – we cannot allow it to fall into the wrong hands . . .' The voices faded as they passed beyond the maid and disappeared amongst the trees.

Sinann waited until she was sure they had gone before

coming out from behind the bushes. The wan sunlight sparkled off her dark hair and highlighted the green tinge to her pale skin. She raised a web-fingered hand and shielded her oddly slanting eyes.

For Sinann was kin to Lir, the Lord of the Sea.

Slowly she walked towards the grove. Even from a distance it radiated an aura of power; of strength held tightly under control. And the crystal fountain was at the centre of the power; it was the protective talisman which linked the seven artificially mutated trees in an unbreakable bond.

The trees were more delicate than normal hazels, their branches longer and the colours of their leaves more vibrant – only the fruit seemed the same. But the fruit of the trees contained the Seven Branches of Learning – the entire knowledge of the People of the Goddess.

And it was hers for the taking.

Sinann smiled, her sharp teeth glinting yellow in the light. With the knowledge she gained, she could vanquish the remnants of the Tuatha and rule the younger, stronger race of Man. And she would be immortal.

She stood beside the fountain touching the blocks.

The crystal was surprisingly warm to her touch and soft, rather like skin, yet the water itself was cold, ice-cold.

The Druids would not leave the grove here; she knew they intended to shift it beyond this world to a Shadowland, a Place Apart, where it would be accessible only to someone with great knowledge and arcane power.

She trailed her hand through the chill water, revelling in the tingling sensation that engulfed her hand and forearm. She could feel the power of the place crawl over her body and raise the short hairs on the back of her neck. With a shiver, she stretched out her hand to pluck one of the hazelnuts ... and her world exploded.

The fountain seemed to erupt in all directions. An icy hand gripped the maid and dashed her against the ground again and again. She retched as foul water forced its way into her lungs, choking her, drowning her. But she couldn't

144

drown, it was inconceivable - she was a water maiden.
Sinann attempted to breathe the water and extract the
life-giving oxygen - and failed.

The maid panicked, her arms thrashed wildly and her legs
scrabbled for purchase. But the grove was gone; the
fountain was gone; there was nothing except a world of ice-
cold water, which paradoxically burned her throat and eyes
like fire. She was lifted higher and higher. She attempted to
scream, but there was no sound, she was deaf. The water
continued to rise, and rise ...

Abruptly, it fell.

The huge wave carried the shattered lifeless body of the
maid south and west, cutting a deep and wide swath through
the lush countryside, until it reached the Western Ocean. It
was a magnificent river and one later generations would call
the Shannon, in memory of the maid.

CHAPTER 7

THE GARDEN OF THE TUATHA DE DANANN

Cathan the Mage raised his alder wand high and cried aloud in the Old Tongue. The wand erupted into writhing eldritch flames, bathing the Mage in emerald light and turning the night into an eerie semblance of day. A ghostwind sprang up, whipping out of the darkness, bringing with it the scent of cloves mingled with the heavy tang of salt, as if it had blown across the seas from distant lands. But he was many leagues from the sea.

Cathan whirled the wand and then struck it against the ground. A single levin bolt exploded from the starlit sky and struck the ground almost directly in front of the Mage. The harsh bone white light lent his thin features a ghastly appearance, like one long dead.

But where the levin bolt had struck, the ground glowed and shimmered in the emerald wand-light, and long tendrils of fog rose from the earth. The fog twisted and coiled in the ghostwind, coalescing into a shifting fogbank.

Cathan spoke again, his words trembling on the sharp night air.

The green light paled and shrank back into the smouldering wand – and out of the fog came a glowing milk-white light, softer than sunlight, sharper than moonlight. Cathan shut his eyes, knowing that to look now would be to destroy his sight forever, for the mind could not comprehend the opening of the Door Between the Worlds.

He waited until the light dimmed against his eyelids, and the warm clove-and-salt scented breeze was blowing steadily against his face, ruffling his long dark hair and then he opened his eyes ... and looked into another world; into the Garden of the Tuatha De Danann.

Cathan stepped forward and looked through the shifting oval of white fog hanging on the night air. The Garden was smaller than he had expected. He could see a small crystal fountain set in the centre of seven small, delicate hazel trees, whose leaves burned with harsh vibrant colours. No insect or bird flew about the trees and nothing crawled about their roots.

It was a dead world.

Cathan stepped into the Shadowland. The shock ripped through his body, leaving him pain-wracked and gasping on the sickly, pale sward of the Place Apart. Almost immediately he became aware of the delicate music of the crystal fountain. The water rose and fell in a graceful arc, each drop of water sharp and distinct on the silent air – for there was no other sound. The noise of the water grew, and grew, until each drop seemed to shatter in the innermost recesses of his mind.

With a groan he lurched to his feet and stood whilst the landscape swayed before his eyes. He pressed his hands against his ears, but he could still hear the falling water. He took a step forward and fell. Slowly he began to crawl towards the crystal fountain, gritting his teeth against the tearing cry of the water. Dark waves rippled across his tortured eyes and his head pounded in unison. With an agonising effort he stretched to his fullest and the tips of his fingers touched the jewel-like water. Bringing his wet fingers back to his lips, he drank. The liquid flowed down his throat like ice with a delicate, almost perfumed taste.

Abruptly he realised the pain was gone – or else he was no longer aware of it. Carefully, he pulled himself to his feet and staggered across to the fountain. The crystal was cool and sensuous beneath his fingers, with a texture that resembled human skin. He dipped a hand in the sparkling water and drank from his cupped palm, savouring the sweetness and delicacy of the liquid. He stared deeply into the diamond studded depths and found himself wondering what he had come here for!

⋅The Mage experienced a brief moment of panic. He could recall neither his name nor his mission. And then he turned and looked back at the way he had come. The milky opalescent wall that surrounded the Garden was rent and torn and through the gaping hold he could make out the tiny points of distant starlight from another world.

Memory returned.

He was Cathan, a Mage, come in search of the fabled Fruit of Knowledge in the mythical Garden of the Tuatha De Danann. And he had found it.

He walked around the fountain and inspected the trees. He could only admire the ancient Druids of the People of the Goddess who had moved this entire grove from their world to this Shadowland, where it would be safe from the curiosity of man. And only when the New Race had gained enough knowledge to breach the defences would the knowledge of the demi-gods be released.

Only once, in the first days of its creation, had the Garden been disturbed and then the waters of the fountain had risen and swept the intruder away.

Cathan gathered the hazelnuts from the seven trees. They were hard and smooth and deep down a slow pulse seemed to beat. He cracked one and bit down hard on the kernel, wincing at the acrid bitter taste. He began to chew methodically ...

When he finished, he sat down with his back to the crystal fountain, the trickle of water now pleasant and lulling. The bitter taste of the nut had faded and his mouth and tongue now tingled as if he had eaten a fresh apple.

He breathed deeply. Strange thoughts flashed across his mind's eye; warriors with flashing swords and clad in gilded armour fought beastmen; sorcerer-Druids fought with fire and lightning from hilltop to hilltop; great armies clashed across sodden marshes; their blood staining the dark earth an even deeper hue; high-prowed ships appeared over the horizon, promising death and destruction. Faces

148

flickered before the Mage's eyes; high-boned, slant-eyed, arrogant faces, with hair as fine as silk and eyes harder than jewels. There were women of incredible beauty wielding swords and spears with the skill of warriors and warriors laboriously working with precious metals and rare gems to create artifacts of delicate beauty.

The Tuatha De Danann.

The Mage shook his head, attempting to clear his head. Gradually, the alien images faded and settled back into his mind, to be called upon if needed. All the images but one ... A face drifted before his eyes, the face of an old, old man. The face solidified, until Cathan could see the iron-grey hair still streaked with black and the curious innocence in the pale, almost colourless eyes.

'Speak ...'

The voice rang hollowly in the Mage's head and, although the image had not moved its lips, he knew it had spoken.

'I ... I have a question ...' he began hesitantly.

'Then ask it.' The image seemed to regard him with some amusement.

'Is ... is there a meaning to this existence?'

The image laughed, a long mellow laugh, that reminded Cathan of a god's. 'Herein are gathered the Seven Branches of Learning of the Tuatha De Danann, the People of the Goddess. Herein is knowledge, and knowledge is power; used correctly it could make you the ruler of your world, or its destroyer. But in all that accumulated knowledge you will find no answer to your question.' The image paused and began to fade. An icy wind blew across the mage and when the voice came again, it echoed from a great distance. 'For there is no meaning.'

And the fountain erupted in all its fury.

CHAPTER 8

FIONN AND THE RED MAN

'And I'll tell you, I'll have a bridge across there if it kills me!' Fionn ripped the side off a nearby mountain, scraped off bushes, small trees and loose earth and pounded it into a rough oblong. 'And we're going to call it Fionn's Causeway.' He pushed the huge rock into the soft earth and pounded it in deeply with his fists.

His cousin Niall shrugged and plucked a nesting eagle out of his beard. 'Whatever you say; only we,' he indicated the rest of the giants with his huge fist, 'want it to be called the Giant's Causeway.'

'Fionn's Causeway!'

'Giant's Causeway!'

The two giants glared at one another across the partly completed causeway of black basalt.

'It was my idea,' snapped Fionn petulantly.

'You only suggested it because you didn't want to get your feet wet every time you crossed to Alba to steal a few cows.'

'I don't like wet cows.' Fionn pounded a large boulder to sand. 'I'm going home,' he said. 'I need the rest.'

Niall turned away in disgust. 'Well good luck to you; and mind you watch out for the Red Man.'

Fionn snatched at a firtree and began to tear off the branches, muttering, 'Red Man, Red Man; do they think I'm afraid of the Red Man?' He stamped his bare foot into the side of a mountain, leaving one large cave with four smaller ones in the solid rock.

But the morning was bright and Fionn soon forgot his

bad humour and set off whistling for Knockmany and his wife Una. He swung the stripped firtree through low copses of trees, beheading them like so many flowers and playfully hefted a rock and batted it from one end of Banba to the other with a single blow.

He stopped only once and that was when a lone figure darted across the horizon. Fionn squinted into the sunlight and thought he could see fiery red hair and beard. He squatted down and contented himself with diverting a stream, and no, he wasn't hiding himself from the Red Man, he told himself; the stream needed diverting ... didn't it?

When he looked up, the figure was gone, lost in the mist which still clung to the west and Fionn hurried on, looking right and left, alert for any sign of movement.

No-one knew who the Red Man was. Some said he was the son of a Banban Giant and an Alban Giantess. Fionn said he was the son of a Banban bull and an Alban Mountain.

He was bigger than most giants and had made it his mission to challenge all the Banban Giants – and had won.

All that is except Fionn.

And if any doubted the Red Man's great strength, he would remove a round disc with jagged edges from his pocket and loudly proclaimed that it was a passing thunder bolt he had flattened as it whipped by his head.

He was looking for Fionn.

It was close to midmorning when Fionn finally reached his fort on Knockmany Hill. The sun beat down strongly turning the rough black stones of the crude fort into a blinding mirror.

'I must do something about that glare,' Fionn muttered shielding his eyes. He snapped a small oak tree in half and rubbed its thick sap experimentally against the wall. He had stepped back to admire his work, when a huge voice roared behind his ear.

'FIONN!'

The giant leaped straight up into the air, to almost three times his own height – which was considerable – and when he came down, the resultant shock waves sent ripples as far as the lonely western islands.

· Fionn climbed out of the hole he had made and found himself staring into the broad peasant face of his wife.

'Oh,' he said weakly, 'it's yourself Una.' His wife nudged a pile of earth back into the hole with a flat foot.

'Now, this is a pleasant surprise,' she said, kissing him soundly on both cheeks.

Across the seas the first of the race of men heard the smacking sounds and prepared for a summer thunder storm.

'You nearly killed me with the fright,' Fionn complained.

'My, and aren't we very jumpy.'

'Ah, but it's good to be home,' he said, quickly changing the subject.

'It's good to have you home. Come on in, and I'll get you something to eat; I've a few cows out in the pen, will they do you?'

Whilst Una prepared the cows, Fionn brought out his collection of weapons and using a boulder sized whetstone began to sharpen his long spear.

Una laid a couple of boiled cows down on the plate and topped it with a small field of corn. She looked at him curiously. 'What are you doing?'

Fionn shrugged and attempted to look nonchalant. 'Oh nothing, just giving the old spear a good cleaning; a warrior should always have respect for his weapons,' he added sagely.

Una looked suitably disbelieving and went and stood by the window as Fionn tucked into a haunch of cow. She glanced over her shoulder at him once, judging her moment. And then she grinned maliciously.

'There is a tall chap with red hair coming up the hill,' she said casually.

Fionn sputtered and choked, spraying half-chewed cow across the room. He tripped over his own feet as he fell, pulling the table and chair down with him. With one blow of his fist he turned the oak table into matchwood and was half way out the back door, before he realised Una was laughing at him.

'Ah, you can't fool me, my boy; it's the Red Man has you terrified.'

Fionn shook his head. 'No, no, I just remembered I've got to see a man about . . .' He trailed off, looking sheepish, and then he nodded. 'You're right, it's the Red Man, and frankly, he frightens the wits out of me.'

'Not that there's many to frighten,' Una muttered. 'Where is he now?' she asked.

Fionn stuck his thumb in his mouth and concentrated. Like many of the giants, Fionn's fingers were gifted with various magical powers; and Fionn's thumb had the gift of prophecy.

'I see him,' he said. 'He's . . . he's just leaving the Dun of Gann - what's left of it.'

'And where's he going?' asked Una.

'He's . . . he's headed in this direction,' he said with a yelp. 'I'm off.'

Una laid a hand the size of a small house on his shoulders and pushed him down. 'What time will he be here?'

Fionn sucked on his thumb until he grew red in the face. 'The second hour passed midday tomorrow,' he gasped.

'Well now, that gives us plenty of time. Be off with you now and fetch me a score or two of salmon for supper, I'll figure out what to do with the Red Man.'

When Fionn had gone, his fishing rod over his shoulder whistling up a storm, a small gale and a cloudburst, Una took nine multicoloured threads from her pocket and murmuring in the language of the gods, wove the nine strands into three cords of Endeavour, Invention and Success, and tied one around her right arm, another about her breast and the third about her right ankle.

When Fiona returned that night, two score salmon dangling over his shoulder and a small cow in his pocket, Una had a tableful of small round loaves.

'Just what I need,' said Fionn, juggling a hot loaf in his hands.

153

'PUT THAT DOWN!'

'Put what down?' he asked, trying to look innocent.

Una staggered in from the kitchen, her arms full of a second batch of loaves. 'If you had taken a bite from that, you wouldn't have a tooth left in your head,' she said. 'Here,' she tossed him a loaf from the tray she had just brought in.

Fionn eyed it carefully. 'What have you done with it?'

'Oh, this tray is right enough, but that,' she pointed at the table, 'has iron griddle baked into it.' Fionn tapped one of the loaves off the wall, and it rang with a dull metallic clang.

'Well have you got anything to drink,' he asked, 'I'm parched.'

Una shook her head. 'I've turned all the milk in the house into curds and whey, you'll have to do with water.'

'Water? Water! Me, the foremost giant in all Banba, having to drink water. Ooh, the shame of it.'

'Well it's either drink water tonight or blood - your own - on the morrow.'

Fionn drank water.

Fionn grumbled at the indignity of having to masquerade as his own child. Una merely ignored him and pulled the bonnet tighter under his chin, felt his cheeks to see if he needed a shave and tucked him into the cradle.

'God save all here,' said a voice with an accent so thick, it could be sliced with a blunt knife. A figure moved through the open door. 'I'm looking for Fionn and I'm told he might be here.'

Una eyed the giant with the wild red hair and a flowing beard to match with some concern. Why, her own Fionn, for all his great strength and prowess was only a boy compared to this monster. 'Well sir, I'm sorry to say he's out at the moment; he's gone off chasing some poor lad . . . the Red Man . . . or something.' She sighed. 'Oh, I pity the lad when Fionn gets his hands on him, he was in a fierce temper.'

The Red Man raised his bushy eyebrows until they disappeared into his hair. 'Why, sure I am the very same

Red Man and hasn't Fionn been avoiding me for the past twelve months.'

'Sure, and wasn't that only for your own good; he didn't want to hurt you. But come on in, sit and have a bite to eat; you can wait for him and you can settle your differences when he comes.'

'Now that's very kind of you, I will.' The Red Man sat by the fire and eyed the piled loaves of bread longingly. His stomach rumbled like a winter thunderstorm.

Una suddenly shivered and pulled her shawl tighter about her shoulders. 'Ah now, will you look at that? The wind has shifted and isn't it blowing straight through the door.' She turned to the Red Man. 'Would you be so good sir, as to turn the fort for me; Fionn always does it first thing in the morning, but he went off in such a temper this morning that he forgot. We like to have the sun in the morning *and* in the evening,' she explained, 'and so he turns the fort to face the sunrise and sunset.'

The Red Man nodded doubtfully, went outside and walked around the house. In one corner he found a crack where, he supposed, Fionn must turn the house. He flexed his right hand and then spat upon the middle finger, the source of his strength. He squatted down and using the incredible strength imbued in his hand lifted the entire fort and turned it almost completely around.

He heard a sound inside the house which could have been a yelped 'help,' but it could equally have been the stones settling.

Una came out and joined him. 'That's a grand job you've done. Now there's one other thing.' She pointed down the hill to a flat rocky plain. 'I've barely a drop of water in the house, but Fionn says there's a fine drop well under all that rock ... and if you wouldn't mind ...'

The Red Man stamped down the hill, tapping his right middle finger against his belt. The more he heard of this Fionn the less he liked the sound of him.

The ground was solid rock, without a crack or cleft in it. The Red Man tapped it, kicked it, jumped up and down on it and cursed. When the avalanches and rockfalls had ceased and the air had cleared somewhat, he found that he had opened a tiny crack in the rock. With a sigh of relief, he got down on his hands and knees, and stuck his finger into the crack and pulled.

The ground moaned, and ripped in a long jagged tear, over a quarter of a mile long and nearly five hundred feet deep, which later generations would call Lumford's Gap.

Out spurted the spring of crystal clear, ice-cold water.

The Red Man trudged back up the Knockmany Hill. 'How is that?' he asked proudly.

'Oh, it's fair enough,' said Una casually, 'fair enough.'

She brought the giant in and set him down by the table, telling him to help himself, but to be as quiet as possible, for she had just got the child to sleep. The Red Man nodded and reached for one of the larger loaves. It was pleasantly soft and warm, and his mouth watered. He bit into it.

The scream brought most of the sons of Man in the Western World awake and preparing to meet their gods and the following day, scores of birds were found scattered about the fields of Banba, killed with the shock.

The Red Man nursed a bloody mouth, whilst on the plate before him lay two shattered white stone-like objects; his teeth.

'Me feet ... me feet,' he moaned.

'What's wrong with your feet?' asked Una innocently.

The Red Man spat blood into the fire. 'Me teeth; I've just shattered two of my good teeth on your bread.'

'What this?' Una picked up two loaves and handed one to the Red Man. 'This is Fionn's bread, on a good day, after a day's lake building or mountain sculpturing, he'll scoff a table full of these. Here, try again.'

The Red Man stuck one in the corner of his mouth and bit ... It sounded like two mill stones grinding together. The Red Man spat two more teeth onto the table.

Una shook her head in astonishment. 'Well I don't know. Why, even the child eats it.' She shook baby Fionn 'awake' and handed him a loaf of bread – this time, one without an iron griddle in it. The Red Man watched in amazement as

156

the child consumed it with relish and asked for more.

'Look,' said Una to the 'child', 'this here's the Red Man; he's come to fight with your father.'

'Baby Fionn' looked the giant over with wide eyes, whilst the Red Man in turn, eyed the enormous 'child' with something approaching fear. If this was only the child, what must the father be like...?

'Here,' said Una, tossing the Red Man a stone and Fionn a ball of curds, disguised to look like a stone. 'Will you play with him for a while?'

'I don't want to,' said Fionn petulantly and squeezed the ball of curds until the whey ran out of it like water. 'Can you do that,' he asked the giant innocently.'

The Red Man grinned weakly and squeezed the rock, but unfortunately he couldn't find the proper leverage for his strength-finger and was unable to crush the stone.

Fionn watched with childlike glee, cheerfully munching on another loaf of bread.

The Red Man dropped the stone. 'It's no use; it's clear I'm no match for Fionn; will you tell him I was here and that I'll trouble him no more.' He watched the child chewing contentedly. Absently he nursed his aching jaw.

'Would you mind if I had a look at your child's teeth,' he asked. 'They must be a powerful set to chew that bread of yours.'

'Ah, they're something any mother would be proud of. Look.' She took the Red Man's right middle finger and stuck it into Fionn's mouth, as far back as it would go. Immediately Fionn bit down with all his strength, shearing off the finger just above the knuckle. The giant swayed on his feet, feeling waves of weakness lapping outwards from his shattered hand. He looked at the child in amazement – and then shouted aloud when the child leaped from the cradle ...

When Fionn was finished, he scraped what was left of the Red Man into a small jar and sent it home to Alba.

CHAPTER 9

THE LEPRECHAUN'S TALE

'Here, hold your whist now and let me tell you about the only time one of the Big Folk ever laid his hand on me.' Sheámus Ban the old Leprechaun adjusted the tiny spectacles on his nose and looked solemnly at the Cluricaune and Fir Darrig gathered about the blazing fire.

Carefully Sheámus straightened his legs, the joints cracking and popping like dried wood. 'Aaah,' he sighed, 'It's pure murder sitting with the old legs folded under you all day - and me with the rheumatics something terrible.'

One of the Fir Darrig pushed his red cap back onto his head and opened his mouth to reply, but then, catching the glint in the old Leprechaun's eye, shut up and said nothing.

'I must have been just a slip of a lad, but even then I was the best cobbler in all of Ireland. Look,' and he lifted up one foot. 'I made these myself about that time.'

Dutifully the Cluricaune and Fir Darrig admired the tiny black boots with their huge silver buckles.

'It was early morning,' he continued, 'and I was sitting under the oak tree down by the stream that runs through Dillon's Farm. I had a fine pair of brogues that needed heels and I was tapping away, at peace with myself and at home with the world.' He stopped and filled a long briar pipe with pungent tobacco. 'Now ...' He puffed vigorously until the bowl glowed cherry-red. 'Now, there I was and not a soul about - or so I thought - and not a sound on the air save the chirping of the birds and the ringing of my hammer. It was a morning to bring a smile to your lips and a song to your heart.' He paused for effect. 'Suddenly, I was pounced upon and held by one of the Big Folk.' He paused again and his audience murmured appreciatively.

'And weren't you afraid?' asked a Cluricaune, sipping some of the clear whisky.

'Ah no, sure don't we all know that the Big Folk are just plain stupid?'

Several heads were nodded wisely and one nodded so vigorously that he banged his head against the wall of the ruined barn where they were meeting and fell down stunned.

'He was a giant of a man,' continued Sheámus. 'He was easily three times my height and with arms on him that could strangle an ox. He was dressed in drab and colourless garments,' - unconsciously the Leprechaun touched his own gold embroidered red waistcoat - 'and over his shoulder hung a basket.'

'A poacher?' asked a Cluricaune.

'Aye, that's what he was sure enough. There was a brace of rabbits and a line of fish in that basket I shouldn't wonder.

'Well, he had me, fair and square and with a greedy look in his eye he asks, "your pot of gold, where is it little man? No tricks now, or I'll use you as fish bait." '

'Of course I pretended ignorance - but he wouldn't be put off, and at last I was forced to relent; but only after he had held me out over the river and promised to drop me in tied to a stone.' The Leprechaun nodded gravely at the frightened whispers that ran around the assembly.

'And it's true, and not a word of a lie in it.'

'What did you do?'

'Well, I'd very little choice, for he didn't take his eyes off me for an instant and so I led him over the bridge and up towards the quarries. I'll tell you - it was a merry dance I led him for most of the morning. By midday he was sweating like a horse - and smelling like a pig.' The Leprechaun paused to relight his pipe.

'But in the end there was nothing for it and I had to bring him to the far end of the quarry. "It's there," I said, and pointed to a flat stone. Well he lifted and tugged and pulled until he was fit to burst, but he couldn't move the stone, and at last declared that he needed a pick and shovel. "And what about me?" I asked. "There's not much I can do for you now."

"Oh, be off with you," sez he. Well as soon as I disappeared, he starts looking round for something to mark the stone with, for if you recall, that end of the quarry is floored with a good many flat stones. And at last he takes up a piece of flint and cuts a cross into the rock. And off he goes in search of a pick and shovel.' Sheámus Bán tapped the ashes out of his pipe and finished the dregs of whisky in his glass and then stood up and made ready to go.

'And what happened?'

'Did he get your treasure?'

'Where are going?'

The old Leprechaun looked disgusted. 'Of course he didn't get my treasure – all he got was trouble. Sure as soon as he was gone, I crept back and cut a cross into all the stones at that end of the quarry!'

CHAPTER 10

THE UNCOVERED LAND

Shea watched the tide slowly receding down Dingle Bay, uncovering the soft wet ground beneath to the early morning sunlight. He stood in the saddle until the waters passed the low watermark and beyond. It had been seven years since he had last witnessed this event – seven years since he had first heard the legend of the Uncovered Land.

Legend had it that the bay had once been part of the land, a broad plain stretching from what was now the Great Blasket Island to Valencia to the south. But when the remnants of the Tuatha De Danann had returned to the land, their magicians had caused the Great Western Ocean to roll across the green and fertile land, whilst they remained safe in their enchanted kingdom of Tir fo Thuinn, the Land Beneath the Waves.

However, every seven years the sea receded almost to the horizon and exposed the elven land to the light of the life-giving sun. And then the descendants of the People of the Goddess would come forth and sing and dance for a short while on the dry land until the tide turned and the magical land was covered for another seven years.

The faery folk laid a cloak upon the ground, a cloak woven of the mists of morning and the spray of a storm-tossed sea and it was this talisman that controlled the sea. And it was whispered that whomever held the cloak could command the waters to stay beyond the horizon, thus gaining lordship over the Uncovered Land.

The sun rose higher in the heavens, shortening Shea's shadow on the ground before him as he waited. The ground steamed in the warm sunlight, wreathing the plain in a heavy mist, through which the silent watcher thought he could hear the faint and distant sounds of music. Shadows moved in the distance and through the thinning coils of mist a figure might suddenly appear, moving in a fluid, graceful dance with an unseen partner.

About mid-morning, as the sun was almost overhead and burning fiercely, the sounds of music and song faded and even the calls of the birds were stilled. Shea, who had been nodding in the saddle, abruptly jerked awake. He leaned forward over his horse's head and stared down into the bay ...

... Into a faeryland.

The mists were gone, revealing a wide, gently sloping plain covered with a grass of emerald green, dotted with large circles of lighter coloured grass studded with jewel-like spots of shimmering colour.

And in the centre of one of the larger circles, Shea could see the small man-like figures lying as if asleep or intoxicated and just outside the circle, lying flat on the ground, was a large square of grey-white cloth: the faery cloak of the sea.

As quietly as possible, Shea urged his mount down the slope and onto the soft moss-like grass of the Uncovered Land. The ground moved beneath his horse's hooves, but it was perfectly dry and it was unimaginable that only that morning it had been covered by the waves.

It took him longer than he had expected to reach the place where the faery folk slumbered within their magical circle and he was surprised when he glanced back to see how far he had come.

Shea dismounted and crept forward. He could see the faery folk quite clearly now. They were taller than he had imagined and their limbs, although long and thin, did not look frail or fragile. Their features were sharp and pointed and their eyes slanted upwards. And he noticed that there seemed to be a thin web of skin between their fingers and toes. There must have been twenty or more asleep in the circle, their faces turned towards the sun like flowers, the harsh light catching tiny sparkles of green and blue in their long fine jet-black hair.

Shea eased nearer the cloak, and 'though there was no wind that morning, the cloak rippled and twitched in a slow regular beat that reminded him of the beat of the sea. Holding his breath, his heart pounding in his chest, he gently lifted the pulsating cloak from the ground and wrapped it about his shoulders. It felt cool and airy, heavy with the tang of salt and its power tingled through his spine. Turning, he ran for his horse.

The horse whinnied as Shea mounted her in one leap – and the cry brought the faery folk instantly awake. He could hear their high, thin, almost musical voices, raised in anger behind him. He fought down the desire to look behind and only dug his heels in, chillingly aware of the need to reach the shore.

He was almost halfway there when he became aware of the low rumble. He felt it coming up through the horse's hooves, vibrating into his stomach and then up into his head until he felt as if his skull was about to burst.

Looking over his shoulder he saw the gathering Tonn Toime, the Faery Wave.

The elven folk had launched their only defence against the thief and the Uncovered Land was rapidly being reclaimed by the sea. The water mounted in a massive wave, gathering strength and height as it came, until it seemed as if a giant grey-white-green mountain was bearing down on the lone rider. The noise was incredible; Shea screamed aloud at the thought of that massive wall falling down on him, but his cry was lost in the roar. He felt a wetness in his ears and across his lips and realised that both his ears and nose must be bleeding. The vibration was almost shaking him out of the saddle and the horse was crazed with terror. But it was that very terror which might save him, for the crazed animal fairly flew towards the nearing shore. Already they had passed the low watermark and he could see the high tide mark clearly. If only he could reach it before the mountainous wave fell ...

And then the sound behind him changed in tone. The

rumble disappeared and was replaced with a sound like glass shattering – but magnified a thousand times. The Tonn Toime was falling! Shea shouted aloud ... and was engulfed in a wall of water.

It hit him like a blow, sweeping him off his horse, battering him against the ground. He felt pain lance through his left leg and wrist; his head felt as if it were being squeezed between two stones and the pressure in his chest was almost unbearable. But the forward motion of the wave carried him far up onto the beach, and 'though it clawed at him with almost tangible fingers, Shea had cheated the faery folk and the Tonn Toime.

He pulled himself along the beach, dragging his left leg and wincing every time his left wrist touched the soft sand. Every time he breathed, pain stabbed into his side and when he coughed, blood spattered the golden sand before his face.

There was no sign of his mount and he felt curiously angry that the elven folk should have claimed even her; she had been a brave animal and had made a gallant effort to reach the beach – and had almost made it.

But he had won, he had the magic cloak and the sea was his to command. Trying to move as little as possible, he reached around to lift the cloak off his back ... and his fingers touched nothing. It was gone. The faery folk had won and it had all been in vain.

Shea lay on the golden sands, a broken man, and wept.

CHAPTER 11

THE SEA MAID

Brendan wandered along the shore the morning after the storm. Long strands of weed splayed like fingers even on the upper reaches of the cliffs, testament to the storm's fury. Driftwood piled against the rocks, rotted and thick with barnacles. Brendan rooted amongst the wood, seeking the firmer, fresher pieces and dropping them into the lobster pot slung over his shoulder.

The waves still shattered against the rocks in the bay, but their fury was gone and this was only the persistent heartbeat of the sea. The foaming white water ran hissing up the rough beach almost to his bare feet as he made his way down the shore to the sand spit where he knew he would find sea wrack.

As he walked out onto the spit, a flash of iridescent green caught his eye. He stopped and squinted into the blinding mirror of the sea. There was a shimmering green shape moving through the water towards him. Dropping to his knees in the wet sand, he threw off the lobster pot and pulled a long knife from his belt.

Perhaps it was a seal ...

The water foamed briefly and a shape slid gracefully from the waves. Brendan almost cried aloud and the knife dropped from suddenly lifeless fingers – for a young woman had risen from the sea. Pressing himself down into the soft sand, he watched and waited.

The maid rose and stretched languorously, running her fingers through a mane of long luxurious black hair glittering with emerald highlights. She was tall and almost painfully thin and clad only in a long cloak of silver-shot green. With long, slim, slightly webbed fingers she unclasped the cloak and laid it down on the sand. She stood and raised her hands to the skies, as if she exulted in the caress of the wind on her naked body and then slowly she sank onto the sand, her face towards the sun.

Brendan squeezed his eyes shut until tears came, but when he looked the maid was still there – he could just make out the dark mane of her hair and the swell of her breasts against the sand. For a moment he had imagined her to be the product of hunger induced delirium.

But she was real.

Brendan struggled to recall what little he knew of the water maids. They were said to be the subjects of Lir, Lord of the Sea, and hail from Tir fo Thuinn, the Land Beneath the Waves, but they were equally at home on land as in water. They could travel from one realm to the next with the aid of a water cloak, a talisman woven of the essence of the sea and the elements of the air, mixed with the spirit of the land. It encased the wearer in an invisible protective sheath.

As the sun moved on towards mid-morning, the wind died, the sea grew calm and a deep, heavy silence fell over the beach. Brendan started awake convinced he had dreamt it all, but the maid was still there, her head thrown to one side, her breasts rising and falling regularly in sleep.

Slowly, carefully, Brendan began to crawl along the sand spit towards the water maid. His questing fingers touched the hem of the cloak; it felt ice-cold and wet to his touch and yet it had lain in the sun for hours. Holding his breath, he began to pull it back towards himself, his eyes on the still-sleeping maid. He almost had the cloak when the maid stirred. He froze. Her eyes snapped open, emerald-green in the harsh sunlight. Slowly her head turned ...

Brendan leaped up, grabbed the cloak and ran.

With a shrill inhuman cry, the maid followed. Brendan ran for the shore, his bare feet sending up spumes of sand and water. The maid's shouts were almost distinguishable and he occasionally caught a word he almost recognised. He

166

glanced back - and fell headlong in the sand. He rolled and pushed himself to his feet - but the maid was closer now and he could hear her rasping breath and smell the heavy tang of the sea. Her long nails scored deep furrows down his bare back. But Brendan had now reached the foot of the cliffs where the going was rougher and the soft sand, which favoured the maid's webbed feet, was gone. Here, there were only hard stones and jagged rocks, and the sea maid soon limped on bruised and bleeding feet. By the time Brendan reached his cottage tucked away in the lee of the cliffs, the maid was far behind.

He was leaning on the half-door when the maid staggered up. Wordlessly she stretched out her hand; silently he shook his head. Again she reached out. Again he shook his head, saying clearly and distinctly, 'No.'

'Why?'

Her question surprised him; he had not known she understood Irish. She spoke it with just a trace of accent and used an archaic variant of the tongue.

Brendan shrugged and shook his head. 'I don't know,' he confessed. And then he added shyly, 'I've never seen anyone quite as beautiful as you.'

The maid coloured, and then, abruptly realising she was naked, attempted to cover herself with her hands. Brendan turned away in deference to her modesty.

'Please give me back the cloak,' she said, 'otherwise I am bound to you.'

'I know,' he said quietly. 'I know.'

The years passed and Murgaine the sea maid stayed with Brendan and in time she bore him a son and two daughters. The boy resembled his father but the girls had their mother's elfin looks and colouring.

As the children grew up and became more and more inquisitive, Brendan was forced to move the cloak from hiding place to hiding place for fear they should accidentally stumble across it. But he could never leave it alone for long and would often start awake from a nightmare in which his wife found the cloak and, taking the children with her, would disappear beneath the waves.

In the long hot days of late summer, Brendan set about thatching the cottage in preparation for the coming winter. He was laying the first layer of thatch when the idea came to him: he would hide the cloak under the reeds, away from both his wife and children and there they would never find it.

The following morning he set off for the shore, the lobster pot over his shoulder, for he still went hunting along the beach for sea wrack and driftwood. Murgaine followed him as far as the shore and stood gazing longingly at the receding tide. With tears in her eyes, she turned her back on the sea and wearily made her way up the rough track. When she reached the cottage she found her young son struggling to raise the short ladder against the wall.

'Brian, what are you doing?'

'I want to look,' he said, his voice carrying a trace of Murgaine's eldritch accent.

She knelt by her son, and stared deep into his emerald flecked colourless eyes. 'What do you want to look at?' she asked gently.

'Why mother, did you not see father laying a shining cloth under the reeds when he was thatching?'

Murgaine felt her world tremble and dissolve before her eyes; her breath caught in her throat in a sob and the sudden pounding of her heart frightened her. With trembling hands she placed the ladder against the wall and climbed up to the low roof. Carefully she parted the bundles of thatch . . . and there was her cloak.

Climbing down, she took her son in her arms. 'It is only an old oil-cloth, perhaps it was the way the light caught it made it shine; it is nothing.' The child looked at her from big solemn eyes and nodded slowly.

When Brendan returned later that evening, he noticed his wife's air of suppressed excitement. She dropped plates, burned herself on the hob and almost ruined the dinner. He smiled inwardly; before she had told him she was expecting their first child, she had been this way.

Murgaine set a large meal down before him and then went outside to draw some water. And Brendan was almost finished when he realised she had not returned.

Outside the ladder and tufts of straw and rushes from the roof gave mute testimony to what had occurred.

He set off for the beach at a run, terrifyingly aware that he had not heard the children playing about the cottage. His heavy meal weighed uncomfortably in the pit of his stomach as he leaped over the broken ground and down onto the beach. He sank, cursing into the soft sand as blind instinct directed him towards the sand spit. He fell, and lurched to his feet, only to fall again. He lay, the sand rough against his face, quelling the urge to vomit and then with a groan, pushed himself to his feet. But when he rounded the bend in the cliffs, his heart lurched and almost stopped.

The sea maid stood by the edge of the waves, the long silver-shot emerald cloak fluttering about her bare shoulders and with her two daughters in her arms. Brian sat on the wet sand beside her, struggling with the laces on his boots.

Brendan screamed and the gulls rose and mocked him with their cries. He ran down the long spit swaying from side to side like a drunkard, his hands outstretched, his fingers hooked into claws.

The maid turned slowly and looked back, the ghost of a smile playing about her lips. She stooped and said something to the boy and he renewed his efforts to pull off his boots.

Brendan was nearer now; he could see the abrupt flicker of fear in his wife's eyes and his son's look of intense concentration as he unpicked the tightly knotted laces. And even as the fear of losing his family ate into him like acid, he could still admire the otherwordly elfin beauty of Murgaine. Almost six years of hard living and bearing three children had not abraded her beauty. She was still as slim hipped and high breasted as the first time she had risen from the sea and her hair, which she had groomed carefully every night

169

and morning, shone with the same metallic green-black sheen. She was beautiful.

He was almost on top of them now – and with a look compounded of both terror and triumph, the sea maid leaped into the waves with her two daughters in her arms.

The boy stood and would have followed had Brendan not thrown himself on top of him and buried his face in the sand so that he might not see the thrashings of his sisters as they drowned.

And the look of horror and loathing on Murgaine's face would haunt him always.

CHAPTER 12

THE FAERY HOST

The silence of the night was broken by the sharp ringing steps of a late traveller on the frost-rimmed road. The young man tucked his head down deeper into his collar and pushed his hands into his pockets, feeling the chill bite through the thin cloth. It was a bitter night and a full moon sparkled on the road, etching it in silver, the harsh light adding to the chill.

He stopped and pulled a hip-flask from his back pocket. The locally-brewed liquor burned its way down his throat and settled in his stomach like hot coals, and the fumes made him pleasantly unaware of the lateness of the hour or the lonely road he travelled.

He had been humming the refrain of an air the piper had played back in the town for some time, when he became aware that his voice was not the only one on the road that night. He stopped and listened. And there, sharp and clear in the distance, he could hear voices raised in laughter and song, with the thin skirl of the pipes and the delicate tracery of a harp hanging on the air.

The young man leaned on the hedge that bordered the road and stared across the fields, but he could see nothing and the night was so clear that the sounds could have travelled some distance. But his curiosity had been aroused and, ignoring all the tales the country-folk told of this part of the west and the warnings never to leave the road, especially at the full of moon, he vaulted the hedge and set out across the frozen fields towards the sounds.

The fields, he knew, were part of the estate of the O'Donnell, the local landlord, an evil man with a dark reputation. A man of whom it was said, bore an uncanny resemblance to both his father and grandfather.

The young man stumbled and fell on the hard earth. He groaned aloud and then screamed as a hand came out of the night and helped him to his feet. He cowered back and stared up at the stranger ... no, not a stranger, someone familiar. He shook his head, trying to clear the fumes and dizziness that made his senses swim.

'You are Colum MacMahon,' stated the stranger.

The young man nodded dumbly, and then recognition dawned. 'You are the O'Donnell,' he whispered, and unconsciously crossed himself.

'Why are you trespassing on my land?'

'I heard the music and singing sir and I just followed it ...'

The O'Donnell smiled and Colum shivered, for it gave his face a skull-like appearance in the bleached moonlight. He recalled the stories whispered about this man and especially the one which said that he had traded his soul and humanity for communication with the Elder Gods and spirits that once walked the land.

'Why then,' the O'Donnell said, 'let us find the source of this merriment.'

He gripped Colum by the hand, and the young man winced and would have pulled away if he could, for although the night was chill, the man's hand was even colder.

The O'Donnell hurried across the fields, his footing sure and certain, never stumbling nor falling, dragging Colum behind him. And if he had not been gripped so tightly, the young man would have believed he followed a wraith, for the man made no more sound than blown smoke and was almost as visible. He was clad all in black, from his high-collared jacket to his black hose, and save for the silver buckles on his shoes and the silver buttons that glittered like tiny stars on his jacket, he would have been invisible.

They marched across field after field, pushing through frozen hedgerows and ice sheathed rivers and streams.

Several times, Colum tried to strike up a conversation with the dark figure before him, but his words hung, forced and empty, on the cold air and the O'Donnell did not deign to reply.

Eventually, they topped a rise and found themselves looking down into a hollow. The depression must have been almost a half mile across, topped on three sides by trees and low bushes. The silver thread of a stream cut across from the left and vanished into the night. And although it was dark in the hollow, Colum could see vague forms moving to and fro.

The O'Donnell pointed down. 'There is the source of your music and laughter. They dance within.'

Colum strained, but the sounds were still as distant as ever ... and who were 'they'? He turned back to the older man, but he was gone, vanished into the night whence he came. The young man backed away from the hollow fully intending to turn and run when he could bear to have the sounds at his back. But suddenly there was movement in the hollow and two figures loomed up out of the shadows.

They were smaller than he and clad in sombre colours of a peculiar cloth which reflected the moonlight like oiled silk. Their features were thin and pointed, their eyes slanted upwards and seemed split-pupiled like a cats'. Their hands, when they reached for him, were long and thin, with delicate, graceful fingers and over-long nails.

Taking him by the hands, they drew the young man down into the hollow. It was as if he were walking under water; all sounds ceased and were replaced with a muffled pounding like the surf on the sands - and which he abruptly realised was the pounding of his own heart. Familiar objects - even the trees - took on grotesque and fantastic shapes; tiny faces seemed to leer at him from their boles, and feral eyes gleamed in the depths of the bushes. Tendrils of white mist - which he had not seen from above - now drifted past his face, carrying the acrid odour of crushed herbs and unfamiliar spices.

Colum tried to talk to the two creatures who were leading

173

him into an unfamiliar world, but although he could form the words, they came out strange and garbled.

The fear and terror he had felt was fading now and the urgency to be away from this place seemed unimaginably distant and unimportant. He felt himself slipping into an easy acceptance of the unreal situation, it was as if he were wandering through a dream – but at some deep, almost unconscious level, he realised that this was no dream. The fog thickened as they moved down into the hollow – and then it abruptly disappeared. Colum looked around in dull confusion. The hollow seemed larger than he had first imagined it to be – it now stretched away to a misty horizon. Buildings shimmered in the distance and the pale silver ball of the moon overhead, now glowed with a wan golden light, like a morning sun.

And the Faery Host had gathered.

They thronged the hollow in a colourful, murmuring mass, like a great swarm of insects. Many were like the two leading Colum; thin, high-featured, elven creatures, dressed in shimmering garments which whispered together when they moved. There were others: small, gnarled, crooked creatures, that seemed neither man nor beast; tiny creatures no longer than his hand who flew on huge butterfly wings, and there were small – but perfectly formed – men, clad in rough clothes of red, green and brown. Some bowed mockingly to the young man as he was led through the mass, whilst others either ignored him, or looked pityingly on him. The low susurration of voices stilled as he passed and the throng backed away on either side, leaving an avenue down which he must pass.

Facing him at the end, seated upon a cloth-draped treestump was a man, crowned like a king and clad in a lord's finery.

Colum stood before the elven lord and stared deep into his colourless eyes; he felt he could drown in them, they were so empty. The king rose – and he was a head taller than the young man – and placed a long-fingered hand on his trembling shoulder. 'I am Illan, Lord of the Elven Folk.'

174

The company murmured their lord's name, as if in benediction.

'You are welcome to this gathering, son of Man,' he gestured about with his right hand. 'Enjoy,' he commanded, and resumed his seat.

The young man was grabbed by two of the elven maids and dragged into the whirling crowd. The faery music began again: two harpers, their instruments the most beautiful and delicate Colum had ever seen, and a piper caressing an instrument which looked impossibly old. The music inflamed him – it was so wild and free, almost alive, not like the poor shadow of sound that passed for music in ... in ... where?

The faint echo of an air haunted the dim recesses of his mind. He groped for it with blind fingers, suddenly realising that it was of immeasurable importance to him.

One of the elven maids pressed a goblet of purest silver into his hands and urged him to drink. He raised it to his lips and the potent vapours made his head swim, but some primal warning urged him not to drink ... no, nor eat the food of faery.

He worked his throat, but handed the maid back the goblet untasted. He refused all food, pretending to be chewing when someone offered him a delicacy.

He danced with many of the elven maids, whirling around and around in a mad swirling that left him dizzy and gasping. Many of the faery folk seemed to want to touch him, as if he were some token or charm and one, an old, old woman, no taller than his waist, wept as she kissed his hand.

The night – if night it was – passed swiftly and as the dawn tinged the eastern sky with pale light, the tiny lanterns were extinguished and, one by one, the faery folk disappeared back into whatever time or place they inhabited. And as they did, the golden moon-sun faded from the skies and sank into the west, the trees and stones ceased to stare and the sounds and smells of faery faded, leaving only the mundane behind.

175

Colum started suddenly. He had been staring into the eastern sky, welcoming and yet regretting the coming dawn, when someone touched his shoulder. It was Illan, the elven lord.

'You have cheated us, son of Man.'

'I don't understand.'

Illan gestured into the east. 'The dawn is almost upon us; the faery folk are gone and by rights you should have gone with them.'

'But why?' wondered Colum.

'Why? Because you were part of a tribute paid to us by the one you know of as the O'Donnell.'

'What tribute?'

'The soul of a baptised follower of the New God, the One you call the Christ. In return we extend the life of the O'Donnell.'

'How old is he?' Colum asked suddenly.

'As we reckon time, four nights - you were to pay for that fourth night, but you cheated us, for you neither ate our food, nor drank our wines and thus we have no claim on you.'

'Four nights is not a long time,' said Colum.

'Time, as we measure it,' said the elven lord, 'differs greatly from your measurement of it. Look,' he pointed into the east. 'The sun arises, I must depart. I wish you well - although I pity you and soon you will wish you had followed us beyond this world, into the Shadowland, the realm of faery. Farewell.' Illan, the lord of the elven folk, moved across the hollow towards the west and as he did so a shadowy figure stepped from behind a tree and joined him. And Colum could have sworn that it was the O'Donnell.

Then they were gone.

The road back to the village was 'wrong'. It was not something he could describe, more an overall impression. He had travelled that road for as long as he could remember, he knew every stone and crack in its rough surface, every tree and bush that lined the winding way, and every lichened-covered wall.

But now they were different.

Perhaps the road seemed wider, the bushes and trees just a little bigger, a little more unkempt than he remembered them. He noticed new bushes and young trees which, he felt sure, had not been there the night before; and there were also gaps where he knew there ought to be a certain bush or a low wall.

He began to run.

The sun came up and his dew-soaked clothes steamed in the hot summer air. *Hot ... summer ... air ...*

But it had been the depths of winter only last ... night.

Filled with a mind-numbing fear, Colum fled towards the village. Everything on the road was so familiar – and yet so strange; so old and yet so new.

The village was much as he remembered it; perhaps the buildings a little more dilapidated and the church slightly more decrepit – but that gilt cross on the steeple was new, it had not been there last night.

The inn was almost unchanged, save that the roof had been recently thatched. All conversation ceased as he entered its familiar dark, low-ceilinged interior, redolent with the heavy odours of strong spirits, stale beer and sweat. Colum nodded to a score of faces he knew – or thought he knew, but they merely looked puzzled and were slow to return his greeting. He ordered a glass of dark beer and lounged back against the smooth wood of the bar.

The locals, their scrutiny of the stranger finished and apparently satisfied that he was one of themselves, turned their attention back to the old man in the corner by the turf fire. His voice was rough, for it had been a long night's storytelling and it was only now coming to an end. He sipped from a heavy mug and resumed.

'From this very spot it was, and sure wasn't it my father – God rest him – who saw him. Out he went and with a few jars inside him, for it was a bitter night and cold enough to crack the stones. And he took the old straight road home.'

177

The storyteller paused and sipped his drink.

'But he never reached it. Oh, there was a search made of course, but sure, he was gone and there was little to be done about it. But,' and the old man paused for effect, 'they found a scrap of cloth torn from his coat just above the faery dell in the O'Donnell's lands. The faeries got him.'

'And who was he and how long ago was this?' Colum asked into the silence.

'Sure, and wasn't he a local lad, Colum MacMahon, and it's nigh on a hundred years since he went with the faery host!'

CHAPTER 13

SAMHAIN EVE

Brian and Mary huddled in the porch of the ancient church watching the rain turn the earth to mud. Thunder rumbled out over the ocean, and lightning flared above the jagged rocks at the mouth of the bay. The angry sea foamed and boiled at the foot of the cliffs far, far below them, sending foaming tendrils of spray high into the salty air, soaking the young lovers. A warm breeze blew in off the ocean and rustled through the bare trees with the sound of muted whispers. Stray leaves whipped through the leaning headstones of the clifftop graveyard.

'I'm frightened, Brian,' whispered the young woman, clutching the shawl tighter about her head. 'Can't we go now?'

'Soon, soon, it's almost time; we'll wait 'til then.'

Mary nodded and shivered in her thin coat, nestling against Brian for warmth. 'What time is it?' she whispered.

Brian glanced up at the heavens, where a full moon was obscured by racing clouds. 'Midnight,' he said, the tension showing in his voice.

They waited, whilst overhead the heavens quickly cleared, the summer storm dying as quickly as it had blown up, leaving the full moon shining sharp and clear in an empty sky. The silence began to grow; the wind died, the rustlings of the night creatures disappeared and even the booming of the waves far below seemed muted. A deathly silence fell over the churchyard and the very night itself seemed to be waiting.

Abruptly Brian stiffened and Mary stifled a scream. A

179

couple climbed the long cliff-face stairway and moved through the silent tombstones and falling behind that another shadow-couple and then a long line winding through the tombs towards the porch. The moonlight glittered on their pale forms, dusting them with silver.

Brian and Mary cowered back as the first of the figures approached. It was the image of a young couple, youths they both recognised as coming from the nearby town. Behind them came the shadow-figures of a young man and woman from the same town. Both shadow couples passed through the heavy wooden door of the church and faded.

'That's Eileen NicMorichue, and Dermot MacBrien,' grinned Brian, 'so they are to be married.' The shadows drifted slowly towards the church and they seemed thinner, more etherial than the rest - or perhaps it was just the brightening skies paling them. As they neared the church Brian gripped Mary's hand tightly and smiled broadly in triumph.

For the shadows were of themselves.

'See, I told you we would be wed this coming year.' He kissed her gently and taking Mary's hand in his set out for the long road home.

The seasons had changed and winter was fast approaching. Once again Mary and Brian climbed the dangerous winding stairway to the ancient church which clung precariously to the clifftop. Every year the sea claimed a little more of the land and often after a storm, shattered headstones and yellow splintered bones would be found on the beach far below.

It was Samhain Eve, one of the great Old Feasts, when the spirits of the dead walked and the borders between this and the Shadowland blurred and time itself rippled and flowed. The country folk avoided the Old Places, the ancient mounds and rugged dolmens, the cairns and faery rings. Most kept to their cottages and only ventured out if it was unavoidable.

Mary was shivering as they made their way through the silent graveyard that was attached to the old church.

'Brian,' she whispered, her voice so low as to be almost inaudible, 'must we?'

Brian squeezed her hand tightly. 'Remember what we saw on Beltine Eve? Who knows what we might see this night.'

'This is an evil night,' she whispered and clutched the small oaken crucifix about her throat. 'Only evil is abroad this night.'

'I'll protect you,' Brian said, with a confidence he did not feel.

They stood in the porch of the church and listened to the night move about them. Tiny rustlings and cracklings seemed unnaturally loud in the silence. Once a barn owl hooted nearby, causing Mary to stifle a scream.

The night was mild and dry; surprising for so late in the year and indeed the summer had been hot and dry and the streams in the district ran low and turgid.

It was after midnight when the lovers became aware of the growing silence. All the tiny noises of the night had faded, leaving only a thick silence. They could feel the tension growing, as if a thunderstorm were brewing – but the sky was clear and the full moon bathed the churchyard in a harsh bone light that contrasted sharply with the ebon shadows. They could feel the pounding of each other's hearts and imagined they must be beating out into the countryside like drums. Abruptly the first of the shadows approached.

This time they came singly and whereas the Beltine shadows were images of people in the full of their health, some of these were thin and wasted, whilst others bore the evidence of wounds, as if they had died by violence.

For these were the shadows of those who would die during the coming year.

The procession was longer than the one at Beltine. Many of the folk, Mary and Brian recognised; some were from their own towns. They passed in a ghostly silent procession and filed through the thick oaken door and into the church.

181

The moon was low in the sky when the procession came to an end.

The last shadows were of a couple. They glided silently through the grave stones and the moonlight turned the milky opalescence of their shadows to silver. As they neared the porch, the young lovers suddenly realised that there was something terribly familiar about the pair ...

As the shades passed, they turned and looked at Mary and Brian ... And they found that they were looking at the shattered images of themselves!

The shade of Brian reached out for Mary, whilst the shadow of Mary reached out as if to embrace the living Brian.

Mary screamed – a long terrified, almost animal-like cry and Brian struck at the outstretched hand of his shade. It was cold – so cold that it burned like scalding steam; he cried aloud in pain, and the image seemed to smile through broken lips.

The lovers fled terrified from the church, stumbling blindly through the headstones which loomed suddenly out of the night and seemed to deliberately impede their progress. Once, Mary fell, pulling Brian down with her and when he glanced back, he could see the ghastly bone-white shades following, their arms outstretched. He dragged Mary to her feet and pushed her out of the graveyard onto the first of the steps. They ran down the rough steps, keeping as close to the cliff-face as possible. Loose stones and pebbles clattered out into space to fall the hundreds of feet to the jagged rocks below.

And then suddenly, Mary stopped and went rigid as a shadow appeared before her. Brian crashed into her and then screamed as a burning cold hand touched his face. He took a step backwards ...

Into space ...

CHAPTER 14

THE BLACK CROSS

The spade hit the wood of the coffin with a solid thud that echoed about the deserted graveyard. Nuala froze, listening. But, save for the slight soughing of the wind through the leaves there was no sound and even the drone of the late-night insects had died off. The young woman glanced up into the skies, watching the dark clouds that threatened to obscure the full moon that rode like a silver coin across a purple cloth.

She hadn't much time.

Nuala dropped down into the freshly dug grave and scraped the earth off the polished wood of the coffin. She pulled a long metal bar from the bag on her back and inserted it into a crack in the thin wood. She leaned on the bar, pressing down with all her stength, and the wood creaked - an almost human scream that set her heart pounding - and then it snapped with a pistol-shot crack.

She looked up out of the grave. The clouds had neared and would soon hide the light of the moon. She must hurry.

Working as quickly and as silently as possible, she levered off the coffin lid and, laying it to one side, grabbed the stiff corpse under both arms and dragged it out of the grave.

Nuala laid out the body by the gaping hole. The moon-light touched its face with shadow lending it character, giving it life. It was the corpse of a young man, not yet into his twenties, who had been buried that morning after a long, lingering illness.

With a short knife, Nuala sliced the threadbare suit from his wasted limbs. Critically, she examined the body.

Although it was pitifully thin, the skin was whole and unblemished – it was perfect. She pulled a tiny knife from her bag and held it up, allowing its razor-sharp and almost hair-thin blade to catch the light. She rolled the corpse over onto its face and, pushing back the lank hair, proceeded to cut a strip of flesh about an inch wide from the back of his neck down to his heel. Calmly, she held the flesh up to the pale moonlight, examining it carefully for flaws or imperfections and, finding none, rolled the defiled corpse back into the shattered coffin, kicked the shredded clothes in after and started to fill the hole.

Her eyes glittered strangely in the silver light; they were hard, cold and metallic. They were inhuman.

Abruptly, the moon was obscured, plunging the grave yard into almost total darkness, and only the sound of falling clay was audible in the night.

Nuala returned to her cottage by the shore as the sun was rising, the wan light touching the waves with pale gold and salmon. In the morning light, her face looked drawn and haggard and there were dark rings under her eyes, but she moved with an almost childlike eagerness, her eyes burning with a frenzied fever.

She treated the skin carefully, washing it in warm water and then drying it inch by inch before the turf fire, allowing the rich smoke to dust the pink flesh a light tan. It was a lengthy process and night was already falling as she completed her preparations.

With infinite precision, she laid the strip of skin out on the cleared floor of her cottage in an intricate pattern that resembled the figure eight. She piled twigs from seven trees and berries from three more in one loop of the figure and then took her place in the other.

A great stillness came over her as she awaited the time to begin the final part of the spell. And while she waited, the tiny question that plagued her during the past few days rose again from the inner recesses of her mind, and this time she

184

could not banish it. The question remained. Was it worth it?

Was it worth destroying her immortal soul in return for earthly pleasures? A tiny voice said no, but another stronger voice answered yes. Soon, soon he would be hers. Soon, she would feel his strong arms about her, soon, she would feel his hot breath on her lips, soon. Nuala shivered in anticipation. Soon.

The spell was old and it was said to go back to the days when the first invaders came to Ireland, when the ice-sheets had retreated leaving behind a blasted landscape and men that were little more than beasts. There were several variations on the basic spell, but one thing remained constant: the flesh of the newly dead.

A strip of skin – in some cases from about the arm, the brow, the groin and breasts or from the head to the heel – was taken from a fresh corpse. If a woman desired the love of a man, then the flesh was taken from a man, and if a man lusted after a woman, he used the skin of a woman. This was then dried and treated and at a certain hour one called upon the Evil One and swore upon the flesh of the dead and the immortal soul, to pay homage to the Powers of Darkness, if one's wishes were granted. And then the strip of flesh was placed about the body of one's loved one whilst they slept. When they awoke, they were lost, captured in an evil web that could not be broken.

Nuala felt the silence of the night deepen and even the lapping of the waves grew distant. She saw the moon move across the cottage's only window. Midnight was approaching.

With trembling fingers, she lit the twigs and berries. They sparked and caught, suffusing the room with a bitter, pungent odour that tugged at the throat and stung the eyes. Nuala began to chant aloud in the Old Tongue, calling upon the powers of Shadow and Darkness, calling forth the Lord of the Night.

Her voice rose in power and strength, taking on a note of authority and command. Thunder rumbled close by, the sound of the gathering storm matching the voice exactly.

185

Lightning flashed, etching the room into deeper night, leaving seared images behind.

And then silence.

The birdcalls awoke Nuala. She opened her gritty eyes, feeling the rough floor beneath her cheek - and the events of the night flooded back like a polluted tide. She sat up, the effort making her head swim and pound, bringing bile to her throat. She looked at the floor and suddenly her discomfort was forgotten. For the strip of flesh, which had been wound into a figure eight had shifted and now resembled a horse-shoe.

The young woman wore the obscene belt beneath her clothing next to her skin for two nights and a day, suffusing it with her essence and aura. And on the morning of the second day, with the belt in her bag, set out for the market-town of Swords - and Donal.

Her excitement mounted as she neared the town overlooked by its round tower and high belfry. It was Wednesday, market day, and a long stream of carts and wagons were making their way through the town, some having come from as far away as Dublin to attend. Cattle ambled through the crowd, ignoring the screaming children who chased them with sticks; dogs herded thin sheep down the main street and the air was heavy with the mingled odours of animal dung and sweat.

Nuala wandered about the small town looking for Donal, eventually finding him in the inn, slightly drunk, with a girl on his arm.

She felt her temper rise, but bit back her anger, nodded pleasantly to Donal and his companion and sat down beside them. The young man squinted through the dim smoky atmosphere.

'Nuala! Nuala, where've you been?' He had to shout to make himself heard above the din. 'I've not seen you for ... for ...'

'A month,' she said sweetly.

'Aye, a month. What'll you have?' Without waiting for an answer, he turned and shouted for the harried barman.

'Porter, a bottle of porter for my friend.'

The barman brought Nuala a bottle of the thick black liquid and refilled Donal's glass.

'Are you not going to introduce me?' Nuala smiled, but only with her lips.

'Of course, of course, forgetting my manners.' He slipped his arm through his companion's. 'This is Mary, a very good friend of mine, and this,' he patted Nuala on the arm, 'is Nuala, our local wild-woman.'

Mary smiled politely, and then turned away and ignored Nuala. The young girl ran her fingers through Donal's unruly black locks and leaned close to whisper in his ear. As she did so, Nuala emptied a small packet of rock-salt into the young girl's drink.

Donal grinned, and then laughed aloud. 'It's a grand idea, let's drink to it.' He raised his glass and emptied half of it in one swallow. Mary drank.

Nuala engaged Donal in small talk for a few moments, watching Mary closely all the time. Abruptly her hand flew to her mouth, and she stumbled through the crowd towards the door, but before she reached it she was violently sick.

Donal suddenly looked disgusted. 'Christ! She can't hold her drink.' He looked away and ignored her. Nuala laid her hand on his, the long nails scratching the weather beaten flesh in a slow rhythm. 'Come outside,' she whispered, her mouth close to his ear.

They pushed their way through the crowd, circling around Mary as if she was not there. Nuala led Donal down through the town and out into the fields beyond. He felt curiously detached, as if the drink had numbed his body, leaving only his mind alert. He knew what was happening even though he had no power to stop it. He knew Nuala was going to make love to him even before she kissed him with a fierce longing. And he knew he would respond.

And when she laid her underskirt on the damp ground

behind the high hedge and slowly unbuttoned her bodice, he knew he was lost.

And he awoke in the morning with a curious belt wound around his waist.

Their's was not a happy marriage. It was dogged by ill-luck and death. They were shunned by their neighbours and their children hated because of their looks. For, nine months from the night when Nuala lay with Donal in the field, she gave birth to triplets. And each one bore a long black mark down his back, from his head to heel and another about his waist - the shape of the black cross.

The mark of Satan.

CHAPTER 15

I: THE MAGIC LINGERS ON ...

'Father, is she dying?' Niall's voice broke and he clutched the old priest's arm and wept.

Father O'Dwyre looked down at the tiny, wizened creature in the bed and shook his head slowly. 'I don't know, my son; I've never seen anything like it and I know of no sickness that would age and change a person so quickly, so thoroughly.' He eased the young man from the bedroom and into the cottage's only other room. Niall went and knelt by the fire and began to feed it rough chunks of still wet turf.

He turned to look at the priest. 'Father, what has happened to her?'

The old priest stood by the half-door, staring out into the misty morning air, whilst behind him Niall wept for the wife he did not know, for the wife he had lost.

Father O'Dwyre couldn't answer it. Barely a month ago he had married young Eileen and Niall and then she had been a bright innocent young girl, just turned eighteen, with a wide-eyed fresh beauty. And yet in one short month she had turned into ... He glanced back at the closed door of the bedroom and he wondered, what had she turned into?

Her clear, unblemished skin had turned leathery, scored with countless wrinkles and it glistened unpleasantly when the light struck it - which was not often, for the creature in the bed detested the light, claiming it hurt her eyes.

Her eyes.

The eyes of the maid Father O'Dwyre remembered had been bright and clear, still full of the wonder of youth - but

189

now those eyes had aged and hardened, glittering with cunning and experience.

It was almost as if ...

Abruptly the priest turned from the door. Niall was still crouched by the fire, staring unseeing at the guttering flame. He started when the priest called his name.

'Niall, I have done all in my power to help you, I can do no more ... except perhaps to make a suggestion which you might find strange.' The priest paused and smiled grimly. 'I am an old man now and have spent over sixty years in the service of God and if there is one thing I have learned in all that time, it is not to take what we call the supernatural, lightly.' The priest lowered himself heavily into the room's only chair.

'I spent many years in the missions abroad,' he continued. 'In India, I saw men do the impossible and in Africa I witnessed the power of the shaman, the Witch Doctors, but it was not until I returned to Ireland that I discovered that the borders between our world and the Other World are not as substantial as they seem. There is something about this land, something we do not feel because we are so close to it and bound so strongly to it. The strangers and visitors here feel it, on the air and in the wind; it is as if the magic still lingers.' The priest laughed quietly. 'You must forgive an old fool, Niall. Here you are heartbroken and me running on like an old woman outside church.' He leaned forward, resting his elbows on his knees. 'Look, you know Nano Hayes in the village?'

The young man nodded. 'They say she is a witch.'

The priest shook his head. 'She is no more witch than I am – and I think I might be able to work more magic than she ever could. But go to her, she is wise in country lore, perhaps she will be able to help. And here,' he took a small bottle from his pocket, 'it is blessed water – just in case you need it.'

Nano Hayes moved slowly around the bed, looking at the woman from every angle. It was just after noon and the summer sun burned from a cloudless sky, but in the room it was dark and close, for Eileen – if it truly was Eileen – could bear no light.

'Well, it's plain enough,' said Nano Hayes, startling Niall, her voice surprisingly youthful for such an old and frail woman. 'Come outside, and I'll get what I need.'

In the other room she ordered Niall to boil a kettle of water and fetch his sharpest knife. But when he asked her what she was doing, the old woman would only smile secretly and shake her head.

When the kettle began to boil, she instructed him to heat the blade of his knife in the flame until it glowed red, whilst she soaked several rags in the scalding water.

And when her preparations were complete, she entered the bedroom. She stood by the foot of the bed, staring down at the wasted creature. 'You know,' she said wistfully, 'I am thinking you're no ordinary maid – I think you're one of the elven folk.' She glanced down at the woman. 'Ah, but sure you're not likely to tell me of your own accord, eh?'

The woman in the bed remained silent, staring at Nano Hayes through slitted eyes.

'Who, no, *what* are you?' asked the old witch – and dropped one of the steaming cloths onto the bed.

The creature in the bed screamed and hissed like a cat, her hard yellow eyes wide in terror and pain.

Nano Hayes reached across and took the heated knife from Niall's lax grip. 'Now if you're not going to tell me,' she began, and waved the heated blade before the creature's eyes, so that she could feel the heat radiating from the knife.

'Stop,' grated a harsh voice, totally unlike Eileen's.

'Who are you,' repeated Nano, 'and what have you done with this man's wife?'

'You may threaten and torture me, but you will never learn the truth.' The creature's eyes blazed with malice.

'Niall,' said Nano Hayes mildly, 'would you open the curtains.'

'No, stop,' the creature shrieked and curled up in a ball in the bed.

'She is a creature of the barrows and of the night, the light

191

of day would surely have shrivelled her,' explained the old woman to the thoroughly bewildered youth.

'I am Fethlin, a banshee, a woman of the Sidhe,' grated the muffled voice of the creature.

'The elven folk,' nodded Nano Hayes. 'And why have you taken the place of this man's wife?'

'Because my lord desired her – I had no choice,' said the banshee bitterly.

'So the faeries have Eileen,' said Niall, in a daze. He shook his head slowly and then looked at the old woman with innocent lost eyes. 'Is she gone forever then, have I lost her?'

But it was the banshee who answered him. 'They ride out of the fort each evening at dusk and your wife is with them ...' And the creature looked at the young man with a smile. 'You could try and take her then – but she is well guarded, for part of the faery host ride with her.' And then the banshee laughed, a hideous cackle, more animal than human. 'And you will never take her from the host – she is lost, gone forever.'

But Nano Hayes patted the young man's hand and said softly, 'Perhaps there is a way, perhaps there is.'

Niall reached the faery mound late in the evening. The sun was sinking and the trees cast long shadows over the hard earth, bathing one side of the fort in warm amber light, whilst the other drifted into dusk. Niall walked around the mound several times, carefully searching the ground for any sign that might tell him in which direction the faery host rode.

But the grass was unmarked and the mound itself showed no sign of a door or opening.

Wearily Niall climbed to the crown of the mound and looked down into the fields ... He saw it almost immediately: on the east side of the mound was a long thin swath of discoloured grass disappearing into the shadows. Niall slid down the side of the fort and made his way to a gap in the hedge through which the host must ride. On one side of the hedge he traced a circle on the grass with holy water and then, slipping the black-hafted silver bladed knife from his belt, knelt behind the hedge and waited.

The sun was slow in sinking for it was close to midsummer, and although the sky deepened to purple in the east and the nightstars began to glimmer dimly, yet the western sky still burned salmon and rose. A few nightbirds attempted a half-hearted song and once a barn owl hooted plaintively. Otherwise the night was still and silent - waiting.

Dusk gradually deepened, softening the harsh outlines of trees and bush, lending a mysterious air to the hedgerows and turning the faery mound to a place of shadowed mystery rather than just a grass covered mound. Niall, glancing out from behind the hedge, shuddered, for he felt he had been transported back a thousand years into Ireland's past.

And then the mound opened.

There was no rumble of earth or grinding of stone, rather it was as if the earth itself had shifted and dissolved. Tiny coloured lights winked far down in the depths of the mound and faint and sharp on the night air came the sound of elven horns. The clear and unmistakable ring of horses' hooves on stone coupled with the jingle of harness.

The faery host rode out.

Niall's first impression of the Sidhe folk was of height, for they seemed to tower above the ground. Their steeds were tall and incredibly thin, with wild darting eyes and long flowing manes, that burned snow-white in the dusk. They were richly adorned and the bits and harness were of silver.

The riders were tall thin creatures from man's past, in silver armour and carrying swords and spears. Their features beneath their crested helms were thin and pointed, with high slanting eyes, pointed ears and flowing hair. Their eyes burned with a strange fire and seemed lost - as if they stared into a dream.

And in their midst came Eileen.

193

Niall caught his breath and for a moment doubted that he was seeing his wife. She was riding one of the eldritch steeds and clad in a long shimmering robe that trailed on the night air and rippled in a breeze not of this world. Her hair had been coiffeured and flowed down her back in long silken waves. About her brow glittered a diadem of twisted silver wire and a matching necklace nestled against her throat. But it was her eyes her husband noticed, for they were flat and expressionless and seemed to stare into another world.

The faery host trotted across the fields towards the gap in the hedge and Niall suddenly realised with a chill that the horses' silver hooves barely touched the dew-glittered grass.

The first of the riders scraped through the hedge, not six inches from the terrified young man. And then another and another of the elven riders followed, bringing with them the chill of the Other World and the sweet, faintly repellent perfume of the barrow.

The next rider was Eileen. Niall waited until she was almost through the hedge and then he leaped for the reins. The horse reared and nipped at him with a click of huge teeth. But he struck the animal with his knife, drawing a thin line of pale liquid from its neck and then he had sliced through the saddle girth. He caught Eileen as she fell and almost threw her into the protective circle he had drawn earlier. And then he prayed.

The faery host attacked with a battle cry that shattered the stillness of the night like breaking glass. But thrown spears shattered about the pair as if they had struck an invisible wall and swords rang above their heads with high musical notes. But the circle held.

Within the circle Eileen stirred and her eyes cleared. 'Elfrann? ... Niall? ... *Niall*!' She buried her head in her husband's shoulder and wept. 'Oh Niall I dreamt ... I dreamt.' Niall smoothed her hair and whispered gently to her, but his eyes never left those of one of the elven warriors, one who remained apart from the rest.

'Your god protects you,' said the elven warrior suddenly, his high musical voice ringing in Niall's head. He came forward and stood beyond the circle. 'It is good to have gods; the gods of the Old Race have long since died – as we should have. But we are tied to this land and whilst it survives, so will we.' With a word the elven prince called off his warriors. The host withdrew and stood staring at the couple huddled within the invulnerable circle on the grass. The elven prince came and crouched just beyond the ring.

'I . . . I cannot say I regret taking her . . . but you love her – you must know how I felt . . .' He looked away and when he spoke again his voice was heavy with emotion and his strange colourless eyes were moist. 'I love her, son of Man,' and then he added in a rush, 'and I need her, for our race is dying. We need new blood. In the elder days the sons and daughters of Man were honoured to join the elven race; they gave us their seed and our children grew strong and the race was preserved. Some stayed with us, but the few that returned to the mortal world where gifted with foresight, the ability to see beyond the veil of their own world or the gift of healing. But it has been a long time since one of the sons of Man bedded one of the elven maids, or one of the daughters of Eve lay with a man beyond the Fields of Man.'

'I have met one of your elven maids,' said Niall bitterly. 'I would not be tempted to bed one.'

'Oh, they are not all ugly and wizened; it is only when they reside in this world for a while that they lose their looks and begin to age rapidly.' And then he laughed gently. 'But if you were to cross the borders into the Other World, then time would not touch you; the years would slip by like days – you would be close to being immortal.' His voice softened. 'I can promise Eileen this, if only you will let her go.'

Niall shook his head. 'I will never let her go – and I would kill her rather than see her go with you.' His voice rose with anger. 'You stole my wife, bewitched her and held her in thrall. You say that you love her – but does she love you? Can you not see that taking a girl just to bear you children is wrong; can you not see that once your spell has worn off, she will do nothing but fear and hate you always? That is not the way.'

The elven lord reached out his hand, as if he sought to touch Eileen, but he withdrew it abruptly with a gasp as if his fingers had been burned. 'She is so beautiful,' he whispered.

Niall laughed gently. 'She is, I'll grant you that; but there are many even more beautiful. But beauty is not everything,' he added.

'In the elven lands, beauty is everything,' said the elven prince.

'Perhaps if you were to woo a maid and she in turn, loved you, then she would willingly go with you into the elven kingdoms and gladly bear your children.'

'Perhaps,' said the elven lord wistfully. 'I think I recall now why the sons of Man gained supremacy over the Elder Folk.' He sighed and his eyes looked back into another age. 'In the end, we grew selfish and we had the power to take what we wanted – and what we wanted we took.' He smiled at the young couple. 'Remember that.' And then he glanced at the lightening sky. 'The night is almost done and we must be gone, but I think we have both gained something this night: you, your bride, and I ... and I, wisdom.' He mounted his wild-eyed steed, and as he led the faery host back into the mound, he turned and called, sharp and clear on the morning air. 'I will take your advice.'

The mound closed as the first rays of the morning sun touched it with bronze and gold.

Niall stood with Eileen in the crook of his arm, staring into the sunrise. 'You know,' he said suddenly, 'the old priest was right: the magic lingers on.'

CHAPTER 16

II: ... INTO THE SHADOWLAND ...

Brigid sat on the banks of the stream, dangling her legs in the cool water - waiting. The sun was sinking behind the low mountains to the west and dusk, the forerunner of the night was rapidly creeping across the fields. But the warmth of the day still lingered and the young girl was content to sit cooling her feet in the stream and listen.

And then as the last of the sun's rays faded and the bird calls died, the music came. It was thin and high and occasionally faded as if it passed beyond the range of human hearing - and it was incredibly beautiful. Brigid listened entranced as she had for the past three nights. She was unable to decide what instrument was playing, whether it was the pipes or a harp. The music had all the delicacy of the harp, but it flowed with that breathless quality peculiar to the pipes. And then Brigid realised that tonight the music was clearer and sharper ... and nearer. Abruptly she stood and ran lightly across the shadowed fields towards the forest and the strange otherworldly music.

It spun a delicate web on the night air, calling, insisting, luring her on, deeper and deeper into the forest that bordered the fields. She paused at the edge of the trees and stood, undecided - the local people told stories about the place, and connected it with the faery mound that rose just beyond the village.

But the music had her firmly under its spell and throwing caution to the winds she pushed on. As she moved deeper into the forest, the music grew louder until it was all about her ... holding her ... pulling her ... pushing ... whirling her around ... and around ... and around ...

She felt the forest spinning ... spinning ... spinning, and she fell.

When she awoke, she was lying by the tiny pool that lay almost in the centre of the forest. The night was far advanced and the heavens sparkled with stars. Brigid sat up suddenly. The time, what time was it? How long had she lain here – and how did she get here? Something moved at the corner of her eye and she stifled a scream.

'You have no need to fear me.' The voice was that of a man, thin and high like the music and it seemed to echo within her head.

'Who ... who are you?' she whispered, her voice cracking with the strain.

The shadow moved closer, until she could make out the outline of a tall thin man. He smiled, his sharp teeth startlingly white in the shadows and pushed back the hood of a long cape. His hair was long and pale and seemed incredibly fine.

'I am Elfrann,' he said. Again the voice seemed to ring in her head and she struggled to make out the accent. It was unlike her own, nor was it like that of the schoolmaster whose accent was harsh and flat, nor was it like Mr Cunningham's, who owned the big house on the hill, but who lived across the water for most of the year. And yet it was familiar – hauntingly familiar. It was soft and flowing and liquid, like ... like the music she had heard.

The music.

'I heard music,' she murmured, 'I followed ...'

The stranger held out a hand harp. 'I often play as the night draws on,' he smiled.

Brigid looked at the harp in wonder. It was carved from a shimmering white wood that seemed to burn on the night air and long wavering lines like script had been cut along its length. Its strings sparkled like silver wire and moaned slightly as Elfrann moved the harp to and fro.

'I have never seen anything like it,' she whispered and stretched out a hand to touch. But Elfrann moved the harp away.

'You cannot,' he said gently, 'it would ... it would burn you,' he explained. And then he added, 'It has been in my family for many years - it is very old.' He glanced at the sky, his eyes burning briefly amber, like an animal's.

'I must be going,' he said and his voice held a trace of regret. 'Will I see you again?'

Brigid nodded dumbly.

Elfrann stood and gathered his cloak about him. 'But I do not even know your name, pretty maid.'

'Brigid,' she murmured.

'Brigid,' he repeated, his strange accent making it sound alien and exotic.

And as he turned to go, he looked her full in the face and his strange eyes caught and held hers. 'But not a word of this to your father or sister - do not tell them about me.'

And then he turned and was gone before she realised she had not told him of her father or her sister.

She met Elfrann the following night in the same place just after dusk. When she came upon him he was playing the harp, the delicate liquid notes hanging trembling on the still night air. And even when he laid aside the harp, the music seemed to linger. He kissed her gently as he greeted her and she felt the blood rush to her face, but the touch of his lips tingled pleasantly on hers and she felt lightheaded and giddy.

Elfrann walked with her through the moonlit woods and although he talked little of himself, she felt she knew him.

And once again he left before sunrise, but not before making her promise not to tell her father or sister.

They met every night after that and the long hot days of summer drifted slowly into autumn and although Brigid spent most of the night with Elfrann, she never felt tired or exhausted the following morning - it was as if she had dreamt it all.

The lingering golden days of September gradually gave way to the colder, wetter weather of October, but Brigid was almost unconscious of the changing days, she lived only for the nights and her lover, Elfrann. She became wan and pale and her eyes grew shadowed and seemed to look into another place or time.

Deep down she knew Elfrann was not human, but he was neither deamon nor devil and she only suspected he was of the Elder Folk, the Faeries.

October passed.

And then on the last night of the month, Elfrann took Brigid to the Faery Fort, the mound that stood beyond the village, and together they climbed to the top and stood staring into the east, where the sky was already brightening in anticipation of sunrise. Elfrann took Brigid's hand in his and looked down into her gentle eyes.

'Tonight,' he whispered, 'is perhaps the last night I will see you ...' he raised his hand and pressed his finger to his lips, stilling her reply.

'No, you must listen to me. Tonight is Samhain Eve, it is my last in your world. I must return.'

'Return?' Brigid frowned and then her eyes opened wide in understanding. 'You *are* of the Sidhe!'

Elfrann bowed. 'I am Elfrann, Lord of the Elven Folk, descendent of the Tuatha De Danann.' He paused and looked down at the mound below his feet. 'And tonight I must return to my kingdom.'

'Take me with you,' she said quickly.

He hesitated.

'Please,' she whispered, 'I love you.'

Elfrann held her tightly, stroking her long red hair. 'Truly? Do you truly love me?'

She nodded dumbly.

'But you know what I am. I am one of the elven folk - I am not human, at least not by your standards.'

'I love you,' she repeated.

She felt him shudder and when she looked up at the elven lord, she was shocked to find tears on his face.

Gently she brushed them away. 'Why do you weep, my love?'

'I weep because once I thought that love was little more than another name for longing. I weep because once I took a woman of your world. I thought I loved her, but her husband taught me what love really was when he challenged the faery host for her – and won. He taught me a lesson.' The elven lord kissed her. 'He taught me that love must grow of its own accord, it cannot be taken or made.'

'Do you love me, my lord?' she asked.

'I love you,' he replied simply.

Together they walked down the mound and stood at its foot. Brigid could feel the air tremble with suppressed power. Abruptly Elfrann laughed.

'What is it, my lord?'

'That man of your world told me that someday I would find a woman willing to wed me, willing to go beyond the veil into the Shadowland, the Realms of Faery.'

The feeling of suppressed power grew and intensified, until the young girl could almost taste it. Lightning flickered across the clear morning sky and her hair rose in long static streamers. The side of the fort trembled and shimmered and then abruptly it was gone and a great door stood in the side of the fort. Silently it swung open revealing a long passage leading down, deep into the depths of the Shadowland. Tiny lights winked and pulsed and on the air came the haunting melody of Faery, a melody similar to the one which had drawn Brigid to Elfrann.

'You know if you come with me there can be no return?'

She held his arm tightly. 'I would not want to return without you.'

'So be it.'

And together they walked from this world into the Realm of Faery.

The pale November sun burned through the thin grey clouds, giving the mound a bleached dusky appearance. Slowly it crept down the side of the fort . . . until it touched the stiff body of a young girl.

CHAPTER 17

III: ... INTO ETERNITY

Nano Hayes sat by the smoking fire, staring deep into the shallow bowl she held cupped in the palms of her hands. She glanced up at the white-faced young woman sitting across from her. The wavering firelight turned the old woman's skin parchment yellow and turned her eyes to points of amber light. With a sigh she tossed the contents of the bowl into the fire, which abruptly blazed blue-green flames. The young woman stifled a scream.

'Now there's no need to be frightened child,' the old woman chuckled. 'I did the same for your mother and your two sisters and haven't they all made a fine match?'

Eithne nodded nervously, clasping her hands tightly together in her lap. She was frightened; the villagers told strange stories of the old woman, some whispered she was a witch and consorted with deamons. But her mother had laughed at the stories and insisted that she see Nano, especially now since she had turned eight and ten years and still with no sign of a husband.

The young girl cleared her throat, but when she spoke her voice was little more than a whisper. She coughed and tried again. 'Who ... Who did you see?' She nodded at the empty copper bowl.

'Why, I saw your husband, dear. And a fine match he will make.'

'Who is he?' Eithne asked, interested now in spite of herself.

'It's Seámus MacMahon - he lives down beyond the stream,' grinned Nano Hayes.

'Isn't he the brother of Niall who married Eileen Ni Sullibhan, who was taken very bad last year?'

'The same.'

Eithne stared deep into the fire, a tiny smile playing about her lips. She looked sidelong at the old woman. 'I've always liked Seámus.'

Nano nodded. 'There now, so you're getting a man you like - aren't you the lucky one? There's some now that have a match made for them and they not knowing the man until they meet him at the altar.'

'I like him,' said Eithne slowly, 'but I'm not sure whether I love him, or whether he loves me.'

The old woman laughed, a dry cackle that sent a shiver down the young girl's back. 'Liking him is good enough for a start, you can learn to love him later.' She glanced at Eithne. 'Do you not believe me? But you wait, love will come.'

'I always imagined it would be different,' she whispered.

Nano smiled at the young girl's romantic fancies. 'I tell you what, I'll give you this.' She handed Eithne a small linen packet of dried and crushed herbs. 'It's a love charm: slip it in his drink the first chance you get, and you can be sure he'll love you and none other.'

Eithne slipped the packet into her bodice. 'What's in it?' she asked.

'It's ten leaves of hemlock I picked on All Hallows Eve from the churchyard; oh, don't look so shocked child, I picked them in the name of the Blessed Trinity - they can only do good. Now if I had picked them in the name of the Evil One, then they could cause only harm and even death.' She stood and reached above the fire, taking down a mortar and pestle. 'I crushed the leaves here, and look . . .' She tilted the bowl towards the fire, and Eithne could see strange flowing letters cut into the hardened clay.

'What do they say?' she whispered.

'It's Greek,' explained Nano. *'"Panta men kathara tois katharois"* - all things are pure to the pure.' She laughed and replaced the ancient objects above the fire. 'Oh, I know I'm called a witch in the village – not that that stops them when they need a cure of some healing herbs – but I've always honoured the True Gods.' She stood and pressed her hands against her back. 'Aaah, but it's old I'm getting.'

Eithne stood and handed the old woman a copper coin. 'It's all I can afford ...'

Nano Hayes took the girl's hand and pressed the coin back into it. 'There is no charge, child; I'll be fully paid when I see you happily wed.' She moved to the cottage's only door and pulled it open with a scrape of warped timbers.

Night had fallen and they both shivered in the sudden chill. 'One last thing,' said Nano. 'When you give Seámus the potion, make sure you say the following, three times:

> You for me
> And I for thee,
> And for none else,
> Your face to mine
> And your head turned away
> From all others.' "

Eithne repeated the charm, and then pulled her shawl up around her head and shoulders. Stooping suddenly she kissed the old woman on the cheek and then set off at a run down the deserted street, her bare feet making no sound on the sunbaked earth.

Nano Hayes stood in the door watching the slight figure disappear into the night, and smiled gently.

It was close to midnight when the old woman heard the muffled hoofbeats and the clatter of wheels coming down the long street. The fire had sunk to a dull bed of embers, barely lighting the single-roomed cottage. She leaned over and stirred the coals. Shadows danced and flickered on the damp streaked walls, and tiny sparks rose spiralling upwards.

A chill wind whipped through the room, fanning the flames, as the door suddenly opened. A tall dark figure stood in the doorway, outlined in stark relief against the yellow harvest moon hanging low over the thatched roofs. And Nano Hayes shrank back, her breath catching in her throat.

For the stranger cast no shadow.

She could feel her heart pounding her chest, frighteningly loud. Blood rushed to her head and she swayed and had to clutch the back of a chair for support. She squeezed her eyes shut, her lips moving in a silent prayer - and when she looked again, she could see the stranger's shadow stretch into the room almost to her feet.

'You are Nano Hayes.' It was a statement more than a question. The voice was male, but was thin and high - almost like a child's - and it seemed to come from a great distance.

'I am,' the old woman nodded. It gave her some satisfaction that her voice was firm and unquavering.

The stranger stepped into the room, the moonlight catching him in profile, painting one half of his high, thin slant-eyed face in wan yellow light, and leaving the other in shadow. His eyes glittered like points of metal.

'I am surprised to find you still up.' His voice rang off the damp walls as if they were metal. 'You were expecting me, perhaps?'

'I was expecting someone,' Nano said carefully. 'I felt someone would come tonight ...' she shrugged. 'But now you're here, what do you want with me?'

'My wife is close to childbirth and she wished to have a ... to have someone with her. I have a carriage without, will you come with me?'

Nano hesitated. Something about this tall stranger chilled her - and although she was close to seventy summers her eyes were still as sharp as a cat's and yet she could not make out his features. And his voice; the more she heard it, the more convinced she became that it rang within her head.

'I will pay you well,' he said, as Nano remained silent.

The old woman dismissed the matter of payment with a wave of her hand and piled some of the things she knew she would need into a woven wicker basket and then followed the stranger outside. He was standing by the open door of a small closed carriage, staring intently into the eastern sky. As he helped the old woman into the carriage, he said brusquely, 'We must hurry, dawn will be early.'

'Where are we going?'

'To my home,' he said and slammed the door. Inside it was warm and dark, the rich odour of polished leather and wood hanging heavy on the air. There were no windows in the coach and when, on an impulse, she tried the door, she found it was locked. She sat on what seemed like velvet, her basket on her knees, clutching it tightly. She knew everyone in the village and many of those surrounding villages along the coast and she knew of no pregnant girl, especially one near childbirth. Unless of course, the child was illegitimate and the parents and families had managed to keep it a secret all these months; but she didn't believe that was possible in such a small close-knit community.

The carriage lurched and moved down the street, the hooves of the strange horses she had only half-glimpsed, sounding muffled and distant.

There was another possibility – a distasteful one. Many years ago she had been called out in the dead of night to attend a birth – or so she had been told. But it had turned out to be nothing of the sort. A young girl of a good family – who had all since emigrated – had found herself to be with child. Her parents would have killed her and the disgrace would have ruined the family, had the father of the child not hit upon a plan. He had brought Nano Hayes to a deserted cottage down by the shore and, believing her to be a godless woman, had told her to get rid of the unborn child. Nano had refused and the couple had grown pleading and threatening in turn, but she had remained firm, despite the threats to denounce her as a witch. The girl never did have the child, although Biddy Early, up in Clare, told her some time later that the couple approached her for a potion to destroy the babe – and she too had refused. Nano Hayes shook her head, someone, somewhere had taken that little life …

The sounds of the carriage's wheels suddenly changed – it

was now running across grass rather than hard earth. Gradually the ground began to rise and then abruptly slope downwards. The horses' hooves now echoed sharp and clear, ringing on dressed stone and off nearby walls. Nano strained and fancied she could hear music and the sounds of merriment growing louder. They must have entered a courtyard she decided, near a large house.

The carriage stopped.

Nano could hear muttered voices outside the carriage and then another voice raised in either anger or command. But the language was strange, although parts of it seemed familiar and she couldn't make out what was being said. Abruptly the carriage door was thrown open. The old woman squinted into the harsh burning light which streamed in, making her eyes water and fill with tears. Someone reached in and gently helped her down, whilst another took her bag. She could see nothing through her tears save a shimmering kaleidoscope of colours and the misty shapes of people as they passed by. An incredibly delicate girl's voice warned her of steps just before they began to climb. Nano paused and wiped her sleeve across her eyes, but they continued to fill with tears and render her almost blind. She heard a lock click, a section of the wall before her swung open and she was gently pushed into a large warm room.

Nano squeezed her eyes shut and blinked and as abruptly as they had started, the tears ceased. She was standing in a large bedroom; to one end of the room was a huge blazing fire, whilst at the other end was a marvellously ornate bed. The high walls were hung with delicately woven tapestries, depicting curiously elfin creatures and strange mythological beasts, whilst the floor was covered with a thick brown-and-ochre carpet, which exuded a musky fragrance with every step she took. There was only one door – the one through which she had come and no windows.

A low moan attracted her attention. There was a young girl in the bed, her face pale and drawn and her eyes tight with labour pains. Nano Hayes frowned; there was something terribly familiar about the girl.

'Hello, Nano.'

And suddenly she knew – the girl in the bed was Brigid Farrell! The old woman felt her blood run cold, for the body of young Brigid had been found at the foot of the Faery Fort outside the village almost a year ago!

The girl smiled weakly. 'Yes, it's me. There's no need to fear – no-one will harm you here.'

'Where are we?' wondered Nano.

'You have passed beyond the Fields of Man into the Realm of Faery; you are one of the few Daughters of Eve ever to have done so and still retained your mortal form. When I came through almost a year ago, I had to leave my body behind.'

'But you are real.' Nano reached out and touched the girl's fevered brow.

'I am real,' she insisted. 'What I left behind was only a husk – a shell of mortal fears and worries, of mundane passions and desires. This is the real me ...' and then she caught her breath and bit back a scream.

Nano Hayes suddenly forgot her questions – she had a young girl in labour to attend to.

'If there is ... anything ... anything you ... need,' gasped Brigid, 'call ...'

Nano looked around, but there was neither hot water nor clean linen. She ran lightly across the thick carpet, the thin odour of musk cloying and catching in her throat. But the moment she opened the door, her eyes filled with tears and once again she was looking through a watery veil.

'I need boiling water and some fresh linen,' she called and slammed the door, lying back against it, blinking her eyes until they cleared.

Almost immediately the door opened and a young maid entered. She was tiny, almost child-like, but perfectly formed, but her eyes betrayed her true age, for they were old and wise with experience. She carried a huge pitcher of steaming water to the small bedside table and laid it down and placed a small bundle of clean white linen beside it. Without a word she turned and left.

Brigid tensed as another spasm shot through her and then another and another. She screamed ...

Nano Hayes washed the child carefully in the still tepid water, wrapped him in a linen sheet and placed him in his mother's arms. Brigid held him as if he were made of glass and looked into his huge black eyes. Tears of joy replaced those of pain which had recently flooded her eyes.

'He is perfect in every way,' said Nano softly.

Brigid pushed the cloth back from the babe's head. His tiny ears were pointed and upward sweeping and both his chin and nose seemed unnaturally sharp.

'He is a child of both worlds,' she said. 'He is beautiful.' And then she looked at Nano Hayes, at the lines of fatigue etched about her eyes and mouth. 'You are tired.' She seemed surprised. 'But I forgot; fatigue is almost unknown here. And you are probably hungry too. But listen to me carefully now. If they offer you food or drink, refuse it unless they can offer you salt with it. If you eat the food of Faery, you will be trapped here for all eternity. You must also refuse if they offer you gold or silver – take nothing above your normal fee; you must take away from Faery only what is yours and yours by right.'

'And what about you?'

Brigid gently kissed her young son's head. 'I am happy here – I came here of my own accord and although I little knew what I was doing, I loved Elfrann, I would have followed him anywhere. But this is my home; my husband is here ... and now my son is here. I cannot leave.'

'But are you happy?' wondered the old woman.

Brigid shrugged. 'Oh, I'm happy ... I suppose. Some of the elven folk despise me,' she added, 'but the birth of my son will silence them. Some said he would be born deformed – that the Elder Race and the newer race of Man could not interbreed and others said he would be stillborn. But this is the first birth in this land for almost a thousand years of your time. My son is the first of a new line of elven lords – he will carry the race on and into eternity.' She ran her fingers across the babe's finely downed head.

The door opened and the stranger who had brought Nano through into the Shadowland entered. He crossed to the bed in long strides and went on his knees beside it. Brigid lifted the child and held it out to him. 'Elfrann, behold our son.'

The elven lord took the boy in his long delicate hands and kissed his wrinkled forehead gently. And then he laughed and held the child aloft as if in offering. 'My son,' he cried and handed the boy back to Brigid, 'Our son,' he corrected himself.

'The race will survive,' she said.

Elfrann shook his head slowly. 'He is the last of the Tuatha De Danann.' He stood and turned to Nano, handing her a silken purse. 'This is but a token – all my treasure could not pay you for bringing this child safely into the world. Now come, you must be famished: there is food and drink prepared.'

Nano shook her head. 'I thank you – but I cannot take this.' She opened the purse and extracted one silver coin.

She smiled thinly. 'Render unto Caesar only what is Caesar's,' she quoted, and handed him back the purse.

The elven lord laughed. 'I did not think you would pay homage to the New God.'

'The New God survives and thrives,' she said, 'and where are the Old Gods of your people now?'

'They are but dim memories,' whispered Elfrann.

Nano gathered up the damp cloths and piled them by the side of the bed. The door opened and the creature with the child's body and the woman's eyes entered and silently removed them. And the old woman noticed how her strange eyes lingered on the babe and seemed to suddenly fill with tears.

Elfrann weighed the purse in his hand. 'I'll wager you will not eat with us,' he smiled.

Nano returned his smile. 'I like my food well salted.'

The elven lord nodded gravely. 'I understand. But before you go, know that you have my thanks and you may be sure I will tell my son of the woman who aided him into the world. And if there is anything I - or indeed he in time - can do for you, then you will need only call.'

Nano thanked him and, taking her wicker basket, stood by the door, whilst Elfrann and Brigid whispered together over their son.

The elven lord led her back through the corridors and rooms of the fort. He had covered her eyes with a silken cloth and he clutched her wrinkled, veined hand in his. As they began to descend the stairs, he stopped and spoke with someone in the strange lilting, musical tongue of the People of the Goddess. He broke off and she could hear the alarm in his voice. 'We must hurry, dawn is almost upon us.' Abruptly, he swept her up in his arms and raced down the stairs, the sudden descent making her thankful for the cloth that covered her eyes. And if she hadn't heard the sound of his bootheels clicking off the echoing stones she could have sworn she was flying.

The sound changed and they were now out into what she assumed was a courtyard. The elven music had stopped and the sounds of merriment had long since ceased.

Elfrann ran on, climbing uphill now, his breath coming in laboured gasps and every now and again he staggered under his burden. At last he skidded to a halt. He called aloud in the Old Tongue and Nano could feel the very air tingle, as if a thunder storm were brewing. A chill wind suddenly whistled past her head and then it was gone and she could feel the fresh morning breeze on her face and taste the damp air.

'I must leave you here,' Elfrann said. 'You have my thanks, now and always.' And he was gone.

She stood listening for a moment, but the morning was silent save for the first tentative calls of the dawn chorus. Stiffly she removed the blindfold and stared into the east, awaiting the sunrise. She looked around, and was not surprised to find herself at the foot of the Faery Fort and almost at the same spot where the body of Brigid had been found. She picked up her wicker basket. Lying on top was a

211

silken purse. She picked it up carefully, feeling the hard shapes of coin through the cloth.

Legend went that whomever was given gold by the faery folk usually ended up with nothing more than lumps of earth or stone. Almost unconsciously her fingers found the draw string and pulled – and a stream of bright golden coins fell onto the dew-damp grass.

Nano Hayes knelt and replaced the coins in the purse. It was the beginning of a new day, a new month and a new season; and a new age for the elven folk, the last of the Tuatha De Danann.

For they had a new lord, a child of both worlds, one who would lead them on ... on and into eternity.

SPRING MOON

BETTE BAO LORD

'A moving first novel . . . a turbulent story
of heroes and martyrs.'
Daily Express

Even as a child Spring Moon was different. She was
too full of life and laughter for the elders. She could
read and write like a boy. And she was the most
beautiful of the many daughters of the great house
in Soochow. A bird in a gilded cage, she longed to
fly to the great outside world of mysterious sorrow
and happiness.

Spring Moon is destined to know the pleasures of
marriage, the pain of loss and the bittersweet taste
of forbidden love before she returns to the home of
her ancestors. Her story spans five generations of
restless change, from the stately days of Mandarin
rule to the death of Mao Tse-tung. Not since
Dr Zhivago has a novel so powerfully conveyed
the hope and torment of love and loss in a nation
in turmoil.

GENERAL FICTION   0 7221 5615 4   £2.25

THE HEARTWARMING TRUE STORY
OF A VERY SPECIAL DOG
AND HER VERY SPECIAL OWNER

SHEILA HOCKEN

(Illus)

Everyone knows the inspiring story of Sheila Hocken and
her wonderful guide-dog Emma, and of the miracle
operation which enabled her to see for the first time in her
life.

Now, Sheila describes her life since the incredible moment
when she opened her eyes and saw the beautiful world we
all take for granted. With freshness and humour, Sheila
tells how each day brought new joys, new challenges and
new surprises.

Emma's life, too, has undergone dramatic changes. She was
no longer needed as a guide-dog but her retirement has
been far from idle. She is now a celebrity and receives her
own fan mail; she has made several television appearances;
she was Personality Dog of the Year at Crufts and is greeted
in the street more often than Sheila is.

'Writing simply, with innate ability to externalise thought,
feeling, experience, she again achieves a lovable intimacy'
Daily Telegraph

AUTOBIOGRAPHY   0 7221 4601 9   £1.25

Also by Sheila Hocken in Sphere Books:
EMMA AND I

ANN DRYSDALE

FAINT HEART NEVER KISSED A PIG

is the unforgettable tale of adorable Ernest, the burglar-proof porker; Snuff, the blackest sheep you ever saw, who arrived at Hagg House just one hour old, shivering and wet; and Dodo, the indescribably ugly guinea fowl . . .

It is the enchanting tale of one remarkable woman, Ann Drysdale, who, with her three children, left the civilised world of London and a career in journalism, to set up home in a North Yorkshire hill farm.

And how, amidst great hardship and even greater hilarity, the Drysdales and their extended family made out . . .

AUTOBIOGRAPHY   0 7221 3070 8   £1.75

A selection of bestsellers from SPHERE

FICTION

TOUGH GUYS DON'T DANCE	Norman Mailer	£2.50 ☐
FIRE IN THE ICE	Alan Scholefield	£2.25 ☐
SOUVENIR	David Kaufelt	£2.50 ☐
WHAT NIALL SAW	Brian Cullen	£1.25 ☐
POSSESSIONS	Judith Michael	£2.95 ☐

FILM & TV TIE-INS

MOG	Peter Tinniswood	£1.95 ☐
LADY JANE	A. C. H. Smith	£1.95 ☐
IF I WERE KING OF THE UNIVERSE	Danny Abelson	£1.50 ☐
BEST FRIENDS	Jocelyn Stevenson	£1.50 ☐

NON-FICTION

WEEK ENDING: THE CABINET LEAKS	Ian Brown and James Hendrie	£2.95 ☐
THE POLITICS OF CONSENT	Francis Pym	£2.95 ☐
THE SPHERE ILLUSTRATED HISTORY OF BRITAIN VOLUMES 1, 2 AND 3		£3.95 each
	Ed. Kenneth O. Morgan	☐

All Sphere books are available at your local bookshop or newsagent, or can be ordered direct from the publisher. Just tick the titles you want and fill in the form below.

Name _____

Address _____

_____

Write to Sphere Books, Cash Sales Department, P.O. Box 11, Falmouth, Cornwall TR10 9EN.

Please enclose a cheque or postal order to the value of the cover price plus:

UK: 55p for the first book, 22p for the second book and 14p for each additional book ordered to a maximum charge of £1.75.

OVERSEAS: £1.00 for the first book plus 25p per copy for each additional book.

BFPO & EIRE: 55p for the first book, 22p for the second book plus 14p per copy for the next 7 books, thereafter 8p per book.

Sphere Books reserve the right to show new retail prices on covers which may differ from those previously advertised in the text or elsewhere, and to increase postal rates in accordance with the PO.